1981

IMAGES OF
ROSE

IMAGES OF
ROSE

ANNA GILBERT

DELACORTE PRESS / NEW YORK

IMAGES OF
ROSE

Chapter One

I woke to hear my sister calling from the window.

"Ellen! Come here—quickly!"

Drowsily turning my head on the pillow, I saw her kneeling on the window-seat. The casement was open. She was leaning out.

"Ellen, you must come. Please. There's a person up there by the cross-roads. I can't think what she's doing."

"A person?"

In a second I was at her side.

"Move up. I can't see."

Across the river there was nothing to see but the pasture, rising so steeply from the water's edge that it seemed almost near enough to touch. But Lucy was pointing to the right where the valley opened out and we could see the signpost, small and lonely on the brow of the hill, its arms spread wide against the sky. We were looking east into the daybreak.

"I can't see anyone."

We crouched together on the broad cushion, gazing up the hill. The air rang with bird song, eerily wild and sweet.

"There."

Among the bracken a lamb bleated, colorless as the hillside. A barely perceptible movement by the signpost might have been no more than a first break in the clouds; or perhaps my eyes had wavered so that for a moment I could almost have imagined a figure.

But in fact there was no one.

"It's too early. There couldn't be."

"But I saw her I tell you. A lady."

"What *was* she doing?"

"She was. . . ." Lucy hesitated and frowned, suddenly doubtful. "Well, I thought I saw a lady—in gray—kneeling beside the signpost, saying her prayers."

I would have laughed at the absurdity of it if the signpost with its outflung arms had not looked rather like a crucifix, and if Lucy had not been staring at me so seriously, her blue eyes wide and a little dazed.

In the candid early light I noticed the transparency of her skin, the delicacy of her still-childish features framed in the long heavy curls. From the frill of her nightdress her neck rose as thin as a lily stalk. She was shivering.

I closed the window, shutting out the bird song and the cool air from the river. We turned back into the dim room.

"You've been dreaming again."

[2]

I laid my hand on her forehead as I had seen Binnie do a score of times.

"Come back to bed. You'll catch cold."

We padded barefoot across the knotted floor and lay in our twin hollows in the goose-feather bed, staring at the ceiling.

"I really did think I saw her, Ellen."

"Dreams are like that sometimes. More real than the things that actually happen. Do you remember when you dreamed that an angel came down in the orchard?"

"And I made you come out with me in the rain to look for it in case it had gone by the time we finished breakfast." She giggled, nestling still further into the depths of the mattress. I felt her relax. "I couldn't believe that it was only a dream. White and shining and *gracious* among the apple blossom. But of course it was winter, as you pointed out."

She yawned and dozed off.

I lay awake as growing daylight restored one by one the familiar details of the room: our two work-boxes on the white painted chest; the two shell-framed mirrors on the wall; the horizontal green bottle on the mantel-shelf containing a replica of Father's barque *Miranda,* perfect in every detail; at one end of the mantel a photograph of Father taken when he was given his first command; at the other, hanging from black velvet ribbons, the miniatures of Mother and Cousin Rose as little girls.

The ceiling shimmered with reflected sunlight from the river below and the room leapt into life. But Lucy had fallen into a deeper sleep. I guessed that her restless night had been the result of too much excitement the evening before.

"She'll wear herself out if she isn't watched," was Binnie's way of putting it; and Binnie had given me a significant look and shaken her head when Lucy launched into the twenty-

[3]

two verses of "The Wreck of the Hesperus," her eyes brilliant as blue glass, her cheeks scarlet. Unconsciously we had grown used to protecting her from the overstimulating effect of her own ardent nature. But last night had been exceptional. Otherwise Binnie would never have let us stay up until after midnight, each wrapped in a pelisse and shawl on the kitchen sofa and fenced off for the sake of modesty by the big square table.

On the other side of the table, eating cold pie and drinking strong brown tea sat Alec, Binnie's son. It was the last night of April, 1883, and Alec's last night at home before he rejoined his regiment to sail for Egypt. He would be away for two years, possibly three.

Binnie sat rocking by the fire, her feet on the steel fender, with Lucy's white cat Blanche on the rag mat by her chair; and she was knitting with a sort of ferocious resolution, relentlessly, round after round, as if she dared not stop.

Could she still be worrying about Mohammed Ahmed ("That Mahdi" as she viciously called him, "stirring up trouble in the Sudan"), even though Alec himself had pointed out to her the distance on the map between El Obeid and Alexandria, where he was to be stationed? Besides, Mr. Gladstone himself had promised that no British troops would be sent to the Sudan; and those were the days, tranquil as a summer afternoon, when the very sun and moon—like the rest of the British Empire—occupied their appointed places only with the approval of Mr. Gladstone and the Queen.

But Lucy and I were almost equally sorry to part with Alec, especially for so long. He was the nearest we had known to a brother, having been brought up at the Mill since the day, eighteen years ago, when Binnie, already widowed, had come to keep house for my parents immediately after their marriage.

The Dutch clock struck one.

"What would Father say if he knew?" whispered Lucy, fluttering her eyelashes in simulated fear. To cast our indulgent father in the role of domestic tyrant was one of our favorite fictions.

We watched Alec eating with the enthusiasm of a man who had walked the best part of seven miles across the moors from Stanesfield. Not that he was complaining.

"It was a bit of luck seeing Tom Amblethwaite from over Kindlehope way," he said as he methodically demolished the pie. "He gave me a lift as far as the Moorcock."

Even so he had been late—so late that Binnie had grown anxious. With not a dwelling between the Moorcock and the Mill, the moorland road was wild and lonely even at this time of the year. Alec had been spending the last day of his leave with Sarah, his sweetheart. As a farewell treat they had gone to the theater to see a play, *The Lady from Locarno*. With a certain aptness it had also been the last performance, a circumstance which Alec and Sarah were inclined to take almost as a personal compliment, accepting the curtain calls and bouquets as a suitable climax to their own leave-taking.

"It was watching the goings-on at the stagedoor afterward that made me a bit late in starting for home," Alec observed. "But it would have been worth walking the whole seven miles just to see their antics."

"You were going to tell us about the play," said Lucy as he put down his knife and fork at last and began to stir the tea in his half-pint moustache cup, "and the dresses." Neither Lucy nor I had so much as set foot in a theater, nor had we seen a play of any kind. But we were perfectly satisfied to enjoy

[5]

the experience at secondhand. Looking back, I marvel at our capacity for enjoyment. The least diversion was enough to arouse in us a delicious sense of the richness and variety of life.

"Well," said Alec thoughtfully, "there was this lady, the one from Locarno. She was the one it was all about. She says to this man. . . ."

"Which man was that?"

"Him with the great big house in Park Lane and footmen in blue silk breeches and white wigs. She says to him: 'I have you in the hollow of my hand,' she says. 'You see, I know your secret.' That's what she said and you could tell he was really taken with her turning up unexpectedly like that."

"What was she wearing?"

"Different dresses all the time. When she said that about the hollow of her hand, she was wearing a sort of plum satin with feathers in her hat. But at the end when she was humbled, kneeling down and praying for his forgiveness, she was all in gray. Must cost a bit the clothes they wear."

"I'd love to be an actress." It was wonderful how much fervor Lucy threw into the words considering how hot we were, wound like cocoons in our pelisses and shawls. "I wonder if I could."

"You'd be good at it, Miss Lucy," said Alec judicially, "the way you recite and dance. I can just see you in a hat with ostrich feathers and one of them reticules dangling from your wrist."

"I have you in the hollow of my hand. You see I *know* your secret."

"You've got it to a T," said Alec as Lucy glared with exquisite hauteur across the kitchen table. Only the informality of her attire prevented her from giving a more extended performance as I well knew. But nothing could stop her from bursting into "It was the schooner Hesperus," with each verse throwing more emphasis and more diverse and remarkable inflections into her rather high voice until Binnie at last stopped in the middle of a row and looked downright uneasy.

Knowing that the twenty-two verses would take approximately four and a half minutes, I settled down to make the best of it.

"Down came the storm and smote amain
      The vessel in her strength.
   She shuddered and paused like a frightened steed. . . ."

I suppose it was a little odd that a sailor's daughter should choose this tragic story as her favorite recitation. As a matter of fact we neither of us gave much credence to the melancholy tale. We were certainly far from identifying our handsome Father with the unfortunate skipper or the birdlike *Miranda* with a mere schooner. In my complacent imagination *Miranda* was always riding out high and harmless seas, buoyant as a cork. There was simply no place for anxiety in our carefree, sheltered world. Even the sharp grief of our mother's death seven years ago had been short lived, though the sense of loss never quite faded. I was just old enough to remember her as a gentle presence in trailing dresses of blue and white with a lingering perfume like the lavender which still clung about her sheets and shawls in the mahogany tallboy in her room.

"Christ save us all from a death like this. . . ."

Lucy came at last to a triumphant halt. Stunned, we gathered ourselves together to applaud.

[7]

"Yes, you've got the gift," said Alec. "That'll be something to remember out there in the desert when we're sitting by the campfire, dreaming of home."

"Dreaming's the word." Binnie got up briskly. "Somebody'll be dreaming all night after this. Not to mention nightmares. Off to bed now, both of you, and you too, Alec."

"I wonder how you do become an actress," said Lucy when she had recovered her breath.

"You may wonder," said Binnie, "but that's as far as you'll get. The stage isn't the life for you or any decent young lady. Actresses! They may look fine enough on the stage with their silks and their feathers. But what are they like off it I ask you? No better than they should be, most of them. People that belong nowhere. You should have more sense than to encourage her, Alec, knowing what she's like when she takes up with an idea."

"No, it's not the life for you, Miss Lucy," said Alec hastily. "You wouldn't have the stamina. They're a penniless lot mostly. Take those we saw tonight. They're no better than bankrupt according to what Sarah heard. You couldn't help but admire them, bowing and smiling over their bouquets with ruin staring them in the face. But it wouldn't do for a delicate young lady like you or Miss Ellen."

"Your place is here at Saxelby Mill," Binnie said, lifting the kettle off the hob and beginning to rake out the fire, "and will be for many a long year. The master'll be home for good after this voyage and he'll want you and Ellen with him after his lonely travels. My, the heat in here. It's something serious."

She dragged the heavy door open and we looked straight out into the scented night, dark and soft as velvet.

"Plenty of things will have happened before I march over

that footbridge again," said Alec as he joined his mother on the threshold.

"Ned Kirkup might have got round to mending it, for one thing," put in Binnie crisply.

"You two young ladies'll be grown up and married maybe," Alec went on.

"I'd be rather a young bride at sixteen," Lucy declared, "but Ellen will be eighteen and quite old enough. She'll certainly have her hair up. But when Father comes home, I don't suppose we shall want to marry. We'll be such a cosy little family living here together, the three of us and Binnie."

"And Alec will come back," I said quickly, seeing Binnie's face, "and marry Sarah and they'll live in one of Southern's cottages. And there'll be Cousin Rose."

"I didn't mention Cousin Rose," said Lucy, "because I have a feeling that if we don't talk about her or think about her even, she may actually come at last."

She used the tone we always used when speaking of Cousin Rose—a tone muted and tense, as when one contemplates the vision of some scarcely attainable bliss. Though we talked of Rose continually, we neither of us really believed in her physical existence.

Only when Alec had climbed the wooden stairs to his room over the kitchen was it seemly for us to come out from behind the table, our crumpled nightdresses hanging a foot below the pelisses.

"What would the Miss Pritts say?" said Lucy saucily.

Binnie had so often made use of the children of her former employer as a yardstick of decorum in bringing us up that they had become a household word.

"The Miss Pritts were never up after midnight and gallivanting round in their nightgowns to say anything. Now I'm not going to tell you again. . . ."

Lucy fled upstairs to the front of the house. I heard her delighted shriek as Binnie pursued her threateningly along the landing to our room.

Lingering by the open door in the fragrance of the spring night, I heard too the stir of young leaves on the chestnut tree by the packbridge, the placid murmur of water sliding over the weir. Two years! In that moment under the solemn stars I felt the power and mystery of time as if I actually saw it stealing away like the dark water under the Mill.

Lives could change in two years. But I saw them changing only for the better, the familiar happiness deepening into a settled and lasting tranquillity.

Chapter Two

Saxelby Mill was a quiet spot in those days, untouched by the sinister reputation that clings about it now. It lay at the bottom of a steep lane, two miles east of Cross Gap and a mile from Saxelby village. My father had come upon it quite by chance twenty years before.

One summer afternoon—he often told us about it—he had been driving a hired gig from Stanesfield to Greater Saxelby to visit friends. At that time of year the narrow turning into Mill Lane was so heavily mantled with overhanging bryony and traveler's joy that he had almost missed it. Then, his attention fixed on his horse as the gig lurched perilously down the lane, he had been surprised to find himself on the hump-backed stone bridge at the bottom, with the Mill unexpectedly on his left.

"Suddenly there it was," he told us, "between the river and the trees. Half as old as time. I got down and stood looking at it. There was scarcely a sound; only the hum of insects and the murmur of water."

I was to know and love it in all its moods, with every variation of light and shade, every change of season; but I see it now as he saw it then: the white lace of water tumbling over the weir: a blaze of crimson berries on the mountain ash sprawling low over the weed-choked mill stream.

"In five minutes," I remember Father saying, "it had become part of my life—forever."

It had long since ceased to be a mill and was then a dilapidated dwelling house, its stone roof-tiles crusted with red and silver lichen, one chimney in ruins, the garden wall crumbling into the river. But its suggestion of permanence, curiously combined with an air of fantasy—as if it had risen quietly from the water or only just detached itself from the trees on the farther bank—these were the very qualities to appeal to Father, in whose own nature romanticism and common sense held an almost equal balance.

Besides, having already proposed to my mother and come into a small inheritance, he was looking for a settled home. He lingered in the village to make enquiries, made the acquaintance of Alfred Southern, the local timber merchant who owned the Mill and half the village as well, fired him with his own enthusiastic plans for renovating the place, and offered to share the cost. The elderly tenant, scarcely able to believe his good luck, was only too willing to move into one of Southern's cottages. Workmen were busy before the end of the week.

After the first moment of infatuation, my father behaved shrewdly enough, giving proper attention to such practical matters as the drains and flues. He resisted the temptation to turn the Mill into a fine country mansion and safely invested the rest of his money in Government Bonds. But it never occurred to him, apparently, to consider whether a house half-buried in trees and with its foundations slipping into a stream was the most suitable place in which to install a delicate young wife with already tainted lungs.

But Lilith our mother was a gentle, uncomplaining creature. Her life at the Mill, from all accounts, was one of utter contentment though much of the time she was alone with her two little girls and Binnie and Alec. My father's leaves were rapturously happy until quite suddenly, according to Binnie, it was all over.

"She just sank like a candle. It was unbelievable how quickly she went. Your father couldn't seem to take it in when he came home that first time after she died. . . ."

Lucy and I had of course idealized her memory to the point of endowing her with almost saintly qualities. Her bedroom at the west end of the house, overlooking the bridge and the valley beyond, had become a shrine.

"Let's go and look at Mother's things," one of us would suggest, an invitation never to be resisted. We would creep along the upper landing and reverently open the door, having first taken off our shoes to save the carpet. The white bed-curtains, the canopy lined with pink tarlatan, the muslin-draped window aroused in both of us a pious awe which we certainly did not feel in church.

Then one of us would carefully pull out the top drawer of

the mahogany dressing table and one by one we would take out the "things," delicately laying them in a row beside the silver-mounted brushes and caskets.

Those cherished relics! A stopperless porcelain perfume bottle with the picture of a shepherdess inset on one side, a handmade purse of silver beads and silk thread, a Valentine with a heart and roses painted on silk in a frame of white lace, a jet amulet on a moiré ribbon, a mother-of-pearl and tortoise-shell needlework box with ivory-handled utensils. Time after time we admired them, held them up to the light, discussed their history, then put them carefully back and tiptoed from the room.

Most precious of all were the gold earrings, each one a pendant flower in the shape of a rose. I remembered my mother talking about them more than once. One of the wires had worn thin and broken so that she had been obliged to put them away. But before that she had worn them constantly and —this was the circumstance we felt to be of particular interest —Cousin Rose had had a pair of earrings exactly the same. In fact she had had hers first; and when Mother had gone as a girl to live at Appleby End after her own parents died, Uncle Adam and Aunt Ann had given her this identical pair, specially made by the goldsmith in Athelby who had made the first pair to his own design for Cousin Rose. They were considered to be quite unique.

Memories of our mother were indissolubly bound up with her stories of those girlhood days at Appleby End—and of Cousin Rose.

"You and Lucy will be just as Rose and I used to be," she would tell me, "except that we were almost exactly of an age and even more alike. We were both light-haired and much of a size."

Uncle Adam had been comfortably off. The girls were "nicely" educated and Aunt Ann conducted her household with more ease and leisure than most farmers' wives could enjoy. I never grew tired of hearing of those far-off days: of the farmhouse with its spacious sunny rooms; the rose-red walled garden; the mulberry tree; the cool dairies with their wide milk pans and well-scrubbed churns. There had been many visitors, musical evenings in the autumn, picnics in summer.

The two girls had played duets together, slept in the same four-poster bed and dreamed of marrying two brothers and naming their daughters after each other. In perfect amity they planned their lives, as closely intertwined as two strands of the honeysuckle round the arbor where they stitched their samplers.

Except that I had been named Rose Ellen, none of those girlish dreams had been realized. Early in her teens my mother had begun to show symptoms of the dreaded consumption which had carried off both her parents. Eventually she was sent to stay with Great Aunt Lumley in the gentler climate of the Isle of Wight, where she met and married my father.

She had never gone back to Appleby End. The journey was long and difficult. Later she had been occupied with her home and children. Meanwhile Uncle Adam's affairs had taken an unfortunate turn. Aunt Ann had died ten years ago, but he lingered on, a fractious old man embittered by financial losses.

"Things are not the same at Appleby End," Mother would say sadly and standing at her knee, I would feel my heart contract with a child's anguished sympathy for the mysterious suffering of grown-up people.

"Poor Rose" had given her life to looking after her father. She had never married. It came to be understood that she had had a "disappointment." I remember an atmosphere of head-shaking and sighs, the clicking of tongues.

But all would be made up to her one day. She would come and make her home with us. She and Mother would be to each other all that they had ever been. . . .

When Mother died, Father wrote to Cousin Rose assuring her that the offer of a home was still open: there was ample room at the Mill for herself and Uncle Adam too: he would be grateful for her help in bringing up his daughters. Rose had replied appreciatively but she had been noncommittal. We had expected her with varying degrees of optimism for seven years. We continued to hope.

More than a year ago had come the news of Uncle Adam's death. Rose was "free at last" and "wretchedly lonely." She would let the house and land and come to make her home with Lilith's girls.

Since then Father had heard from her once, at Christmas. There were difficulties; it was not easy to find a tenant; lawyers were unbelievably slow.

Lucy and I persisted in expecting her daily. Each night she figured prominently in our prayers.

"We beseech Thee, O Lord, to let Cousin Rose come soon," was my modest request.

Lucy was more insistent.

"We ask Thee, O Lord, in Thy infinite mercy, to let Cousin Rose come *tomorrow*."

Often in the morning when we had given regard to the weather like true sailors' daughters and calculated in our own highly inaccurate fashion Father's probable position on the high seas, Lucy would say: "Not a very good day for Cousin Rose to travel if she *should* be traveling today," or "What a lovely day for Cousin Rose! I think it quite likely that she will come today."

Inevitably Rose had drifted into the realm of superstition. We envisaged her coming as an ethereal visitation. She would appear from the larger air like the martins that nested in our eaves, one day long absent, the next miraculously there. We would look up from the garden and see her, smiling on the bridge.

Liberally endowed with our father's romantic imagination —a faculty increased in us no doubt by the secluded nature of our life at the Mill—we had bestowed on Rose all the good qualities of both our mother and herself. When Lucy hung over the pictures on the music covers of pensive, large-eyed maidens in lace fichus, I knew that she was thinking of Cousin Rose, while I saw her as wise, good, and beautiful, bringing one day to the Mill all the mellow charm of Appleby End.

Meanwhile we were marvelously content without her. She gave us the one thing we lacked: something to long for.

"I don't know what to make of you," Binnie once said. "Your two heads are in the clouds most of the time and there's not much to choose between you for airy-fairy ideas. You mustn't expect too much from your cousin, supposing she ever comes. Times change. And people change. From what I can make out she's had a trying life, nursing her old father and losing her expectations—and her hoped-for husband too according to what your mother said. You never know how a disappointment will take people. She was a girl when your mother knew her. She isn't as young now as she used to be by any means. Look at me. I was as thin as a wand once and a regular tease to the men. . . ."

"Mother loved her," Lucy protested. "She must be nice."

"I'm not saying she isn't. But your mother always saw the best in people. She didn't know the world. Not that I'm saying anything against your Cousin Rose—Miss Warden I should say. But you talk as if she was an angel from heaven and that's what no human being is. Some more like the opposite which I won't name. Now out of my kitchen, there's a pair of doves, while I make up the oven for pastry. No, angels don't walk the earth, not these days. At any rate not in these parts."

It was after this that Lucy had her dream about the angel in the orchard.

But in the confidential depths of the goosefeather bed—or swinging in our hammocks in the orchard—Lucy and I had not neglected the interesting question of the "disappointment." We were wiser now, but in our younger days the nature of Cousin Rose's trouble had been entirely mysterious. It was when the word arose in one of our spelling lessons with Miss Southern that Lucy first put out an exploratory feeler.

"What exactly happens, Miss Southern, when a lady has a disappointment?"

"That is scarcely a subject we need to discuss now, Lucy, if you please," said Miss Southern with rather less than her usual vague sweetness and Lucy subsided in blushes of shame. No need to remind her that such a question would never have crossed the lips of a Miss Pritt.

But Lucy was inclined to persevere and it was she who raised the subject with Nancy Kirkup, the girl from Mill Cottage who came in to help with the rough work and washing.

Nancy's reaction was more straightforward.

[18]

"A disappointment? Oh, you mean like Cissie Pellow. Terrible, isn't it, what it does to them?"

Our hearts sank. What unspeakable misfortune then had befallen Cousin Rose? But we were intrigued too. That very afternoon we took our walk along Plum Lane in the direction of the Pellows' cottage. It was a bright October day, I remember. Lucy must have been about ten years old at the time. At any rate we were young enough still to enjoy scrambling up and down the high banks on either side of the lane to look for late blackberries, and the oak tree beside the Pellows' cottage had shed such a wealth of acorns that in gathering them to make a doll's tea set, we almost forgot what we had come for.

But as we stooped for the nuts, through a gap in the hedge I caught sight of a figure fluttering in the sunlight among the gorse and bracken of the sloping field.

"Look! There's Cissie Pellow."

We knelt down to watch her, framed in the yellowing hazel leaves; a thin woman, hatless, with a quantity of light fluffy hair. She wore an outlandish dress in the Dolly Varden style more than ten years out of date: an overskirt of chintz, very short in front and bunched out in panniers over a petticoat of faded blue cotton. Worn with thick country boots and black stockings, this costume struck even my innocent eye as vaguely unsuitable, and there was something odd in Cissie Pellow's haphazard way of moving among the gorse bushes.

Whether she was searching for eggs or for a stray hen I cannot say. She looked not unlike a stray hen herself as she hurried forward in sudden awkward spurts and then stood stock-still, plucking at something on her skirt.

Presently we knew that although we had kept quite still, she had seen us. She had turned her face in our direction. It was a rather long, pale face; and I saw its expression of vacant silliness change to a complacent smirk. In a moment she made off toward the cottage with the same erratic and fluttering walk, and before we had time to take in the fact of her disappearance, she had emerged again from the doorway and come waveringly back to within a few feet of the hedge.

This time she was carrying, cradled in her arms, a shabby bundle, and looking down at it with an expression of exaggerated tenderness. Then she began to rock it, gently at first but more and more wildly until I felt Lucy grip my arm in concern.

"It's a doll," I breathed, scarcely finding reassurance in the amazing fact.

"But she's quite old."

"I know. But I think she must be a little . . . crazy." And suddenly we leapt to our feet and fled down the lane, slithering on the acorns and stumbling over ruts and stones. Nor did we slow down until we were safely back within sight of the Mill.

"Did she think it was a baby?"

"I don't know."

It had been a disturbing experience; so much so that we scarcely discussed it though many a time afterwards we walked past the cottage, half-hoping, half-dreading to catch sight of Cissie Pellow again. And we carefully refrained from connecting her in any way with Cousin Rose.

As we grew taller, our vocabulary increased. Occasionally we referred to Cousin Rose as having been "crossed in love"; the expression having a dignified sadness more worthy of her; or we wondered about her "unhappy love affair."

But on the whole we did not think about it very much as we dawdled happily through the days. In the mornings we walked to Saxelby for lessons with Miss Southern. In the afternoons we roamed the woods and river banks or gathered fruit in the orchard. In the evenings we played and sang or wrote to Father; or sat in the shadowy kitchen listening breathlessly to Nancy's lurid tales as she cleaned the knives, tales of suicides and sudden deaths, evil omens and blind beggars, mysteries and vanishings, until Binnie packed her off home in the twilight and we settled down to play draughts or Beggar-my-neighbor by the fire.

So the innocent days slipped by until that May morning when the world began to change.

Chapter Three

Alec went off in Morton's milk cart at seven o'clock. As he stood bareheaded under the chestnut tree saying goodbye, his buttons glittering, his belt pipeclayed to the whiteness of snow—there was an unexpected solemnity in the leave-taking. We shook hands almost in silence, overawed by the splendor of his scarlet coat and the realization that he might after all be going to fight for the Queen—perhaps even to die for her.

As the horse pounded up the steep lane and round the curve, we stood each with an arm round Binnie, waving our handkerchieves; and even through the remorseless whale bone of her stays I felt her take in a long breath and release it in a single despairing sigh.

But almost at once she said, "You two must have your breakfast. I want to get on." If the skies fell, Wednesday would still be baking day. We went indoors and down to the kitchen where our porridge was keeping hot in the oven and the table was set with the blue Staffordshire ware and a jug of the goat's milk which Father insisted on our drinking for our health.

Later in the morning Lucy and I went to Cross Gap to see the crowning of the May Queen. It was one of the occasions when we liked to wear our best clothes. Apart from our rare trips into Stanesfield with Father, and the weekly attendance at church, there was nothing more formal than an invitation to tea at Miss Southern's to give us an excuse for dressing up. Yet with a superb disregard for practical realities, Father persisted in bringing us home china-handled parasols, feather muffs, mother-of-pearl fans, and similar frivolities.

"I thought you'd like them," he would say helplessly. "They might come in useful. . . ."

And indeed we did like them, however unsuited to our way of life. Sometimes on wet days we would dress up in all our finery and mince up and down the landing, bowing distantly to each other as we passed in a wave of potpourri.

"Are not umbrellas of great antiquity?" Lucy would enquire in a fair imitation of Miss Southern, who must have been the last surviving adherent of Mangnall's questions.

"Yes," I would reply as we simultaneously unfurled our lace-edged parasols. "The Greeks, the Romans, and all eastern nations used them to keep off the sun. 'Ombrello' in Italian signifies 'a little shade.'"

We were not so scatterbrained as to take the lace-edged parasols on our two-mile tramp to Cross Gap; but we did venture for once to wear our white stockings with the red clocks (already, had we known it, several years outmoded). We also wore our blue polonaise dresses, matching velveteen hats with upturned brims, black shoes and kid gloves, and we each carried a linen bag containing a buttered tea-cake and a horn cup.

We reached the gate as Mr. Southern drove past in his dogcart. We knew that he was going to London on business and would be away for a month. He gave the reins to the groom and walked up the hill with us.

"You are looking very fine if I may say so," he observed, with the sort of unsmiling humor that was the nearest he ever got to unbending and he told us to be good girls while he was away. "Though you're almost too grown-up now to get into mischief," he added with a stiff movement of the lips that was almost a smile.

"I wonder if Mr. Southern is going forth to seek a bride," Lucy said as we watched the dogcart travel along the highroad and we giggled all the way along Plum Lane at the thought of a man almost as old as Father having such romantic aspirations.

All the same we were flattered by his attention and sorry that as usual there had been no one about to witness it.

"The trouble with us is that we're neither one thing nor the other," panted Lucy, aiming a blow with her bag at Pellows' gander as we scurried past. "We aren't really ladies like the Miss Pritts and yet we aren't village girls either."

We had faced the dilemma before. Our father's connections were good; he was the son of a family whose ancestral home was Barrow Hall in the Lake District; but we had long ago conceded the social palm to the Miss Pritts who, according to Binnie, had said "Papa," whereas we said "Father." They had also "come out" at eighteen and gone to balls in white dresses with "clouds" on their heads. No such prospect awaited us so long as we lived at the Mill, though we had hopes that when Father retired from the sea there would be more visiting and company.

"Just at present," Lucy went on, "I think I'd rather be one of the village girls."

"That's because you'd like to have a turn at being May Queen, isn't it?"

"There's absolutely no hope, I know, but I'd like it more than anything. Of course even if we went to school with the other girls, they might not choose me but at least there'd be a chance—and we could plait the ribbons and dance instead of always just watching."

"I'd rather watch."

Coming out into the sun again from the shadow of a hazel copse, we heard music—the faint, tinny notes of the school piano.

"They've started. Hurry!" Lucy sprang forward, her fair ringlets swaying, her scarlet clocks darting back and forth above the sky-blue puddles. "Oh, Ellen, there's a fiddle. Old Mr. Hicks must have got over his bronchitis. Hurrah!"

She careered down the grassy path toward the village—a cluster of gray cottages round two sides of a level green by the river; at one end the church and school and beyond, green slopes rising between dry stone walls to a dark line of moor. Then she waited for me, suddenly demure, and we went together to the wooden seat by the school gate where the children were already forming in twos for the procession.

Old Mr. Hicks arranged his beard, caught the eye of the lady at the piano and struck up with "Butterfly." Well scrubbed in their clean shirts and pinafores, the children followed the new Queen to her throne, a tall school chair decorated with flowers and ribbons, where she knelt—lucky Daisy Marshall—to receive the crown of primroses and forget-me-nots from last year's Queen. Two small girls with funereal solemnity arranged her train and handed her a posy. Safely installed, Daisy suddenly flushed and smiled with relief. The children bowed and curtsied.

"Isn't it lovely?" Lucy breathed.

The music changed to "Come, Lasses and Lads," the children scurried to take the ribbons dangling from the Maypole and the plaiting began.

Lucy nudged me.

"Look. He's there. The Wild Boy."

I had already seen him five minutes before, climbing over the wall with long-legged ease as he always did, his coat over his shoulder and his face flushed with exercise as if he had walked a long way. I had watched him with the same feeling of surprise that I felt every year, surprise that he should bother to come quite deliberately to see the schoolchildren dance round the Maypole.

Yet there was never any doubt that he did come deliberately. He was leaning against the wall watching with a pleased intentness as if he really enjoyed the colored pattern of ribbons, the solemnly circling children, the thin harmony of piano, fiddle, and murmuring river, all cupped in the sheltering green hills.

Almost from the first I had noticed in him a special quality of ease—the natural poise of perfect self-confidence, despite his odd and unconventional appearance. His clothes were always shabby, as rough and practical as a farm laborer's. Last year for instance, he had worn a sleeveless waistcoat and a blue striped shirt such as no gentleman would wear—with a battered wide-awake hat. But he stood erect and looked round with a lively awareness by no means typical of an uneducated countryman.

Our acquaintance with him was one of those slow-growing relationships familiar to all who live in the country. He always came to the May Walk but we never saw him from one May Day to the next. And we had never spoken to him until last year when, after the dancing, he had come over to us, raised his hat and said, "Good morning. I should like to show you something."

Before our astonished eyes he had thrust his hand inside his waistcoat and drawn out a white kitten.

"Oh, how lovely!" Lucy had put out her hand impulsively. "Please let me hold it."

He gave her the kitten and she laid it in her lap.

"I brought it for you."

"For me?"

"Yes. Would you like it?"

He stood looking down at her indulgently. Now that he was close to us I noticed that he had a pinched look. There was a whiteness about his mouth that made me wonder if he had enough to eat. He would be about seventeen, two or three years older than I. He clearly thought of Lucy as a pretty child and indeed there was a perfect aptness in the choice of gift which dispelled at once any feeling that he was a stranger.

"Mine? To keep you mean?"

Lucy's eyes were like stars.

"I should love to have it. Oh, Ellen! A white kitten of my very own. I shall call it Blanche. That means white, you know, in French."

"I thought you'd like it. I wanted it to have a good home."
He was obviously pleased. We talked about the kitten for a
minute; then he made a slight bow and went away. As Lucy
fondled her new pet, I watched him stride across the wall and
up the hill among the new green bracken.

We had gone home full of the incident.

"He'll be one of the Aylwards," Binnie said at once, "from
Kindlehope Grange. In fact there's only one boy and the old
man living up there now."

"What sort of people are they?" I asked.

"The Aylwards? It's hard to say. This boy now. He'll be
Mark. His mother died years back. She was from the South.
His father's dead too. Enough to eat? Sakes, I should hope so.
They own all the farms at Kindlehope. But I don't know who
looks after them now. Likely they'll have a couple living in to
do for them. Old Mr. Aylward's a great scholar, they say, always reading and studying and he's been a magistrate for
years—chairman of the Bench. They were always people that
went their own way, the Aylwards. . . ."

The conversation had drifted to other things. But the gift
of the kitten, the few details of his history and our growing
familiarity with his appearance had gradually cohered into
something like a friendship, so that all at once, catching his
eye across the green, I smiled.

He came over, raising the still more battered wide-awake
which the intervening year had turned into a very old hat
indeed.

"Good morning."

I had forgotten the unusual husky quality in his voice. We
all looked at one another—familiar, yet because twelve
months is a long time when one is very young—strangers

again. For one thing, he had grown a good deal and seemed now more of a young man than a boy. Though still thin, he had lost something of his wild look. Apart from the battered hat, his appearance was more spruce. He wore a white shirt and corduroy breeches and gaiters.

"Blanche sends her respects to you," Lucy said.

"I trust she is well."

"She's grown beyond recognition. You'll be interested to hear that she has had her portrait painted."

"By you—or your sister."

He smiled, with the look of friendly attentiveness I had first noticed in him.

"Neither. By a real artist."

I explained how one morning we had suddenly been aware of an artist seated on the bridge with his easel and canvas already set up.

"We knew that he was an artist because of his slouch hat and red tie," said Lucy.

"Not by what you saw on the canvas?"

"That was later. I mean when he first appeared."

"You give the impression that he dropped from the clouds," said Mark.

"It's a curious thing," I told him, "but it was rather like that. From the windows or the garden we can only see the bridge, not the lane on either side—because of the trees—so that people do have the air of appearing by magic."

"And the artist?"

"He was painting the Mill," I said. "Perhaps you know it. People think it rather picturesque. We went out to watch him and when he saw Lucy holding the kitten he said she would make a charming subject. Father was not at home but fortunately Mr. Southern had called to pay the wages. He's Father's closest friend—and he keeps an eye on things while Father's away."

"Both eyes," said Lucy.

"He said that he didn't think Father would mind. Lucy wore the dress she is wearing now and sat in a little wooden chair by the lavender hedge with one of the windows open behind her."

"And then he folded his easel and went away, taking the picture with him?" He smiled regretfully, knowing how we had felt.

"We thought he might have left us a sketch. Father would have liked it."

"Still, we must be thankful that Blanche is to be among the immortals," Mark said.

"Oh dear, not for a long time yet, I hope," said Lucy in consternation.

We laughed. For me it was a moment of dreamlike happiness. The hazy brightness, the lilting music scarcely as resonant as the bleat of moorland sheep, the muffled beat of children's footsteps in the grass, the moving rainbow of ribbons all combined to arouse in me a tingling sense of life, as though I breathed it in with the pure upland air and felt it revolve round me with the throb and dazzle of a spinning top. It would have been no surprise if the straggle of watching mothers and babies, the church and the entire circle of hills had begun to revolve too, leaving our three selves fixed forever in the center, bound together in an enchanted stillness.

We shared our lunch with Mark. He ate ravenously and filled our horn cups for us at the pump. He himself drank from his cupped hands and wiped the drops from his chin with the back of his wrist.

The dancing was over. Miss Blewett the schoolmistress was marshaling the children in front of the Rector before dismissing them to their dinners and a half holiday. We stood up too and Mark took off his hat. Hands together, eyes closed, the children sang their grace.

> "Be present at our table, Lord;
> Be here and everywhere adored;
> Thy creatures bless and grant that we
> May feast in Paradise with thee."

When the Rector had given the blessing, we waited, in one of those awkward moments of transition from the elevated to the mundane, for there had been something touching in the children's voices, husky and sweet.

"A Christian blessing on a pagan festival," Mark said.

"Pagan?" I was not sure what he meant.

"The crowning of the Queen, the flowers, the Maypole—they're as old as fairy trees and wishing wells. We've been wise enough—or lucky enough—to purge them of unwholesome magic and lodge them safely within the bosom of the church."

He might almost have been quoting from a book or one of the learned articles in the Cornhill magazine, but there was no mockery in his tone.

"That reminds me." He suddenly dropped his scholarly manner. "I'd like to show you something."

Remembering the conjuring trick he had played last year, we were instantly attentive as he put his hand into his breeches pocket. But this time it was no kitten or guinea pig that he held out.

"What is it?" Lucy sounded frankly disappointed.

Stepping nearer, I saw what seemed to be a perfectly ordinary gray stone about the size of a large cameo brooch—a piece of flint—one of hundreds turned up by a plough perhaps, and not worth stooping to pick up.

Then I saw that the stone, instead of being solid, had a hole apparently bored through the middle, a perfect circle in the dead center so that I saw a segment of the lines on Mark's palm as through a spy glass.

"How did you make that hole in it?"

"I didn't make it. I found it. It's a thing you find once in a lifetime, with luck."

"Are there others?" I asked.

"You don't know? It's a hagstone."

He spoke in a lowered voice, almost with awe; and his seriousness impressed Lucy and me so that we both gazed at the stone, trying to discover in it some quality remarkable enough to account for his manner.

"Do you mean—something to do with witchcraft?" I asked, seeing Lucy's eyes widen.

"It's a protection against witchcraft and other sorts of evil," he said. "I found it on our land—one of thousands and thousands of useless stones."

"And you knew at once what it was?"

"Of course. Belief in hagstones is as old as dancing round the Maypole. Do you wonder?"

He held out the stone with its perfect circle, so exquisitely shaped as surely to have been contrived by a craftsmanship beyond human achieving. For a second I caught the blaze of

[32]

a scarlet ribbon through that mysterious eye, before he placed the stone again in the palm of his hand.

"I think it must be because of the mystic power of the circle," he said thoughtfully. "The magic center, like the Maypole, you see."

"It's a very precious thing," I said, meaning really that it was precious to him.

"Yes." He glanced up, his eyes a flash of blue. Now that the flush of exercise had faded, his face was pale; and though his tone was half-teasing, he was serious too. "You must take great care of it."

"Do you mean that you are going to give it to us."

Instinctively Lucy had almost held out her hand.

"Yes. But this is for your sister."

"For me?"

"For Ellen?"

We spoke together.

"Yes. For Miss Ellen."

"Of course."

Lucy spoke a little too eagerly. I knew that she was abashed. Mark knew it too. He smiled.

"Your sister will need it more than you."

"Do you mean that she will need it to keep away evil spirits? But Ellen is so good."

"That's why."

He must have been joking, of course, but I felt embarrassed, and when Lucy said at the top of her voice, "What exactly does evil mean?" I remember looking round quickly, feeling conspicuous. But the green was deserted. Everyone else had gone home.

"I know that evil is something to be delivered from," Lucy

went on. "Is it something worse than bad luck? It sounds more serious."

"I'm not sure," Mark said. "It's the absence of everything good, I suppose, so that there's a sort of vacuum and the other sort of things take over."

"The other sort of things?" Again Lucy's voice rang out like a challenge.

I saw them in a series of disquieting images, the things that had frightened me as a child: the tearing blood-stained beak of a sparrow-hawk, the beating of wings among the cobwebs in the coachhouse rafters, the weed-choked depths of the old mill race. But now the scenes reshaped themselves harmlessly with no power to disturb me, dazzled as I was with happiness.

"Do you think there really are evil spirits?" Lucy was saying.

"I'm sure there are good ones," Mark replied. "Why shouldn't there be evil ones too?"

"Not here," I protested, watching a lamb suddenly leap off the ground with its four feet in the air as if in response to a subterranean drum beat. "One doesn't expect to find anything evil in a place like Cross Gap."

"Not here," said Mark. "Where else but here in the very heart of England? It was here in these valleys, remember, that they kept to the old ways even when the new religion came."

"Is there a new religion?" Lucy asked.

"I mean Christianity."

"Oh, I see. You're talking about a long time ago."

"Not so long in the life of these hills."

"I wonder what the old ways were like," Lucy observed, speaking, I knew, out of a bottomless ignorance.

"Savage and cruel, I'm afraid," said Mark. "There would be human sacrifices, perhaps, and local devils and covens of witches."

"Oh, if it's witches you're talking about," said Lucy confidently, "they had one in Saxelby not so long ago. Nancy's grandmother knew her."

"Hush, Lucy," I said, "it isn't a thing to joke about." I had always found it one of the more uncomfortable of Nancy's stories. I had first heard it when my head was just level with the kitchen table and the dreadful words seemed to come from on high, to the hypnotic accompaniment of a blade flashing back and forth on the knifeboard so that it might have been the reek of brimstone I was breathing in instead of bath brick; for Nancy was always most eloquent when she was cleaning the knives.

"They drove her out of the parish. Still in her white apron she was," Nancy would say, her face shining in the firelight, her wrists strong and purposeful as she pressed hard on a knife. "They weren't havin' the likes of her. She had the evil eye, you see. Honest! My grandma told me. She was running, with a stitch in her side—right past the crossroads and all the women after her, banging their pan lids and fire irons. Eh! The noise! My grandma said. . . ."

"The Saxelby witch," Mark was saying. "I wonder what became of her."

"She just vanished, I suppose, as witches do," I said and was suddenly aware of Saxelby Crag squatting like a huge toad just below the horizon to the east and looking black as night even on this spring morning.

"She chose a rather inhospitable stretch of country to vanish into," Mark observed.

"It wasn't exactly choice."

"No." He laughed. "The women of Saxelby roused to vengeance would be a pretty compelling force."

"And yet she was probably quite innocent," I said. "So far as I know she had done nothing wrong."

"At any rate she's gone. The last of the witches!" declared Lucy with a touch of regret.

"I don't know," said Mark. "It wouldn't surprise me if there were still one or two of them about."

"Now you're teasing."

But to my surprise he went on quite seriously: "It seems to be more or less accepted that there are individuals through whom sinister forces can work. It may not be of their seeking. They become, so to speak, helpless instruments. . . ."

He must have enjoyed the way we hung on his words. Certainly we made a perfect audience, as gullible a pair of country cousins as he could have found. But I don't think he was trying to impress us, and I was to remember the conversation in very different circumstances. "Suppose this woman was such an instrument. Their idea of dispossessing an evil spirit was sound enough, only they chose the wrong way of going about it."

"But they certainly got rid of her."

"For a time perhaps."

"You don't think she might come back?" asked Lucy eagerly.

"She—or another? Who knows? But the evil forces might well have lingered. You can't drive them out by violence. You'd be more likely to make them worse."

[36]

"Then how?"

"Only by exercising a stronger influence for good. That's the whole principle of exorcism—casting out devils. The hagstone would be of no use on its own." He smiled and held it out to me. "But it might help."

"No, really," I protested. "You found it and you ought to keep it. It's such a very unusual thing. You'll never find another."

"I want you to have it."

Reluctantly I took it. Mark's hand was warm on mine for a second but the stone felt heavy and cold.

"Thank you," I said. "I'll take great care of it."

And because the awkward hesitation I felt was shot through with a sense of the sweetness of his words, "I want you to have it," I felt my voice tremble and turned my head away. But the same adventurous lamb came trotting up and then stopped dead, its wedge-shaped white face turned toward us with a look of such ridiculous innocence, that I burst out laughing.

The cracked bell in the church tower struck twelve. After that there seemed nothing more to say. We wished him good-bye and he walked away over the wall and up the hill through the bronze and green bracken.

"How kind he is!" Lucy said as we climbed the field path, "giving us presents when we scarcely know him. I suppose it was all right to accept them. It simply never occurred to me not to take Blanche. After all, a kitten must have a home. But when he gave you the hagstone I had the most extraordinary feeling. . . ."

"What sort of feeling?"

"That it was important. He didn't in the least mind parting

with Blanche—but that old stone—he seemed to want to keep it."

"I wish he had kept it," I burst out. "I didn't want it."

"But he wanted you to have it as much as he wanted to keep it. More. He was *torn,* you see. He's an unusual person, isn't he? Ellen, let's give him a present next year. I wonder what he'd like."

She prattled cheerfully about knitted watchguards, pen wipers and bookmarks as we trudged along the lane in the noon-day sun.

The hagstone lay heavy in my pocket, and always against my warm hand, it felt cold.

Chapter Four

The moment we entered the hall I saw the letter lying on the brass tray. It was addressed to me. My first thought was that it was from Father. Then I saw the writing.

"It's from Cousin Rose."

"Open it quickly. If she's written to you instead of to Father, it must be because . . . Oh, can she possibly be . . ."

For once Lucy's frenzy scarcely exceeded my own. My hands shook as I opened the envelope to find, sure enough, the long-awaited news that she was coming:

> . . . all the arrangements here being now complete. I cannot recollect whether I wrote to you about the tenants. They are

Colonel and Mrs. Graham, home from India and wanting a place for their retirement. They move in on Saturday and I should be with you on Tuesday or Wednesday of next week.

Here she had evidently paused. The next paragraph had been written in a different ink; and in a different mood perhaps? The writing was less even, as if the hand had trembled slightly—with haste—or another kind of agitation.

It has not been easy. I have hardly felt equal. . . . Everything seems to be coming to an end and perhaps after all that would be for the best. Another life. . . . [The words had been crossed out and she had gone on more prosaically,] Of all things I detest a railway journey and having remained at home so long, I find the prospect almost too much. So tired. . . .

The last two words were curiously affecting as if a sigh of utter weariness had arisen from the very page. But Cousin Rose had concluded primly enough:

Trusting to see you soon, I remain your affectionate cousin, Rose Warden

Altogether the letter was not what I had expected. I reread it thoughtfully. Of course she had not told us about the tenants. We had not heard from her for nearly six months. Then I had expected Cousin Rose to be more precise about the details of her arrival, more competently in command of the situation than the unfinished sentences and the disjointed style of the letter suggested; though why this should be so when I had never met her, had known her only through the interchange of two or three letters and faint memories of Mother's stories of her girlhood companion, I could scarcely tell.

The note paper had a dog-eared look, as if it had been folded and unfolded several times or had lain about for a while before being put into the envelope. Had she even at the time of writing been uncertain as to whether to come or not?

"Cousin Rose hasn't dated her letter."

I made the discovery with a touch of alarm. Lucy, who had been swinging rapturously on the banisters, returned abruptly to an upright position.

"When was it mailed?"

The envelope too had a grubby look as if it had been dropped and trodden on so that I could not make out either date or postmark.

"Is that a six? April 26 perhaps?"

"You don't suppose she meant last Saturday?"

"In that case she could be arriving today. Binnie, Binnie!" Lucy was already half way down the back stairs. "Cousin Rose is coming."

I followed her into the kitchen where Binnie, having just set her loaves to cool in their upturned tins, was looking startled.

"It's just that she doesn't say which Tuesday or Wednesday," I said soothingly, handing her the letter.

"It's my belief," Binnie reddened with annoyance as she read it, "that Tom Leish has been up to his tricks again. Ten to one he forgot this letter or sat drinking in the Moorcock and couldn't be bothered to come as far as the Mill. I thought he had a hang-dog look when he shuffled in here at eleven o'clock making pleasant conversation about the weather and the smell of bread rising. Like as not you should have had this days ago."

"She could be here any minute," said Lucy dramatically.

"And the bed not aired—and nothing to eat in the house."

[41]

As we gazed at each other in consternation, there came through the open door the rumble of wheels from the brow of the hill. Unprepared for the mighty event now that it had come so precipitately upon us at last, we all three stood as if paralyzed. Then we heard the shout of a driver: the slurring sound of a brake being applied: heavy hooves on the loose surface of the road.

"It's more than a cab surely." Nancy had come in from the scullery, all agog. "It sounds like one of them big drays."

Recovering ourselves, we rushed to the gate in time to hear the snapping and tearing of boughs as a station wagon drawn by two Clydesdales rounded the last bend.

"Saxelby Mill?" called out the man holding the head of the leader.

"Name of Westerdale?" The driver mopped his brow, evidently relieved at having brought his team safely down to the bridge. "There's a load of luggage here. Somebody's coming to stop for a bit, I should say—and I don't blame them, getting here being what it is. . . ."

There followed a confused and strenuous hour while the men unloaded the luggage. Binnie, in a state of distraction, even panic, took out sheets and pillowcases and Lucy and I lugged our own mattress along the landing and made up the bed.

It had been decreed long ago—by Mother, I suppose—that Rose was to have the south room, one of the sunniest in the house, overlooking the orchard. Besides the usual bedroom furniture it had an ample tiled fireplace with a low brass curb: a velvet upholstered chaise-longue: and an adjoining dressing room, hardly bigger than a closet, with an arched window looking into the room and a door opening on to the back

[42]

stairs. For years the room had been used as a passage, giving easy access to the back of the house.

But already it had become Rose's room and there was no doubt whatever that she was coming. When we had lit a fire, cleared the drawers and put flowers on the dressing table, we stood looking in a state of dazed disbelief at her belongings, which covered every inch of the floor and overflowed into the landing: two black trunks; two wicker dress baskets; a bass bag; two portmanteaux; three or four objects sewn in hessian, probably pictures; and an unmanageable bundle consisting of long slats of wood which Binnie identified as quilting frames. Each item bore a clearly printed label, "Miss Rose Warden, Care of Captain Westerdale, Saxelby Mill, Saxelby."

The wagon lumbered off to Saxelby, the jangle of its horse bells dying away into an uneasy silence. Lunch was forgotten. Binnie and Nancy closeted themselves in the kitchen. We roamed restlessly about the garden, cutting enough flowers to fill every vase in the house. Twice we toiled up the lane to look along the empty moorland road for a cab. (Cousin Rose would travel by rail to Stanesfield and thence by road.)

"Now that we know she really is coming," said Lucy, "I wouldn't mind if she came tomorrow instead, or even the day after."

We had come temporarily to rest on the terrace outside the front door.

"Of course I'm delighted that she *is* coming."

"I know. It takes a little time to arrange one's feelings. It's going to be different."

"Much nicer of course."

"Oh, much nicer."

But as the afternoon wore on, Cousin Rose began imperceptibly to slip back into the realm of fantasy where we had learned to deal with her. I wandered down to my favorite nook in the herb garden where the last three steps led down to the river. Here the wall had crumbled away, its fallen stones mingling with the gray boulders so that the garden seemed to subside gently into the water.

I sat down, recognizing the onset of evening in the cool air from the river. The sun was low. Between the shining water and shining sky curved the dark arch of the bridge. I heard Lucy crooning to herself somewhere in the garden. A blackbird in the rowan was in full song. Feeling something heavy in my pocket, I drew out the hagstone and traced with my finger the outline of its strange smooth circle as Mark had done. Then childishly I put it to my eye, spy-glass fashion, and saw like vignettes in its tiny frame a glint of yellow gorse on the steep pasture, a drift of golden cloud, a spray of alder leaves, a black shape on the bridge.

The blackbird flew straight in front of me, sounding its alarm note. Lucy too had stopped singing. I put down the hagstone and looked at the bridge, seeing at first only an extended darkness above the parapet. Someone was standing there. A tall figure.

I think now it must have been a foreboding, that sinking of the heart.

"Ellen! She's here. Cousin Rose is here." Lucy's shriek would have wakened the dead as she hurled herself up the steps to the gate and out on to the road. "Cousin Rose. Cousin Rose. You've come at last."

Running through the garden, I saw her fling her arms round Cousin Rose in a first rapturous embrace. When I joined them, she was looking up at her, her face shining with welcome.

Cousin Rose was still standing with her left hand on the parapet, leaning on it with the whole weight of her body. I felt at once her utter exhaustion, as if she could hardly summon strength to open her lips. At her feet lay a bulging carpetbag.

"I'm Ellen. And this is Lucy. Welcome to Saxelby Mill, Cousin Rose."

"You were expecting me?"

Her voice was low and rather beautiful but she spoke as though, behind her veil, her lips were stiff, her teeth clenched. I noticed how she drew a great breath to make the simple remark as if it cost her an effort.

"We weren't sure of the day. Your letter came only this morning. But your room is ready."

I picked up the bag and had to take two hands to lift it. In stooping, I saw that the pleated frill at the bottom of her dress and even the two rows of ruching above it were gray with dust.

"But how have you come, Cousin Rose? You surely haven't walked from the Moorcock? Your bag is so heavy."

She gave a half humorous shrug, almost of despair.

"A carrier of some sort. . . ."

"You must have come with Babbitt," cried Lucy. "It isn't his day for Cross Gap but he'd have brought you here, Cousin Rose, if you'd given him a shilling extra."

"The station cab would have been best—or we could have sent Reg Morton with the pony trap if we'd known. . . ."

Again she shrugged as if the matter were scarcely of interest. The veil shrouded her features but I thought she was smiling. She wore a stylish little hat with a bunch of magenta feathers at the front, matching the revers of her black jacket. No wonder she was tired: her tight-laced bodice and narrow shoes were not designed for walking; yet her long tramp in the dust had not robbed her of an elegance of carriage which impressed me at once.

At last she raised her hand from the parapet and allowed Lucy to lead her toward the house. It was as though she were beyond caring whether she came indoors or stood forever on the bridge.

"Your luggage is all here," Lucy told her. "You'll feel quite at home with your own things around you. We've put you in the south room as Mother always said. . . ."

"You'll feel better when you've had tea. Do be careful, Cousin Rose. This handrail is rather loose."

We were so well used to avoiding the sprawling boughs of the mountain ash which overhung the footbridge that I did not think of warning her of them too. It was unfortunate that a spray of half-opened leaves should catch at her veil so that we had to stop and free her, breaking one of the threads in the process. She gave an exclamation of annoyance and pushed up the torn veil from the lower part of her face. Her lips and cheeks were deathly pale.

By this time Binnie, flushed and breathless, had emerged from the kitchen door.

"Miss Warden. You're welcome, I'm sure, as the master would tell you if he was at home. Binnock's my name and if you'd like me to show you to your room. . . ."

Whether it was Binnie's nervousness or the rather formal manner in which, after a moment's hesitation, Rose held out her hand, I cannot say, but for the first time I saw Binnie as a servant and not as the infallible, maternal power she had always seemed. Beside Cousin Rose's tall figure she looked small and stout. There was a trace of flour in her hair. Nancy was already running upstairs with a copper can of hot water; but even with Lucy and me on either side to support her, Cousin Rose was too weary to climb the second flight of stairs and seemed thankful to sink on to the sofa in the drawing room.

"She's ready to collapse, poor soul," muttered Binnie as, having lit the shavings in the fireplace, she despatched Nancy to fetch wood and hurried down to the kitchen to make tea. While I set a tray with the best Rockingham cups, Lucy fetched a pair of slippers and reverently undid Rose's shoes, then bathed her hands with a wet flannel and dried them on one of the best linen guest towels.

All this willing service Cousin Rose endured almost without a word, rather with a curious detachment as if she scarcely saw us. But we needed no encouragement. Once having grasped the fact that she needed to be looked after, we rapturously assumed the role of bond slaves, positively purring with satisfaction when, propped up with cushions and revived by her second cup of tea, she at last gathered strength to unpin her hat.

A little color had come into her lips. She had a full expressive mouth. Later on when she talked more freely, I liked to watch as she spoke and to listen to her vibrant, beautiful voice. When she took off her hat I saw that she had gray eyes, tending toward turquoise or even green according to the fall of light upon them. Now they were dark circled with weariness and as she began, naturally enough, to look round the room in an exploratory way, I had the oddly contradictory impression that although there was restlessness in those darting glances at the ornaments on the mantelpiece, at the window, Lucy and myself, there was at the same time a lifeless quality— as if the details of her new home were not quite real to her. Altogether her face was more defined, less tranquil than the dim visage of the Cousin Rose I had imagined. Carefully dropping sugar into her third cup of tea, I realized that that saintly and ethereal creature had been rather dull. . . . For better or worse, she was gone forever.

For better, surely. Gratified, I watched Cousin Rose's white teeth sinking into another wafer-thin slice of bread and butter. Apparently she had not eaten since morning. From under the window came a frantic clucking and flapping as Nancy caught a chicken and I hoped that Binnie had everything well in hand below stairs.

Meanwhile I enjoyed presiding over the tea things. It was a pretty room, the walls white paneled, with gilt sconces and mirrors in the Regency style. Our parents had not changed it except to add chintz-covered chairs and a sofa, a walnut piano with pink-ruched candle-shades, a canterbury for music, and a painted firescreen.

As always it felt a trifle damp and the fire was slow to draw in the long-empty grate, but at last the polished steel firedogs shone red, the aromatic scent of cherry wood filled the room and the mirrors, green with reflected leaves, were suddenly stippled with the gold of sunset.

A sense of familiarity stole over me. This was as I had dreamed it would be. Here at last at the Mill I felt all around me, recreated, the social grace of Appleby End—of ladies talking and drinking tea. I loved the rosy gleam of the china, the blue flame of the spirit burner, the whole scene shrunk to the proportions of a doll's house and reflected in the burnished silver kettle.

Already Lucy's color was hectic. She sat at Rose's side, pouring out a stream of information about Father, Binnie, Nancy, Alec, the Southerns. . . .

"You're talking too much, Lucy," I said. "You'll tire Cousin Rose. Do you think Lucy is like Mother, Cousin Rose?"

She turned her head and looked at Lucy with a touch of surprise as if she had only just appeared. We waited expectantly.

"Of course you never really knew Mother when she was grown up, did you? But I don't think she changed much."

Suddenly, with one of the abrupt changes that we were to find characteristic of her, Cousin Rose's expression relaxed into one of utter tenderness.

"Lucy is very like her mother as a girl," she said, and stretching out her hand languidly, she patted Lucy's cheek.

Lucy and I exchanged glances, deeply satisfied. For the first time I knew what I had always longed for: a sense of continuity; of belonging to a feminine world of relations and family talk; the world of our dead mother, whose place only Cousin Rose could fill.

Chapter Five

At first Rose spent most of her time resting on the sofa in the drawing room, scarcely speaking, often lying back with her eyes closed, occasionally smiling vaguely as we crept in to bring her a glass of milk or a cup of tea.

"It's all the packing up and worry," Binnie said, "and the sadness of leaving her old home. It'll take time . . ."

She was certainly in no hurry to begin unpacking, seeming almost dazed by the conglomeration of luggage. Several times I saw her standing feebly on the landing, eyeing the trunks and boxes as if she could not summon the strength to open them.

"So much," she murmured. "I didn't realize . . ."

More than once we offered to do the unpacking but each time Rose shook her head or half-lifted her hand in protest and let it drop again like a dead weight.

"Not just yet, dear. In a day or two."

It was not only that she was tired. The impression persisted that she scarcely saw us. She had at times the vague, abstracted movements that I imagined a sleepwalker might have and there were moments when she put me in mind of a story I had once read about a spellbound traveler to whom shadowy figures appeared, offering food and drink.

Somehow the word "ordeal" came to be used a good deal.

"She's been through such an ordeal," Lucy said more than once in a sage, maternal fashion.

It was only gradually that I began to consider exactly what the ordeal had been: years of genteel poverty; of keeping up appearances even if it meant doing without essentials like food and fire and servants; years of attendance on an old man whose ailments and disappointments made him ill-tempered and disagreeable.

But after all he was her father. I tried to imagine myself sentenced to a long term of nursing my own father and in my ignorance could feel only a thrill of happiness at the prospect, no matter how sensibly I told myself that the nicest people could grow old and tiresome and even physically repulsive like old Michael Shaw who sat coughing and spitting on the porch of his son's cottage in Saxelby.

And then at the end, when Father died—my eyes filled at the thought—how could I bear to leave the Mill and make my home with strangers? Yet that was what Rose had had to do. Besides I was forgetting her unhappy love affair, her hopeless devotion to a man who had, presumably, married someone else. The agony of it! Poor Cousin Rose! It had all been too much for her. How dark her future must seem!

With a sense of guilt I went into the garden to gather a fresh posy for her room.

Unpleasant memories of poor Uncle Adam may have accounted for her extraordinary behavior toward old Solomon, the traveling draper who paid us a visit one morning at about that time. He must have been one of the last of the pedlars who tramped the country lanes with a pack on his back, selling laces, buttons, needles and stockings. His visits were a welcome diversion. Over the years Lucy and I had grown quite fond of him and usually helped Binnie to ply him with food and drink, enjoying the gossip from the local farms. But he was a repulsive-looking old man, short, squat and far from clean with a thick neck and gross red face.

The sun was warm on the courtyard outside the kitchen door. Solomon had already walked seven or eight miles and was glad to sink on to the stone bench. But before he could unroll his pack, he began to cough and heave until the tears rolled down his cheeks and his face grew mottled and purple as if he would choke.

"Come now, you've been overdoing things," said Binnie, and in her practical way she undid his filthy collar and sent Nancy for a glass of water.

"I'm getting old," Solomon wheezed as soon as he could draw breath. "It's no good. I'm getting past it."

His hand shook as he drank. I remember the pathetic look of his great broad boots, worn and dust-covered, and the thick veins on his pudgy hands as he began to cough again into a grimy handkerchief.

I think I was the only one to see Rose. She came languidly

through the garden, irritably pushing aside the purple sprays of lilac, and stood in the shadow of the west wall. Blanche was with her, sinuously rubbing herself against her skirt.

"I'm getting past it." Solomon wiped his rheumy eyes. "But I'll have to keep on till I drop. We must all come to it sooner or later. One of these days they'll find me dead in a ditch," he moaned. "And I won't be the first. Queer things happen, I can tell you. Not a hundred miles from here either."

It was not a hint that Lucy could resist.

"What sort of queer things?"

"Didn't you know? They've found a body up there." Solomon jerked his head in the direction of the crossroads. Then to prevent any misunderstanding he added, "A corpse."

Naturally we were startled. I saw Rose turn her head.

"When was that?" asked Binnie sharply.

"A day or two ago. Tom Amblethwaite could tell you. He found her on Cross Gap Fell not above a mile from the crossroads."

"Who was it?"

"There's no tellin' except that she was a woman—once."

"Do you mean—she had been there a long time?" Lucy asked.

"Could've been, judgin' by the state of things. The bracken was growin' green round her when she was found."

"Funny we didn't hear of it."

"Seems as if the clothes last longer than the flesh, up there at any rate," said Solomon.

"What was she wearing?"

With a sudden movement that made us all jump, Rose stepped out into the sunlight. Blanche too was startled. She arched her back, her pale eyes flaring.

[53]

"Who is this horrible old man?" Rose demanded.

"Ssh! He'll hear you," said Lucy.

"Hear me! I should think he will. Send him out of here at once."

"But he isn't well," I protested.

"Then he should be in the workhouse." She used the unmentionable word without hesitation. "Such people shouldn't be at large. I won't have him here I tell you."

There was an awful silence. With a shaking hand Solomon put down the glass and made an effort to fasten his collar. His little eyes, usually lively and kind, were hard with misery.

"Nancy," I said in a low voice. "Let him go to your house. We'll bring him something to eat."

"God bless you, Miss." He heaved himself to his feet and leaning against the back of the bench, turned on Rose quite deliberately. "And as for you, the devil damn your eyes, you frozen-faced hussy." He spoke with surprising energy and with a calculated ill will such as I had never heard before. In fact his voice vibrated with sheer hatred.

Rose's face had also darkened. Her brows were drawn down—and her eyes! How could I ever have thought them gray? They were green as grass. She seemed transformed. Her sudden transition from listlessness to a sort of reckless violence was so unexpected that I felt my hands hot, my heart race. And yet when Solomon had trudged away with Nancy, she stood leaning against the wall—very pale now as if she had exhausted herself.

There must have been talk in the village about Tom Amblethwaite's discovery of the remains of an unknown woman on the fells but at the Mill we heard none of it. Nancy, our usual source of news, was quite ill at the time with a toothache, poor girl, and in no mood for gossip. So the macabre incident never became familiarized through the medium of homely talk and conjecture. Instead it took on, for me at least, a strange, isolated significance. The enfolding hills lost something of their power to reassure, as if the land-scape had darkened.

How sad, to die up there alone! And who could she have been? Not a local person. We should have heard if any one had been missing. Yet who would be traveling alone in those unfrequented parts.

Altogether it was a disturbing morning.

There was no doubt that Rose's nerves were in a delicate state. We were careful not to refer to Solomon or the dead woman in her presence; and there were to be other areas of silence.

One morning we came back from our lessons to find her door ajar and saw her at last languidly unpacking one of the bags which had stood unopened with the other luggage for almost a week.

"May we help you, Cousin Rose?" (How tired she must have grown of her two unflagging attendants!) "We could put the things in the drawers for you." She gave an indifferent shrug; and since she did not actually forbid it, we insinuated ourselves into the room, already littered with the small articles one would pack at the last minute and unpack first, a work-basket, a bundle of knitting needles, a letter case, a pin cushion.

Lucy was in one of her flighty moods, pirouetting about the room with each object as Rose took it out of the bag, and placing it with a flourish on the dressing table or in the cupboard—her enthusiasm in marked contrast to Rose's lacka-daisical manner of looking dully at her things as if they meant nothing to her.

A watercolor sketch in a carved wooden frame brought Lucy to a temporary halt.

"This must be Appleby End. Look, Ellen, isn't it pretty?"

It was just as I had imagined it—a long low house of flint and rose-red brick with latticed windows.

"Did you paint it, Cousin Rose? It's very good."

Rose made the now familiar deprecatory movement of her lips in a half-humorous pout as if the subject bored her.

I pored over the picture, identifying each detail, the warm red of the garden wall, the spreading tree at the gable end. Was that the famous mulberry? For a moment I imagined myself walking down the brick path to the front door, pausing to look in at the open lattice and seeing, seated at the table with her sewing, Mother. Forgetting that she had been only a girl when she left Appleby End, I saw her as I remembered her. At the same time there revived in my mind the infant memory of a song she used to sing, an interminable ballad about "Broom, Green Broom," so that almost, as I dreamed, the half-remembered presence took visible shape, here in the beautiful lost world of Appleby End where Mother had been a girl. And Cousin Rose, too, of course.

A feeling of surprise—it was like mounting a staircase and finding a sudden gap where the next step should have been—made me look up and across the room at Cousin Rose. With a curious, swift sense of loss, I saw the object in my hand as no more than an amateurish sketch. Mother was dead. And Cousin Rose? I shivered, feeling all at once the cold breath of change.

By this time Rose had sat down on the bed and Lucy was herself taking out of the bag a whole collection of gilt-framed photographs. I looked over her shoulder at the likenesses, of a young girl in her teens with a long curl over each shoulder; a middle-aged woman with an immaculate center parting disappearing into a lace cap; a family group.

"Who are these?" Lucy asked.

She turned over the last of the photographs, one of a man no longer young, with dark whiskers and eyebrows and a rather heavy chin above the high stiff collar fashionable twenty years ago.

"Now let me guess," said Lucy. "This must be Uncle Adam."

I heard Rose draw in her breath. She gave a short exclamation, something between a gasp and a protest, then gradually the strangled sounds formed themselves into words, mounting in an ever-rising pitch to become subdued screams.

"Leave me alone. Leave me alone, I tell you. Why do you torture me with questions—always asking, asking? Stop it! Stop it!"

I thought she would go on forever, her screams growing louder until the phrase, endlessly repeated, seemed to lose all meaning, and she began to beat her hands on the bed and drum her heels on the floor, her movements increasing in violence until the heavy bed shook and I knew that this must be hysteria.

Horrified, penitent, Lucy carefully laid down the photograph. Together we tiptoed out of the room. I saw Rose fling herself back against the pillows as I gently closed the door.

"Whatever is the matter with her?" asked Lucy, white-faced. "What did I say?"

I put my hands on her shoulders.

"We must never, never talk to her about Appleby End again, do you hear? Not unless she mentions it first."

"No, of course not. But I wonder why . . ."

"Never mind. I think she must have had some sort of shock. Perhaps some day she'll talk about it."

Strangely enough it was a relief. I found that Appleby End was the last thing I wanted to talk about.

When luncheon was ready, I tapped at Rose's door. She was lying on her bed in her petticoat with her stays undone, staring up at the canopy. The room was littered as before, the bag still half unpacked.

"Would you like me to bring you a tray up to your room, Cousin Rose?"

She half-lifted her head and nodded feebly.

For the first time since her arrival Lucy and I ate luncheon in the kitchen with Binnie, of whom we had naturally seen less than usual while we devoted ourselves to Rose. Meals were now laid in the little dining-parlor on the ground floor. In the afternoons and evenings we sat in the drawing room.

It was perhaps inevitable that Binnie should have grown more irritable. The presence of an extra adult and one who was little better than an invalid, made many demands on her well-filled time. When we began, "Cousin Rose seems upset," Binnie put down a dish of potatoes with a slight thud and said, "She's best left alone then and if I were you, I'd let her have a little more time to herself. You've been running after her for a week now. There's moderation in all things and only fools go to extremes. It's high time you got back to a normal way of doing things."

Subdued, we ate almost in silence and afterwards went for

one of our long walks. I think we both found it a relief to be out of doors again. I remember feeling with the freshness of novelty the scented May breeze on my face and noticing the fully opened pink blossom on the chestnut tree, as if I had been away for a long time.

I wonder now how Rose actually passed the days at that period. She appeared to have lost interest in the embroidery in which she had excelled as a girl. Lucy and I regularly got out our work in the afternoons and evenings but Rose sat idle or played the piano a little, breaking off in the middle of a tune to walk to the window and drum with her fingers on the ledge. Sometimes she sat for half an hour at a time on the window-seat, staring up the valley, until twilight blurred the fields and hills, and only the outline of the bridge remained above the dark water. Yet there was no one to see: a whole day might pass without a soul going by.

One interest she had, I remember; and now of course I can see the significance of so many little things, unregarded then. Somehow she established first claim on the newspapers and we got into the habit of sending them up on her breakfast tray. Every day she would skim through the Gazette, put it down and ten minutes later, as if unable to resist it, flick through the pages again. But any newspaper appealed to her. She would even read through the piles of old newspapers in the cupboard at the top of the cellar steps, or unscrew a piece of paper from the unlit grate, read it, then drop it back just as it was.

She was interested too in the souvenirs and knickknacks in the drawing-room cabinet. When we took them out to show to her, she would take each one in her hands and look at it with absorbed attention. Cupboards of any kind seemed to arouse in her an almost childlike interest. I have seen her loitering about the rambling passages, occasionally stopping to open a cupboard, and spend several minutes gazing at its contents. But her interest in housekeeping went no further. I had always imagined that she would gradually assume a gentle authority over the preserves and linen: but she let the soft-fruit season go by without so much as snipping a currant or a gooseberry, and she never went near the kitchen.

Cousin Rose was not talkative: I can recall very little of what she actually said, but as the days went by she seemed increasingly to enjoy an atmosphere of talk and gossip. Perhaps she had been starved of feminine chatter in her latter days at Appleby End. There was something almost luxurious in the way she would lie back among the cushions, listening, half-smiling, occasionally asking a languid question while we talked.

I have the impression that we sat for hours in the drawing room or parlor—the three of us—when Lucy and I would normally have been out of doors. Needless to say it was Lucy who did most of the talking. When family news failed her, she would embark on one of the lurid tales in which Nancy specialized, stories of drownings and disappearances, unexpected windfalls, hauntings and suicides.

"Lucy, you've talked enough," I would say. "Cousin Rose doesn't want to hear of such things."

But Cousin Rose did. I remember particularly the day Lucy treated Cousin Rose to her version of the story of the Saxelby witch. It was when Nancy's grandmother was a girl in the early years of the century that there had come to live in the village a woman who was a stranger. She had lived alone and for some reason had never been accepted.

"Chantry Cottage, that's where she lived. We'll take you there, Cousin Rose." Lucy spoke as though the tumble-down place were one of the local sights. "She rented it from the Rector of all people. Of course it's close to the churchyard. Perhaps that was the reason."

"The reason?"

"Why they thought she was—a witch." Lucy's sense of drama did not fail her here and Cousin Rose looked startled. "They were ignorant people, you see. For that matter they still are, if Nancy is anything to go by."

"And what she says is hardly worth repeating," I put in ineffectively, insincerely too, for the story was in fact irresistible.

"What happened?"

"They let her stay for a year and a day and then—they drove her out."

"They?"

"All the women of Saxelby. They came at twilight with their pots and pans, rolling pins and pokers and washboards and skillets, making a tremendous noise. You could hear them as far away as Plum Lane, according to Nancy's grandmother. She—the woman—was sitting by the fire in a ladder-backed chair and they dragged her out, still in her white apron." Lucy lingered over the last phrase and indeed as children we had both felt an extra poignancy in the idea of the unfortunate stranger hurrying between the hedgerows in her apron, without hat or shawl. "Mrs. Shaw's great-grandmother was the first person to lay hands on her."

"Was there no one to stop them?" Rose asked. "What about the constable?"

"Not a soul," said Lucy firmly. "She was a solitary, friendless creature. They followed her along the lane, down to our bridge and up the hill, banging and rattling their pan lids and iron spoons, right up to the crossroads. That's the parish boundary. And then she was seen no more."

"What happened to all her things?" I remember feeling that it was not the question I myself would have asked first.

"I don't know," Lucy confessed, a little deflated. "I must ask Nancy."

"Not now," I said. "Let's talk about something else."

"It was horrible," Rose shuddered, coming belatedly to the heart of the matter. "What became of her, I wonder? What was her name?"

But no one seemed to know, if any one had ever known. From Lucy's expression I half suspected that she was making up her mind to ferret it out even at this late date. Her reaction to the story had always differed from mine. She regarded it, I think, as a triumph for the women of Saxelby, like the successful expulsion of a wicked fairy. But my own sympathies had been more confused and wavering, settling finally upon the hapless stranger. There was something repellent in the picture of those avenging housewives, united (and that in itself was remarkable enough) in superstitious frenzy, to ravish the quiet lanes with their furious din.

"What had she done to annoy them?" Rose asked.

"I don't know that she had done anything actually. But don't worry, Cousin Rose. There aren't any witches now. Mr. Gladstone wouldn't allow it. Besides, we would have nothing to fear. Ellen would save us with her hagstone."

I had forgotten all about it. Involuntarily and to my embarrassment, I smiled, remembering Mark Aylward's voice, recapturing for a second its exact husky quality, as he said, "I want you to have it."

Soon after I made an excuse and went to my room to feel in the pocket of my blue polonaise. But the stone was not there.

I felt put out, distressed even, out of all proportion to my regard for the token itself. Remembering with what reverence Mark had handled it, I felt ashamed of having treated it so lightly. It seemed to me that I had laid it down somewhere; but though I searched in the bottom of the cupboard and in all the drawers, I could not find it.

"It would be of no use on its own," he had said, teasingly. "But it might help."

The sudden longing I felt to talk to him, to feel again the warmth of his hand holding out the hagstone, arose perhaps from an instinctive feeling that now I needed help. Altogether the loss depressed me. It brought the first ripple perhaps, of a growing disquiet which was to come mainly from other causes.

Chapter Six

Once in those early days we persuaded Cousin Rose to walk to Saxelby to look at the church. The outing could not be called a success. She found the walk tiring and soon lapsed into one of her long silences.

It was on the way back that Lucy insisted on doing the honors of Chantry Cottage. She was quite prepared to borrow the key from the sexton, but having peered through the windows and pointed out the exact position, as she conceived it, of the famous ladder-backed chair, she found the door unlocked.

"To think that we are standing now on the very spot where

she wreaked her evil influence." Radiant in her blue-ribboned hat, she addressed us from the doorway. "Or should it be wrought?"

But her efforts to wrest every ounce of drama from the visit were lost upon Rose, who stood dispirited in the middle of the path, and no wonder, for although the day was sunny, an inexpressible air of sadness lay about the nettle-grown garden.

We went cautiously down two steps to the kitchen. It was bare of all furniture now, the floor oozing damp. A square of window at the back gave a glimpse of the churchyard. Stooping, I looked up at a huddle of graves.

Rose sat down heavily on a low stone shelf in the recess by the rusted stove and I had joined Lucy on the threshold again when Mary Shaw went past the gate and wished us good morning. For Lucy it was not an opportunity to miss.

"Mrs. Shaw, do please tell us about your great-grandmother, the one who first laid hands on the witch."

Mary Shaw was a serious young woman, Nancy's friend, who had done well for herself by marrying the butcher. She came up the path and rested her basket on the step.

"Well now, Miss Lucy, I don't know that my great-grandma ever said much about that. Only that she was a bad'un."

"How did they know she was bad?"

"Oh, they knew that all right, even if it hadn't been for my great-grandma's sister, that should've been my great-great-aunt."

"Should have been?"

"Drowned they found her. In Fuller's Reach."

"But mightn't she have . . ."

"As pure as the day she was and her not known to any man.

[65]

There was no reason. Nor was she the first. There was another young girl frightened into fits until she lost her reason entirely."

"But what made them think it had anything to do with the woman who lived here?"

"They knew, sure enough, her being a total stranger in these parts. A tall woman she was, my great-grandma did say, with a crooked mouth. You could tell, she said. They packed her off all right."

"It was rather cruel, the way they did it," I ventured.

"What else could they do, Miss? It was only according to the Bible. 'When thine eye is evil, thy body also is full of darkness,' and then again, 'If thy right eye offend thee, pluck it out and cast it from thee.' That's what it says."

During this conversation Rose had not moved. I turned and looked down into the kitchen. In the dim light her face was colorless; her eyes were strangely luminous. It was like looking down into a grave and seeing one of the dead gazing up. She had the look of one of the lost souls in Father's book of engravings from Dante's *Inferno*—one of the guilty.

For a moment I forgot altogether who she was and saw her only as a white-faced woman in the grip of some totally compelling circumstance, in her whole expression and posture a quality of . . . surely it was desperation. Somehow the superficial concern I had felt for the woman who had lived here deepened; and always after that when I thought of her, I saw her with Rose's eyes and features, and with the same tilt of the head.

Then Rose languidly picked her way over the damp floor and emerged into the daylight.

Mary Shaw was too stolid to look surprised, but she did

almost flinch at Rose's sudden appearance. I saw her blink as she stepped back.

"For pity's sake, let's go home," Rose burst out peevishly. "How could you think of bringing me to such a dreadful place? But it's just like you, Lucy, to be so wrapped up in yourself that you have no feeling for others."

"I'm sorry, Cousin Rose."

I was struck by the deliberate manner in which Mary Shaw, having glanced at Lucy's downcast face, stood looking steadily at Rose before she picked up her basket and walked away. I thought her rather an impressive person.

We were all rather quiet on the way home and Rose vowed that she would never again walk all that way in the heat.

Chapter Seven

There was no repetition of the hysteria. We scrupulously avoided any reference to her old life, treating Cousin Rose as if she were as fragile as one of the china shepherdesses on the mantelpiece, and gradually she regained her strength and spirits. While we were at Miss Southern's she began slowly to unpack. One by one the baskets and boxes were carried away to the attics and somehow their contents stowed into drawers and cupboards.

She became absorbed in arranging her clothes and possessions. We would hear her moving about her room after we had gone to bed and we grew used to seeing her at her table sewing.

"So many things needed a stitch and I've had so little time," she would explain, holding up a skirt with a torn flounce or a bodice needing a dart. "I seem to have lost a little weight."

Her recovery seemed to date from the first time she changed her dress. She had worn her traveling clothes, brushed and sponged, day after day, and when at last she came down in a brown summer dress, I remember feeling suddenly happier. The long, close-fitting bodice in vogue at that time was flattering to her tall, slender-waisted figure and there was something in the tilt of her head and the carriage of her shoulders that gave her a modish look whatever she wore; but I thought she looked more settled, more at home in the simple dress, worn with one of the aprons of which she had such an assortment— lace-frilled, printed silk or beaded.

One afternoon Miss Southern called with her brother. Lucy and I were standing at the drawing-room window when the barouche drew up at the gate.

"Isn't it providential that we're wearing our white dresses?" Lucy breathed, enraptured at the prospect of callers.

Rose had just come into the room. Ever since the outburst of hysteria I had felt a slight tension in my attitude toward her, a suppressed anxiety resolving itself into relief when nothing went wrong. But the novelty of her appearance had not yet worn off and we were proud of our new-found relative. She was wearing a dress of cinnamon foulard with lace at the neck and wrists; and she had washed her hair and dressed it carefully, being one of those fortunate women who are skilful with tongs and comb.

"Where shall we all sit?"

Lucy danced round the room. "Cousin Rose on the sofa. I

on the stool. Miss Southern here." She dragged forward one of the spoon-backed chairs and flicked a foot-stool with her skirt. "You, Ellen, on the sociable with Mr. Southern." She giggled delightedly.

"I should put the old gentleman in your father's chair," said Rose.

"He isn't so very old," I began but Binnie was already showing in the visitors.

I made the careful introductions.

"Miss Southern, may I introduce my cousin, Miss Warden? Cousin Rose, this is Miss Southern and this is Mr. Southern."

Cousin Rose seemed taken aback as Mr. Southern took her hand with his usual stiff gravity. He would be about seven and thirty then, nearly twenty years younger than his half-sister. We had not thought him interesting enough to describe to Rose beyond defining him as our landlord and owner of the successful timber business he had inherited from his father. In any case we were so familiar with his intense dark eyes, his thin, unsmiling mouth that we scarcely noticed them. We respected him, knowing how highly Father valued his friendship, but we were both a little in awe of him, even Lucy, whose relations with people were freer and more effortlessly friendly than mine.

We sat down in our appointed places, Lucy and I with our ankles crossed, hands folded in our laps, in what we supposed to be the appropriate attitude.

Miss Southern made kind enquiries about Rose's health— whether she enjoyed the country at this time of the year, whether she did not find the heat a little too much, though to be sure it was deliciously cool here by the river. . . .

Rose replied that she found the weather delightful, that she was now quite rested and that she looked forward to knowing the district better.

As soon as the polite skirmishes were over, Lucy burst out, "We have had such disappointing news from Father. *Miranda* has been ordered to Sweden to load timber as soon as they have discharged the cargo in London."

"I have had a letter too," said Mr. Southern. "That was one reason for our calling, besides the wish to become acquainted with Miss Warden."

"Do you suppose this will be a long trip?" I asked.

"No, no. Not more than eight or ten weeks, I dare say."

"And you know, Ellen," Lucy said, "Father has promised to be home for your birthday, winds and tides permitting."

That was the proviso applied to any doubtful venture ever since we were children.

"Which will be the fifth of August, I believe," said Mr. Southern. "Ellen's sixteenth birthday."

I was surprised that he should have remembered my birthday, even though he had known me all my life: and yet it was like him to have got it right and to state the fact without any of the jocular remarks some men might have felt tempted to make. He had no lightness or small talk.

"When Father wrote," Lucy went on, "he had not received our last letter and yet he knew that Cousin Rose was here. You must have written to him, Mr. Southern, before we did."

"I wrote to him in care of the agent at Valparaiso and also to Doughty and Son in London on the day after Miss Warden arrived."

"You knew at once then," Lucy said. "The Kirkups would spread the news, I suppose. Not that one could keep anything secret in Saxelby."

"I met Miss Warden's luggage, so to speak, when I was driving into Stanesfield on my way to London. It was scarcely possible to avoid seeing the labels."

It was then that I noticed the change in Rose. She was sitting bolt upright, more alert than I had ever seen her. The languid air of half-attending had quite gone.

But before I could establish in my own mind exactly what it was about her that was different from usual, Miss Southern had begun on her favorite topic, the difficulties of shopping in the country.

"Such a tiresome distance from Stanesfield, though in fine weather it is a pleasant enough drive over the moors, but of course you know it already, Miss Warden. I buy my hats at Ebury's. They always have a good selection of Heath hats. For country wear there is nothing in my opinion to equal a Heath hat, particularly their felts. Though this straw is, in fact, a Heath."

"Ebury's you say. In Stanesfield."

Rose turned to her with a vivacity that astonished me. There appeared no end to the questions she wanted to ask about the shops in Stanesfield. Shoes, it seemed, were what she chiefly needed. Indeed ever since she came she had worn the same pair. The pointed toes were crumpled now, the heels worn down. Not even the graceful arch of her long, slender feet could distract attention from their shabbiness.

"Dickens and Jones will send a selection of boots and shoes," Miss Southern said. "I have been well satisfied with a pair of glacé kid I had from them for lighter wear. I send a pair of my own shoes as a guide to size. One must be comfortably shod. We do so much walking and the roads . . ."

"Are you fond of walking, Miss Warden?"

The question was surely inoffensive enough: yet it was unlike Mr. Southern to ask it for the sake of adding to the conversation. Moreover his manner of asking had a deliberate forthrightness, even a sharpness, that visibly affected Rose. She hesitated.

"Walking? Why I . . ."

"I do not think many people can like walking," put in Miss Southern, "especially when there is so much dust. The last month has been so dry—and Miss Warden, we must remember, has been greatly in need of rest."

Indeed, as Rose sank back against the sofa cushions, she seemed suddenly tired. Her face had lost its animation and color. It was almost as if she were on the point of relapsing into the exhausted creature she had been on the day of her arrival. With some difficulty, almost unbelief, I remembered her leaning on the parapet of the bridge, her cheeks gaunt, dark smudges beneath her eyes, her skirt gray with dust.

Fortunately at that moment Binnie and Nancy brought tea upstairs quite in the new fashion. Instead of placing the tea things at Rose's sofa as I had expected, they unhesitatingly put the tray before me and Binnie gave me a firm nod before I could demur. But Mr. Southern came to my side, ready to hand round the cups; and when in my nervousness I poured tea into one of the saucers, he whipped it up, emptied it into the bowl and returned it to the tray with surprising dexterity. Glancing up to thank him, I found him looking down at me with such kindness that I felt a sudden glow of confidence, as if more than the tiny mishap had been involved.

Afterwards, at his request, Lucy and I sang the songs we were practising for Father's return, chosen with great care for their suitability: "Down by the riverside I stray" was Lucy's choice and mine, "I dreamed there was a garden gay." Mr. Southern turned the pages. Lucy he complimented on "a sympathetic rendering" and suggested that she should take one or two phrases more softly. "The Garden Gay" he found "very pleasing and tasteful."

When I returned to my seat the two ladies were chatting amicably about lace and I was able to indulge my favorite activity at that time of watching Cousin Rose. Looking from her to Miss Southern, I thought how unlike they were, naturally, since there was a great difference in age. It must have been Miss Southern's faded complexion and inconspicuous clothes that accounted for her rather negative quality. She seemed to recede, almost to become invisible, so irresistibly did my attention fix itself upon Rose.

Rest and country air had rounded her cheeks. She talked more than I had ever heard her. The tea seemed to have revived her and she was evidently stimulated by the company. I felt a sort of magic in her beautiful voice, in her red lips, the lower one full and pouting, in her white, even teeth; and in her eyes, changing from green to gray as the light changed.

And yet my admiration for Rose, my pride in the white-paneled room, the china and flowers, my pleasure in the visitors, together did not quite fuse into a mood of perfect ease. At the Mill we never knew the steady blaze of full sunshine. Always, even on that summer afternoon, it was a subdued light that crept into the room through the green twilight of leaves; and in the same way there hovered over us as we sat talking, a kind of shadow.

Was it something to do with Rose? Looking at the two women, I saw that Miss Southern's quality was not after all a negative one. Faded and aging she might be, but I recognized

[74]

in her the quiet confidence that comes from being in perfect harmony with one's surroundings. And Rose, by contrast . . . For the first time I noticed how alert, how active Rose's eyes were. Yet I had thought her such a dreamy person.

Puzzled, fascinated, absorbed as I was, it was some time before it came to me that I was not alone in studying Rose. Mr. Southern sat in silence, his dark eyes fixed upon her and upon Lucy on the stool at her side, with such intensity that Rose must surely have been aware of it.

"It has been a great success, hasn't it?" Lucy said with deep satisfaction when the Southerns left.

"Yes."

I picked up a handful of fallen rose petals from the carpet and crushed them in my hand. Their perfume seemed to stir memories of a by-gone sweetness, remote and melancholy.

Later on Rose played the piano and Lucy and I danced. It was better than dancing to the musical box. Rose's mood had changed to one of exaggerated brightness, almost merriment, as she played "Sunshine Waltz" rather loudly with the pedal down so that the jangling music floated out into the quiet garden with an unaccustomed effect of gaiety, as if a whole band were playing.

"A sympathetic rendering," she broke off to say, drawing down the corners of her mouth in imitation of Mr. Southern. "Very pleasing and tasteful," and then when neither of us laughed, she launched, with a little pout, into "Belle of the Village."

Lucy, infected at once by the noise and the rackety rhythm, danced with such vigor that she was soon out of breath and collapsed on Rose's shoulder, her hair-ribbon untied, a quick pulse beating in her throat.

[75]

"Let me tie it for you?" Rose produced a tiny comb from her pocket and began to pat and coax the thick hair into place. "Why don't we comb it over your forehead a little, like this?"

The effect was soft and pretty. While Lucy admired herself in one of the mirrors, I said, "Show me how to do my hair differently, Cousin Rose. You're so good at it."

She looked at me appraisingly, then shrugged.

"It doesn't matter how you do it," she said. "With your features it simply doesn't matter."

I felt rebuffed. Unable to control my quivering lips, I ran to the door and up the half-flight to our bedroom. Was I so plain, so homely then? As I went across to the looking-glass, Lucy came rushing along the landing and into the room to throw her arms round me.

"Ellen, you're crying. I know what you thought and you're quite mistaken."

"She said it didn't matter. What is wrong with my features?"

"She meant it as a compliment, you dear goose. Only she didn't bother to explain. She could have. It doesn't matter how you do your hair because you're so beautiful. Father says your features are far better than mine. Pure, he said. He said you were the beauty of the family."

"Father said?"

"I heard him say it to Mr. Southern. Look."

She dragged me to the chest of drawers. I tilted the glass, aware in its mottled depths of my unsmiling face, my brown hair drawn tightly back, relieved that Father didn't think me plain.

But I was not really seeing my own reflection at all: I was seeing only Lucy behind me, thin, panting, flushed, her hair too long and thick for her slender neck. I turned and looked at her. It seemed to me that in the blue depths of her eyes there was a shadow I had not noticed before.

"Let's go to bed," she said. "I'm tired." She pulled off her sash. "You know, Ellen, it's funny. I never thought Cousin Rose would be so . . . noticeable."

It was an odd word but perfectly appropriate. Long after Lucy had fallen asleep I lay awake. The familiar rhythm of her breathing, the drowsy softness of the bed, for once failed to soothe me to sleep. Somewhere close at hand an owl shrieked, and at once there flashed into my mind every detail of the scene outside: wooded valley, humped bridge, white lane climbing to the cross-roads, and beyond, the Roman road running straight to Stanesfield. I pictured the wagon with Rose's luggage—and Mr. Southern driving by. What else had he seen? Instinct told me that something had been—not quite as it should be.

After warm days I was used to hearing small sounds from the ancient beams and warped floorboards as the house settled for the night. I heard them now, sometimes for whole minutes together, like slippered feet on the stairs and in the attics above. For the first time in my life I was afraid, in my own home, in my own bed.

I watched a finger of moonlight steal to the green bottle on the mantelpiece so that the tiny ship inside took on a ghostly radiance; and I wished with all my heart that Father would come home.

Chapter Eight

It was a warm dry summer of langorous days made interminable by the long anticipation of Father's homecoming. We spent them chiefly in the garden or the shady orchard or by the river.

It was gratifying that Cousin Rose could rouse herself to show an interest in Father. Lucy had the happy idea of reading his letters to her and she not only listened attentively but actually asked to have some of them read again.

She seemed almost to enjoy Lucy's chatter about *Miranda*. "One of the fastest clippers of her class. She's a barque of 896 tons register, Cousin Rose" . . . about her painted figurehead with long fair hair, her teak deckwork and all aloft painted white, though we had neither of us so much as set eyes on her, how Father would never put to sea in a steamkettle, only he disliked general trading and thought it especially demeaning to carry coal for refueling the horrid dirty steamers.

"It's an insult to *Miranda* really. Ellen and I think that's why Father won't mind leaving the sea, though he loves it so much. And this being his last voyage, he'll have been driving *Miranda* all he can, trying to make a record run. Believe it or not, she once made the homeward run in eighty-four days, but last time she took ninety-three days from Sydney. They were unlucky in the Trades of *all* things. . . ."

"What will he do with himself all day?" Rose asked. "It will be quiet for him here after being at sea."

"He'll go out shooting and fishing with Mr. Southern, I expect, and he has ever so many plans."

We explained that Father had the option on a piece of land and would probably do a little farming. He had always wanted to raise pedigree cattle.

Rose's first initiative came when she announced one morning that she must go into Stanesfield to do some shopping.

We looked up hopefully.

"Shall we ask . . ."

I knew that Lucy was going to say, "to be excused from lessons," but before she could finish Rose broke in:

"Yes. I was going to ask you to order the pony and trap for me as you pass Morton's. I should like him to take me at once, this morning, but if he can't manage today, then tomorrow."

"Yes, Cousin Rose."

"I expect she thought there wouldn't be room for all of us, with the parcels," Lucy said regretfully as we set off for the village.

Rose returned from the shopping expedition with a number of packages: shoes, one of the new waterproof mantles, and a very becoming summer hat, the wide brim lined with lace and pearl-colored silk, and tulle streamers to tie under the chin.

She was wearing the hat when Father came home.

Neither winds nor tides prevented him from keeping his promise. It was in fact the day before my birthday when he came. We were all three in the orchard, Lucy rocking in her hammock with Blanche at her feet, I leaning against an apple tree with a book in my lap, Rose in a low wicker chair, her eyes often closed, the pale tulle streamers and pearl-colored silk softly framing her face.

There came the sound of Binnie's voice, raised just sufficiently to make me sit up, suddenly alert; a shadow on the grass between the trees; a familiar voice.

"Ellen."

"Father."

Time has not dimmed the happiness of those longed-for reunions. His living presence was always more than I could believe. I remember his boyish pleasure at having once again surprised us; how he literally caught Lucy in his arms as she cascaded out of the hammock, and held her up as if she were still a baby; while I clung to him, to my astonishment, in tears.

Then I remembered.

"Father, this is Cousin Rose."

As Rose looked up, I saw him as she was seeing him, blue-eyed, trim-bearded, bronzed, smiling, broad-shouldered in his dark-blue reefer, authoritative. It was the authority that I loved best, the way orchard, Mill, woods, river—instantly became his domain again so that I always felt an exquisite relief.

"Rose. At last."

He took her hand. With a swift change of vision I saw Rose as he was seeing her, a graceful figure under the trees in the softened sunlight, her cheeks gently flushed with the late summer warmth, rounded with health and leisurely living, shaded by the pale oval of that most charming of hats. I saw the bow-shaped lips part in a smile of welcome to reveal white, even teeth. Her eyes were gray and large and soft as I had never seen them before. I saw for the first time that she was beautiful.

I scarcely remember the rest of the day. I believe there were meals, untouched in the excitement, the usual glorious unpacking, a litter of shawls and trinkets, for Lucy a canary in a gilt and green cage, a minaret of carved ivory for me—and for Rose . . . ?

"If only I had known sooner." He looked down at her with whimsical regret. "But she can have it all." His gesture seemed to embrace not only the overflowing bags and chests but the entire Mill—and they smiled at each other.

"What a homecoming!" There was a new, jubilant note in his voice. "And to think that this time it's for good. It's all over—the hard tack, the dried peas, the salt meat, the cold, the heat, the wet . . ." He strode over to the window and looked down at the water. "A trout stream at the bottom of my garden. Better than all the oceans of the world. 'Here is my bourne, my absolute content. . . .'" Father, among his many gifts, had a fine sense of occasion.

We helped Binnie to clear up, then stood aimlessly outside the drawing-room door, hearing Father and Cousin Rose talking inside, or rather Father talked and Rose murmured and laughed occasionally.

"It doesn't matter if we don't hear all about the voyage tonight," Lucy said, "now that Father's home for good. We shall have plenty of time to talk to him."

"It's nice for him to have someone else to talk to—someone of his own age."

"How old do you suppose Cousin Rose is?"

By this time for no accountable reason we had wandered into Mother's room where the evening light had turned everything to gold. Beyond the muslin curtains the trees rose heavy and motionless in full summer foliage. Some disposition of light and shade gave an additional air of stillness to the scene, as if here at least nothing had changed or could change.

"She's the same age as Mother," I calculated. "It's seven years since Mother died and she was twenty-nine."

"Then Rose is thirty-six. Is that old—for a woman?"

"No, of course not. It's quite young."

"It's odd that I never thought of her age before."

For a silent minute or two we thought about it.

"You wouldn't call Father old, either," said Lucy tentatively.

"Goodness gracious, no. He's forty-five."

With the absurdity of youth I saw him suddenly diminished, as though by having an age like other people he had become less rare. It was not just that I had regarded him hitherto as immeasurably superior to other men. It had simply not occurred to me that comparisons were possible. To see him as a man at all was still beyond my powers.

I stretched out the muslin curtain with both hands and looked through it at the summer world outside, seeing as though through a veil the blue-green layers of foliage, the curve of wooded slopes; and I tried to decide whether they were more beautiful like this, muted and blurred through the softening medium of the muslin.

"Ellen." Lucy was sitting at the dressing table. I turned my head and saw her through the glass, her eyes wide and serious. "You remember Cissie Pellow?"

I put aside the curtain. Unveiled, the trees assumed a firmer outline, not harsh in the bloom of evening, but more insistently themselves. Hollows dimpled the dark water where fish were rising. I pushed open the window and heard the rustle of birds, smelt the cool river as it slid under the bridge, where we had first seen Rose, a pinpoint of darkness against a golden sky like this.

"What about Cissie Pellow?"

"What really happened to her?"

"I don't know. Nancy said it was a disappointment. Loving someone who didn't marry her."

"Like Rose."

"I suppose so."

I considered, but the mental effort of finding some point of resemblance between Cousin Rose and the witless woman with the doll was altogether too much for me.

"It made her crazy—Cissie, I mean," said Lucy. "It doesn't seem to have affected Cousin Rose like that."

"People have different sorts of feelings," was all that I could summon up by way of solution to the problem. "Perhaps we'd better go down. Father always likes music on his first evening."

I had scarcely spoken when we heard the piano, and Rose's voice, soft, vibrant, intimate—in the first notes of Lucy's song, "Down by the riverside I stray . . ."

[83]

Presently Lucy pulled open the top right-hand drawer of the dressing table. I went and stood beside her, looking down at Mother's things—the scent bottle, the beaded purse, the trifles of jewellery. Then without a word Lucy held out her pinafore. One by one I took out the cherished relics and placed them in her lap. When the drawer was empty, I closed it. Lucy gathered her pinafore to her; we went out of the room, carefully closing the door, along the landing and into our own. In the same silent ritualistic fashion, I emptied the top right-hand drawer in the painted chest and in it laid Mother's things.

With our arms round each other's waists, we went downstairs. The last notes of Rose's second song died away as we came in. She sat with her hands resting on the keys, Father leaning on the piano. It was a moment before either of them spoke. Then Rose closed the piano gently with just a touch of reluctance.

"Ellen will want to put out the chessboard," she said.

"Chess!" Father's heartiness did not deceive me for an instant. "Come along, Ellen. I've a new opening for you"; and as I went to the cabinet to take out the box he leaned over the sofa where Rose had seated herself and said, "How did you know? Come, girls, tell me how it is. Your cousin knows our ways as if she had always lived here. I believe . . ." He dropped his voice; the words—something about magic power —were meant only for Rose.

As if there were anything left for her to learn about us— anything that Lucy had not poured out in one or other of her endless monologues!

Somehow we never had our game of chess, neither then nor for many evenings to come. Those hours after dinner had always been the most precious part of Father's leaves and now that he was home for good their pattern did not change. In some ways the evenings became even more festive. Now that there were four of us, it was easy to generate a mood of gaiety, as though every day were a holiday, every gathering a party. The old rooms had never rung with so much noise and laughter. More than once I told myself how happy I was now that the Mill had miraculously flowered into the sort of home I had always dreamed of.

How strange then that looking back I can scarcely recall what part Lucy and I played in those evenings, can summon up no memories of the two of us more vivid than if we had been two shadows sitting quietly together by the open window; no images more constant than those of the martins swooping over the darkening water or the bats fluttering under the trees.

It is Rose who dominates the scene: at ease against the chintz cushions, her laugh grown rich and mellow, a new confidence in the gestures of her slim white hands, a new warmth animating her eyes, her lips.

If she was fascinating to me, to Father she must have been irresistible. Seeing him talkative, high-spirited, full of plans, I realized that we had never seen him happy before, not with this fervent, vitalizing happiness—this ardor. How handsome he seemed to me in his velvet jacket and rather full necktie (he affected a mildly Bohemian style of dress)—wearing in his buttonhole one of the flowers presented to him daily by Lucy or myself.

And how he talked.

"Did I ever tell you," he would begin, "about that time in '79—three days out from Taltal—the cruelest place in God's universe?" And there would follow a hair-raising description of *Miranda,* her decks awash with heavy seas, heeled over till the yard-arms dipped the water; of seamen in drenched oil-skins and sodden seaboots standing on a mere loop of rope to haul in a billowing mass of canvas. "I'm afraid it's always been my way to keep on every stitch of sail to the last possible minute. It really grieved me to have to hand her over to old Golightly when I signed off. Oh, he's competent enough but far too heavy-handed for *Miranda.*"

Now that they lay behind him forever, he told us more about the hardships and perils than he had ever done, inspired perhaps by a new and always attentive listener. We heard of the icebergs, the furious gales and unnatural gloom off the Horn; of strange visitations; ghost ships; the weird phosphorescent things that clung to the backstays and shone gently in the dark like the souls of dead sailors; and we listened enthralled as a yellow moon rose above the elms and the blue twilight deepened.

Then Father would take out his watch; Lucy would reluctantly say goodnight and go to bed; and presently I would follow, sensing their impatience to be alone, feeling, though I knew nothing of passion, the fervor of longing which drew them together.

It was not the first night but it cannot have been long after that I lay in bed reading until the candle went out. As the flame guttered and died, I heard the drawing-room door open, footsteps, low voices, the rustle of Rose's dress. A door along the landing opened and closed. From within I heard Rose's laugh. It seemed to my weary fancy to fill the dark Mill, to be the only sound in the world.

Chapter Nine

I want to talk to you," Father said one morning at breakfast. "The fact is—I have a surprise for you."

As if we had not guessed! Even so, watching him as he fidgeted with his napkin, looking first at Lucy and then at me, I felt suddenly breathless. Lucy sat as still as a statue on the other side of the table.

"I hope you'll be pleased—and I believe you will."

"What is it, Father?"

"It's Rose." He looked young, almost shy. "Rose has—I have asked her to be my wife and—in short, it's all settled, my dears."

Neither of us spoke. Too ignorant and inexperienced to

find refuge in conventional phrases, too unaccountably awk-ward to get up and put my arms round him as I had done on scores of trivial occasions, I sat dumb. Lucy too seemed paralyzed.

"You're pleased?" His sudden anxiety was unbearable.

"Yes, Father. Of course."

"Very pleased."

"I wondered if you had guessed how Rose and I feel about each other."

"Not really . . ."

"In a way . . ."

What did it matter what we said? His happiness must have been of that impregnable kind, beyond misgiving or doubt, that sets the rest of the world at a distance. I could feel the gulf yawning between us as surely as if the white tablecloth had become a snowy sea.

"It has all turned out so extraordinarily well. I can scarcely believe it. It was always our intention to give Rose a home. Your dear mother wished it above all things. Leaving you alone here for so long has been a great anxiety to me. Oh, Binnie does well enough, I know, but she is hardly a suitable person to give you the sort of upbringing I want my daughters to have. Young girls need a pure and refining influence. All these years I have looked to Rose to provide it. And then to find her such a person as she is!" He jumped up, went to the window, took a deep breath and came back, holding out his arms. "It's almost too much, my darlings, to have you and Rose as well!"

Of course we kissed and clung to him though we were both still speechless.

"You'll go to her, Ellen, won't you—and tell her how

pleased you are? She wasn't sure how you would take it, though I told her how you'd always longed to have her here. As little girls you even prayed for her to come. Remember?"

"Yes, Father. We'll go at once."

It was a relief to know what was expected of us, a relief to leave him. I tapped at Rose's door. She was reclining against the pillows in the sun-drenched room in a tumble of lace, her hair loose.

"Your father has told you?"

"We came to say how pleased we are, Cousin Rose."

"How sweet! Come and kiss me."

One on either side of the bed we kissed her.

"You'll be like daughters to me."

Somehow we got ourselves away to our own room.

"It's strange," said Lucy, "but when something really wonderful happens, like this, you don't feel like dancing about and—well, rejoicing. I feel quiet and far away as if it were happening to someone else."

"We aren't used to it yet."

I was looking at the twin miniatures in their gilt frames of Mother and Cousin Rose as children. The characterless little faces were almost indistinguishable from each other; two pairs of short, thick ringlets, two pairs of light eyes and childishly rounded cheeks. There seemed nothing to choose between them.

"It's better than if Father had married a stranger," I said. "In a way we've always known Rose."

"And Mother was devoted to her."

"It couldn't be more suitable."

"What relation shall we be to Rose?" asked Lucy. "Shall

we go on calling her Cousin Rose? I know, let's call her Mamma."

Suddenly we both laughed, equal at last to the Miss Pritts. The wedding was to be at the end of September.

"Rose wants everything to be done very simply," Father told us.

"The quieter the better," Rose said. "Your father can't bear a fuss. Personally I dislike a tasteless display."

Naturally she had to do a little shopping. She and Father made several trips to town and came back laden with packages. Parcels were delivered by post too; lace sets, underwear, half a dozen pairs of gloves, two dozen pairs of stockings.

One morning I ran upstairs with a dressmaker's parcel. Finding the south room empty, I laid it on the bed, intending to leave at once. But Rose had been burning something in the grate. A screwed-up paper had fallen on the hearth and was filling the room with smoke. As I took up the tongs to put it back, among the unburned letters in the grate I recognized a childish script, my own, on a letter written to Rose years before at Appleby End.

I glanced indulgently at the carefully formed letters, the stilted phrases. Yet the sentiments were affectionate and Rose had replied affectionately. Kneeling on the hearth, once again I had the feeling of returning to a lost world.

It was typical of Rose that she had not even made a success of burning the papers. I saw that there was also a crumpled sheet of newspaper. Seeing the words "Cross Gap Fell," I straightened it out and read a brief account of the coroner's inquest on the remains of an unidentified woman.

I remember feeling a faint surprise that Rose should have

bothered to keep the cutting. (It was in fact the entire sheet, but I could see nothing else there likely to have interested her.) But its effect was chiefly to revive memories of that embarrassing morning with Solomon in the courtyard. The recollection of Rose's heartless words, the violence in her manner, reinforced my impression of the change in her since she had come to the Mill. I felt that in the old days at Appleby End she must have been quite a different person.

I got up to go. The cupboard door was open. Across the entire bottom stretched a row of shoes; eight or nine pairs, I suppose. It seemed an immense number. Yet it had been shoes that Rose had declared herself positively to need.

An empty shoe, more candidly than any garment, reveals the defenceless personality of its owner. If I had picked up one of Lucy's shoes anywhere in the world it would have asserted with a small stamp the name "Lucy." But now looking down at Rose's eighteen or twenty shoes, I was struck not only by their lack of elegance but by some quality in them that I had never associated with Rose: a roundness in the toes: an unexpected smallness: a kind of humility and usefulness: a country look. They were well polished and oddly at variance with the rest of the room, which—I could not help noticing with distaste—had lapsed into a state of bedraggled untidiness.

Naturally I am giving now a specific form to what was then no more than an impression. It was like listening to music and hearing not just a change of key but an entirely new kind of sound. The quiet dresses—dove-gray, faded blue, all long unworn—hung wistfully, waiting, like hostages, to be rescued.

[91]

I closed the door quietly, feeling that I had spent a few minutes at Appleby End.

Once, seeing two or three dress boxes in the hall, Father stood for a moment looking thoughtful. Then he suddenly said, "You'll see that the girls have something pretty for the wedding, Rose?" and rather awkwardly taking out his purse, he shook out some sovereigns.

"Indeed I will. We must talk about your dresses, girls. What would you like? We shall do you credit, Jonathan, I promise you."

Casually—indifferently—she held out her hand and as Father dropped the gold into it, Lucy nudged me and mouthed the word, "Ten," then pursed up her lips and nodded, deeply impressed—consoled too, because I am sure she had cherished hopes of being a bridesmaid, only Rose had said there was no need of anything of that sort.

Father insisted on staying at the Southerns during the weeks before the wedding; that is, he slept there and walked home for breakfast each morning. Perhaps that was why we saw less of Mr. Southern than usual.

But one morning he and Father sat smoking together on the white seat in front of the house overlooking the garden and river. I was cutting late roses and did not see them at first, nor did they see me; so that I felt no obligation to join them.

They had been bickering amicably about Gladstone's policy with regard to the Sudan. Father believed that we should send a force and drive the Mahdi out. Mr. Southern supported Gladstone; the Sudan was no affair of ours. But they had arrived comfortably at an agreement—that only Gordon could handle the situation and should be dispatched there at once.

Presently I was aware of some change in Father's voice.

"Upon my word, Oliver, I don't quite take your meaning."

"I think you do. It isn't my way to wrap up my meaning. Tact is usually an excuse for not coming to the point."

"It can also be a way of seeming to mind your own business."

Mr. Southern was silent.

"My regard for you is such, Jonathan," he went on at last, "that I believe I have come to think of your affairs as being my business."

"Well," Father sounded mollified, "heaven knows you've every right to think so. What should I have done these last seven years without you and Miss Southern? I should have had to send the girls away to school to be made into bread-and-butter misses, I suppose. It's been a comfort to me when I've been on the other side of the globe to know that you were here to keep an eye on them—and the old Mill. You know how I feel. Gratitude is too cold a word."

"Never mind that. But I've come to know you all pretty well and that gives me the confidence to speak even if you don't like what I say."

"Very well. Go ahead then. Say your piece and I'll take from you what I wouldn't take from any one else."

"It's just that you're rushing things. Why can't you wait? You've always gone full tilt at things without looking at them from every side. Look at the way you set about renting the Mill. If we'd cared to sell it, you'd have paid every penny you had for it, just because you wanted it."

"By God, you're right. And it would have been worth it. Instinct didn't lead me astray that time, old man."

"Perhaps not, but you'd have been a poorer man than you are. And unless you take care, a poorer man you'll be. Keeping a wife with a taste for fine clothes isn't the same as keeping two young girls."

"I'm not short of money if that's what you have in mind. You're surely not suggesting that I can't afford to keep a wife."

"Of course not. Especially as she'll have something of her own, I dare say."

"Then it isn't my marrying that you object to?"

"Object isn't the word. A man marries to please himself, not his friends. All I'm suggesting is that you should wait a while."

"What difference would that make?" Father demanded.

There followed a long silence. Through the rosebushes I saw Mr. Southern staring across the river, his black brows drawn down, his lips clenched, as if he never meant to speak again.

"You think I might change my mind?" Father took the pipe from his mouth with a touch of eagerness that made him seem the younger of the two, despite his seven years' seniority. "I won't change. What's more, I can't go on living under the same roof as Rose unless I marry her. What's that you say?"

I had not caught Mr. Southern's remark either but I heard him now as he said brusquely, "That was your mistake, bringing her here without making her acquaintance first. I tell you there's something . . ." It must have been the soothing effect of Father's presence that dulled my awareness of what Mr.

Southern was trying to say. Even so I dimly recollected his first meeting with Rose and her uneasiness under his dark gaze; but now the prick of anxiety was missing. Nothing was wrong, nothing could be wrong with Father there.

But Father broke in. "Ah now, there I was rash. I admit it. Lilith's cousin was the obvious person to have a hand in bringing up the girls, especially as she was alone in the world, except for the old man. But I confess that I hadn't seen the implications of having her here in the house. I suppose I'd always thought of her as some kind of dim, spinsterish, even elderly relative. I can see now that even if Rose and I hadn't —well, if we'd been indifferent to each other—it wouldn't have been suitable for us to be together en famille, so to speak. But as it happens Fate has rescued me from what could have been an awkward situation; in fact played into my hands with a generosity I don't deserve. Rose's influence can do so much for the girls, especially Ellen, now that she's growing up."

Mr. Southern gave an exclamation of annoyance.

"There was nothing wrong with the way Ellen was growing up. In fact if you ask me, the influence would be better working the other way round."

"You've formed some sort of prejudice, I can see. Don't let it come between us, Oliver. When you get to know Rose better, you'll understand. The trouble is you're such a cool customer that you don't realize how a hot-blooded fellow like me can feel about a woman. Wait until your time comes."

"You underestimate me, Jonathan."

"You mean—there is someone. Come now, you're a dark horse? Who is it? Tell me. I had no idea."

"Unlike you I can keep my feelings to myself. But believe me, if a man's affections are strong enough and deep enough, and if the object of them is as good and sweet a being, and as beautiful as this life is likely to afford him a chance of knowing—he can wait a very long time; forever if necessary. Even if it's a vain hope, to hope can be enough."

It struck me that there had been some unusual quality in his last speech and Father was plainly astonished; but my mind was still more than half on the roses and I filled my basket before going along the flagged path to where they were sitting.

"Here's one for you, Father." I tucked into his lapel his favorite old-fashioned yellow tea rose. Then, the recollection of what Mr. Southern had been saying made me feel a little sorry for him and I offered him one of the white roses.

His whole expression changed.

"Thank you, Ellen."

He took the rose and fixed it clumsily in his buttonhole. It was the first time I had seen him actually smile. Something must have pleased Father too—or perhaps the rose served as a peace offering. At any rate when I left them, he sat there positively beaming at Mr. Southern and twice I heard him say, "Well, well, Oliver, you certainly have surprised me."

Their difference of opinion cannot have impaired their friendship for Mr. and Miss Southern came to the wedding and afterwards to the Mill for bride cake and wine. They were the only guests.

Of the wedding day, which must surely have been a highlight in our quiet lives, I have only fitful recollections. I remember Rose coming downstairs in her dress of ivory lute string and a wide hat with an aigrette of osprey feathers; and following her with Lucy to the carriage.

During the mile-long drive through the haze of the September morning, she scarcely spoke but sat with her head high, her eyes fixed on the distant hills, so that gradually we too became quiet, even Lucy, and the three of us rode to Saxelby church in almost unbroken silence.

But my most vivid recollection of that morning is not of Rose but of Binnie. When we came home after the ceremony Lucy and I ran down to the kitchen to show ourselves off. Binnie had been harassed and low spirited for some time. Alec had been moved to Cairo and there was no knowing what that might lead to, though we had not then heard of the terrible massacre of the Hicks Expedition by the Ansar. Now she was plainly in one of her moods. I recognized the danger signals at once. But she put down the cutlery she was polishing and gave her critical attention to our dresses (cream barege with draped overskirts, worn with matching Gainsborough hats), lifting the hems to examine the wide stiffening of white muslin underneath and turning Lucy round to adjust the grosgrain bow below her waist.

"Oh yes," she said at last. "There'll be all of forty shillings-worth there."

"Don't you like our dresses?" I asked.

"They'll do and you look ladies every inch. I'll say that for you which I wouldn't say for everyone. Fine feathers don't make fine birds, however, though osprey feathers may try."

"You're cross, Binnie," said Lucy. "Are you tired? Shall we help to put out the wine glasses?"

"No, love, that's all done and there's Nancy in her best apron to give a hand. But I'm put out, that I'll admit. It's your Mother's silver bonbon dish. I can't lay my hands on it and I've ransacked the house looking."

"It must be at the back of a cupboard somewhere."

"That's what I said to Nancy. I remember Alec helped me to put the silver away after the last big cleaning just before he went. I've racked my brains trying to remember if I put it somewhere special. . . ."

"Does it matter?" I said. "There are plenty of other dishes."

"None so pretty. Your mother was so fond of it. Solid silver and pierced—with a fluted edge. We had it out for both your christenings, and she'd have wanted it out today." Then abruptly breaking off, she clapped her hand to her mouth. "What am I saying? And her cold and forgotten in her grave." And as suddenly as if her legs had given way under her, she slumped into a chair and began to cry. Lucy and I promptly melted into tears of sympathy, while Nancy, coming in with a tray, stopped in her tracks, round-eyed and solemn.

It was in this mournful state that Father found us as he came downstairs on his way to the cellar.

"What in Heaven's name is the matter?" he demanded.

"Binnie can't find Mother's silver dish," gulped Lucy.

For almost the first time we saw Father explode into anger.

"Pull yourselves together this instant and stop that sniveling," he commanded. "Have you taken leave of your senses? Is this the way to behave toward Rose on her wedding day? Ellen, Lucy, go upstairs at once. Miss Southern will be here presently."

"Yes, Father."

The gloom cast by this incident seems to have obscured the details of the rest of the day. The next thing I remember is standing on the bridge to wave goodbye as Father and Rose drove away on the first stage of their journey to London. It was beginning to rain as they left. Lucy and I ran to our room to watch them pass the cross-roads but already the mist had come down so that we could see no farther than the trees at the water's edge. It was one of those evenings when the Mill seemed to shrink deep into the valley and to draw closer than ever to the river so that there was nothing in the world but water and stone.

"It's the end of summer," Lucy said.

But I felt an unexpected lightness of heart. A red fire glowed in the kitchen grate. Binnie had a brown dish of apples baking in the oven. With Blanche asleep on the mat, we sat in our old places and talked over the events of the day. Binnie read us Alec's last letter while soft rain fell on the windowpanes, shutting us in, safe and warm and untroubled as in the old days.

Chapter Ten

It was in that autumn of 1883 that I discovered the joys of reading. Hitherto Lucy and I had taken our lessons lightly, but Father had tactfully suggested to Miss Southern that I might be ready for a richer mental diet than Markham's *History of England* could provide. The study of some famous biographies might, he thought, extend the range of my experience.

Accordingly I had been introduced to Macaulay's *Life of Pitt* and Lockhart's *Nelson* and *Scott*. It was the last which led me to the *Waverley* novels. All unaware of the lasting delight they had to offer, I strayed into the world of books and found myself at home there, so deeply absorbed that sometimes after a long spell of reading, I would look up and find myself back at the Mill with a sense of unfamiliarity as after a long journey.

One Saturday afternoon, having reluctantly come to the end of *Guy Mannering*, I made a sudden decision to walk to Saxelby to borrow another book from the Southerns. Lucy was confined to bed with a feverish cold. I could look forward to several hours of reading in the evening. As I put on my hat and jacket, I thought with active pleasure of the rows of green and gilt volumes of Scott in the Southerns' back parlor where we had our lessons.

I was a little embarrassed to find Mr. Southern reading by the fire. Miss Southern, apparently, was also suffering from a cold and keeping to her room.

I explained my errand.

"You must let me help you," he said. He knew the novels well and loved them. We discussed the merits of *Rob Roy* and *The Bride of Lammermoor*. His own preference was for the historical tales. *The Heart of Midlothian* appealed to me for its title, but he took it from me and put it back on the shelf as "not quite so suitable for you."

"It's a great pleasure to find that you enjoy reading, Ellen. There are plenty of books here for you to borrow and more in the study. Help yourself whenever you like."

Though, as always, restrained and quiet in manner, he was more animated than I had ever seen him. When we talked of characters and scenes, his dark eyes were alive with interest; he spoke fluently; his ideas surprised and stimulated me. To know that he found Colonel Mannering and Meg Merrilies as intensely real as I did was strangely exciting. By some imaginative sleight of hand I succeeded in transferring him from his own back parlor to the romantic world of gypsies, smugglers and strange prophecies where I too in a sense belonged.

So that by the time he saw me out, clutching *The Bride of Lammermoor,* the constraint I had been used to feel in his presence had quite gone. Thinking of him, I forgot too the foolish distaste I had for walking through Saxelby alone. It was perhaps some forgotten experience in my childhood that accounted for the irrational fear I sometimes felt of the two bleak rows of houses facing each other across the steeply narrow street, enclosing it like a tunnel of stone. The doors were always shut as if the secret life of the village went on elsewhere. As a little girl I had imagined watchful eyes behind the flower-pots in the shrouded windows; and still worse, halfway down the hill at the corner of the humped churchyard stood the ivy-covered ruin of Chantry cottage, dark as a decaying tooth.

In fact, the only object in the village to inspire confidence was the Southerns' own square-built house with its white paint and looped chains protecting the well-washed gravel stretch in front of the windows. Today as I looked back up the hill it was to see Mr. Southern standing at his gate and watching me. He raised his hand in a salute which had in it, I oddly felt as I had done once before, a quality of reassurance.

Father had always said that Oliver Southern was a remarkable man whose gifts of personality he had felt from the beginning of their acquaintance. He had been only twenty-one when Father had come to Saxelby. A few years later he inherited the family business, a flourishing concern employing twelve men, which from the age of eighteen he had chosen to carry on personally instead of going to the University,

[102]

though his record as a brilliant classicist at Stanesfield Grammar School promised him an academic or at least a professional career.

Instead he had stayed on at Saxelby and had extended his business to include a highly successful venture in cabinet-making. He was himself a skilled craftsman, almost an artist, specializing in the heavily carved chests and chairs which the revival of taste for the Gothic demanded. We had an oak chest of his in the hall and a fine pair of the Plantagenet chairs which had made his reputation, not only locally but even in London and the South.

With all these gifts there was something else, a special quality which I can recognize now as an almost rigid integrity. For him life was a serious affair. It was difficult for him, I believe, to take anything lightly, so that in manner he often seemed stiff and severe; but as I walked home on that crisp October afternoon under a pale blue sky with the robins singing, I thought only of the way he had talked about the ruined castle at Ellengowan and felt delighted that his feeling for it coincided with my own.

It was a long time before Lucy threw off her cold; in fact she seemed languid and prone to feverish attacks throughout that autumn. Consequently I often went to the Southerns alone. If I had recently discovered a new enjoyment in lessons, it was not only because my studies had become more rewarding but because the Southerns' quiet parlor now seemed a refuge more tranquil than the Mill, where I sometimes felt overwhelmed by the interplay of personalities, all of them more dominant, I suppose, than my own.

But here, absorbedly writing at the table to the tick of the marble colonnaded clock, I felt both peaceful and confident.

Sometimes Mr. Southern would drop in when we were having our midmorning glasses of milk and slices of Madeira cake. Once he took me into his workshop and showed me the chest he was carving. I could feel his enthusiasm for the work as he stroked the intricately carved leaves and flowers as if he loved them.

"One has the illusion, you know, Ellen, that by making a thing of beauty, one can defeat time."

The light in his eyes, the eagerness in his manner as he got out two similar designs and asked me my preference, made me see him all at once as much younger than I had supposed.

One very wet day he insisted on walking all the way back to the Mill with me, holding up an enormous black umbrella and when I told him our joke, "Is not the umbrella of great antiquity?" he actually laughed and assured me that this one was forty years old. "More antique than either of us," he said quite jovially.

Under his influence I began to grope my way to a new awareness of other things besides books. Gradually there emerged with new clarity the features of my own world: a country of boulder-strewn moors and deep valleys: of cottages as rugged as the outcrop stone thrusting through heather and bracken, so that human dwellings had the same unchanging character as the hills themselves. And not only the dwellings.

"You see that woman," Mr. Southern said one afternoon as we walked down the village street.

She was gathering apples from two or three low-leaning trees in a patch of green behind the last house. It was Nancy's friend, Mary Shaw.

"She's typical. These people don't change from one generation to the next."

I saw at once what he meant. She was a statuesque young woman with a natural rhythm in her unhurried way of stretching out for the apples and stooping to lay them in the basket. In her blue dress and brown hair, in the red apples and the autumn sunlight on the long grass, I recognized a touch of poetry. It was as though she were outside time, one of an endless line of women gathering apples from similar trees for countless decades.

"I'll wager she's the image of her grandmother," Mr. Southern said.

I said tentatively that I rather liked the idea.

"Physically? That's well enough. You'll find plenty of girls like Mary in these valleys: big-boned; full-necked; masses of thick hair. But the type is too persistent. There's been too much intermarrying. And in their outlook they do not change. They haven't progressed much beyond their forefathers in the Middle Ages: the same narrowness of mind; the same prejudices and superstitions."

"Do you mean . . ." I hesitated, half-recollecting a conversation with Mark Aylward (How long ago it seemed!), "that in similar circumstances they would behave in the same way?"

"In response to the same stresses—and fears, perhaps? Yes, I think they might. Have you any particular circumstance in mind?"

He was so rational, so enlightened. How could I even mention the particularly lurid circumstance I associated with Mary Shaw's great grandmother?

[105]

"Not really," I said, and lost an opportunity never to be regained.

"It's education they need, Ellen."

And he went on to talk about the Mechanics Institute in Stanesfield of which he was a founder member.

Whether through natural affinity or because my unformed ideas readily took the shape of his I cannot say: but again and again I found myself agreeing with him, seeing through his eyes, and I felt my mind expand and my imagination quicken as new worlds of thought opened before me.

"When we were small," I told him, "we came across the word 'sage' in a story and had to look it up in the dictionary. It said 'A person accredited with profound wisdom.' In a flash I thought of you. 'Like Mr. Southern,' I told Lucy."

He laughed.

"You think I should fit quite well into a tale of the Arabian nights or one of Aesop's fables?"

We were standing on the hearth rug. The Webster in my hand had reminded me of the incident.

"I thought so then," I said, "but then I had very strange ideas."

"Do you remember when you were afraid of the Vikings?"

I turned to look at them, mounted on their curveting bronze horses at either end of the mantelpiece and brandishing their dreadful spears. He took one of them down and considered it critically.

"It's a monstrosity," he said as he replaced it. "I wonder my sister can endure the things."

"They were terrifying," I said, "when one looked up at them, but now . . ."

"You are almost tall enough to confront them, face to face."

We looked together into the pier glass, both smiling. My head was level with his shoulder.

"We have known each other a long time, Ellen."

"All my life."

"All sixteen years of it."

He had turned to look at me directly so that I saw his face in profile through the glass. There seemed a touch of sadness in the droop of his mouth when it was in repose. I waited, hoping to see his face light up again with one of the playful remarks I had come to expect but he said no more, and fearing that I had kept him from his work, I put on my things and went home.

The autumn leaves had burned themselves out and the trees were bare before Father and my stepmother came home. Their short stay in London had been extended several times and then Rose had "begged for a trip to Paris." It was November when the telegram came, announcing their arrival.

The evening was mild, the valley full of the soft afterglow of sunset, the air spiced with the smell of wood smoke from Kirkup's bonfire. Impatient to see Father, I put on a shawl to walk up the lane, but I had gone no farther than the bridge when through the leafless hedgerow I caught sight of a figure at the top of the pasture.

Then he had not forgotten his old trick of taking us by surprise. The familiar thrill of happiness in seeing him sent me flying through the gate and into the field, too eager to wonder why I should have thought him changed.

"Father! Father!" Racing up the hill, I flung myself into his arms.

"Ellen, my darling. It's been too long. Are you both well?

Where's Lucy? How is Binnie? She won't like this news from El Obeid."

Arm in arm we went down, lurching on the tussocks of grass, gray now in the twilight, stumbling and laughing as we had done a score of times.

"There's so much to tell you," he said. "It's been a wonderful experience, naturally, for Rose. To see her pleasure in everything—and I must say Rose is feminine to the core in her love of bright lights and people and dresses and all that sort of thing—to be able to give her a little taste of gaiety after all those drab years; believe me, Ellen, it's been worth every penny of the expense."

I was struck by something in his manner. Was it a touch of overenthusiasm, a need for justification?

"So many times I wished that you and Lucy were with us," he went on. "Lucy would have loved Paris—the parks, the cafés, the shops. I should have liked to show off my daughters. Rose will tell you all about the fashions."

He talked of the art galleries, the palaces . . .

"But I'm determined that you shall enjoy it too, the whole world of art and culture. I mustn't keep you buried here at the Mill. Somehow I've got to do that for you." Then as I protested,—"No, I'm serious, Ellen. You must meet people and widen your experience. Too narrow a life can create a lack of balance. Besides, you must learn enough of Vanity Fair to know its emptiness."

"It would be wonderful," I said, wondering at his seriousness, "but I don't feel the least bit buried."

We were halfway down the pasture, right above the Mill. With one accord we stopped, each discovering the familiar scene afresh, he after weeks of absence, I stimulated by his presence, seeing together the pale smoke rise between bare branches, the windows warm with lamplight, a new moon over the chestnut. Together we heard the unending murmur of water falling over the weir.

"It's so beautiful," I said.

"You think so? You do really?" Again his eagerness struck me as disproportionate: he must know that I loved it. "You understand what it was that appealed to me when I first saw it? I can't tell you how often I've thought of it, dreamed of it, looking just like that: still, tranquil, secure, with you and Lucy waiting for me."

Attuned as I was to all his moods, to every inflexion of his voice, I sensed in him some need of reassurance though I could not tell why.

"We'd rather be here than anywhere in the world," I said, "and especially now that you're back."

"That's just it. But we'll talk about it later."

Hearing the carriage wheels in the lane, we hurried down; but the stillness, the soft sky sprinkled with stars, above all the rapture of having him home again, had given me a moment of happiness so pure that it has served ever since as a guerdon, a glimpse of perfection.

And then, with unbelievable suddenness it came to an end. It seems to me now incredible that knowing him so well, I could have been blind to his intentions. If only I had been older, more observant! If only we had talked more, I might have dissuaded him. But the winter passed for me in a swift sequence of busy days. Absorbed in my books, in looking after Lucy, whose cough and languor kept her mostly indoors, in helping Binnie, I saw little of Father except at breakfast and dinner.

Rose seemed in good spirits after the honeymoon. But when she had shown us her new clothes—a sealskin jacket and muff, a mantle trimmed with passementerie—and when she had told us about the shops in the Burlington Arcade, and installed her possessions in the west room which she and Father were now using, she relapsed into her former habits, silent much of the time, generally idle, often restless. She complained of the cold and spent all her time by the bedroom or parlor fire.

One morning in March, I was finishing my hour of piano practice before breakfast when Father came into the drawing room.

"I want to talk to you, Ellen."

He had a sheaf of papers in his hand. I noticed an entirely new frown between his brows and wondered with ridiculous terror if he were growing old.

We sat down on the windowseat.

"The fact is that I've come to a painful decision. No, don't be alarmed. You see these. Most of them are bills. Well, there's nothing very unusual about that. They'll be paid of course. But the expense of running the house is proving to be greater than I had thought. And it isn't likely to get less, with two growing daughters."

Sitting with downcast eyes, I caught sight of the unpaid bill uppermost of the little pile, a bill from Ebury's in Stanesfield. "Item: to supplying material and the making of two dresses in cream barege, £5/5/0. Item: Two Gainsborough hats . . ." I remembered the chink of the ten gold sovereigns and Rose's hand held out casually to take them.

"Then Rose would like a carriage some day. We certainly need a conveyance of some sort. That will mean having the stable and coachhouse put in order and engaging a man . . ."

"Can we afford it?"

"We aren't poor, my dear, but I've come to the conclusion that I shall have to go back to sea—for a few years. It was a little too soon to retire."

The decision was reasonable enough, yet it took me entirely by surprise. I felt all my energy roused. My whole being woke into passionate resistance.

"No. No. You mustn't."

He must have thought me hysterical but I rushed on, "You mustn't go. It isn't necessary. We don't need a carriage or a coachman. It doesn't matter about clothes and company. We've been perfectly happy without them. Thousands of people are living on the verge of starvation. Why should we have so much?"

Father laughed.

"You're quite right. I don't think I've ever heard you express yourself so forcibly. For a moment you reminded me of Southern. He talks like that sometimes. But I've worked it all out and I'm afraid there's no doubt that this is the most sensible course to take. I wrote to the Company and had this letter from them this morning. It's the most tremendous piece of luck."

He spoke with his old, boyish enthusiasm.

"You remember old Golightly. Well, it seems he's had a heart attack, poor old fellow. I'm sorry of course but it fits in extraordinarily well with my plans. The fact is she was too tender a ship for him. I never thought he'd manage her."

"They've offered you *Miranda* again?"

"My old berth—for a few more voyages. Providential, isn't it? I shall be able to look at those investments in the Australian mines and see a broker in Sidney. In some ways it'll be a good thing to feel the timbers under my feet again. Oh, and by the way, it's back to the wool trade again and a chance of record runs. No more general trading."

A darkness settled upon my heart as I listened. Already his imagination had kindled to the old life as surely as if the stream outside had swelled to a salt tide, the blackbird in half-song become a screaming cloud of gulls.

His enthusiasm carried him through the bustle of packing and arranging his affairs. We had scarcely grown used to the idea before he was gone. It was on the first of May that he left, exactly a year since Rose had come.

Chapter Eleven

That year for the first time the martins did not return to their nests under the eaves. Their absence troubled me. For as long as I could remember, the flash of their white bodies and black wings had been part of the very essence of a summer day, their unfailing return a miraculously forged link with the wider world.

I pointed out the empty nests to Rose as she came out of the dark hall but she only shrugged and walked away through the garden and over the wooden footbridge to the gate. These short walks were becoming a nervous habit. Sometimes she went through the gate and on to the stone bridge where she would lean against the parapet and look first up the steep incline in the direction of Stanesfield, then up the gentler slope toward Saxelby. After a few minutes she would saunter back to the house.

Perhaps after Father went away she became more isolated from the rest of the household. It is as a solitary figure that I chiefly remember her, standing absently in the garden or, with a shawl round her shoulders, looking up the lane, or leaning out of the drawing-room window, gazing down at the river.

Her interest in gossip had evidently flagged. The impression that she scarcely noticed us persisted and deepened. It must have been about this time that I began to sense in her apathy something more positive than a dreamy absent-mindedness. Her lack of feeling for things—and people—made me, more than once, almost afraid.

Even in summer we could rarely sit in the drawing room without a fire. One evening Lucy, who soon felt the cold, had put on another log and drawn her stool closer to the hearth. Almost at once Rose complained of the heat on her face, went up to her room and returned with a hand screen—an exquisite thing of ivory silk in the shape of a shield, embroidered with green and gold water-lilies and mounted on a slender handle of rosewood.

"What a lovely, lovely thing!" Lucy exclaimed as Rose flung herself down on the sofa and held up the screen between her face and the fire. "Is it an heirloom, Mamma, or did you buy it in the Burlington Arcade? That's satin stitch, isn't it? May I see?"

I was sitting on a low chair between them. As Lucy stretched out her hand I had a swift glimpse of Rose's expression. She was looking at the screen with a total absence of pleasure, almost with distaste.

The impression could only be momentary, for as Lucy leaned forward somehow—I cannot tell how it happened—the screen slipped from Rose's hand into the fire. Impulsively Lucy reached out as though to snatch it back; her stool tilted forward; in another second she would have toppled into the flames. As it was I caught her by the collar of her dress and held her, one of her long curls dangling an inch from the bars.

I felt the heat on my face, I smelt the scorching silk as it shriveled and vanished, one water lily lingering pale and cool for an instant until a yellow tongue of flame seized it and it too disappeared.

"It was such a pretty thing," Lucy whispered as we watched the softly polished rosewood char and blacken.

Sick and faint with terror and relief, I felt too a sinking sense of foreboding. The delicate structure of ivory and gold had gone, in an instant, forever. With the sudden sharpness of a searing flame, there seized upon my imagination to haunt it for many days after, a vision of Lucy, her pale skin and golden hair scorched and shriveled too.

"That was a silly thing to do," I said sharply. "You might have been badly burned."

I was still clinging to her convulsively when Nancy came in with Lucy's bedtime drink of black-currant cordial and I suppose there must have been a feeling of tension in the room because I noticed, to my further annoyance, that Nancy was staring inquisitively and taking her time in going out.

But in the midst of my nervous distress I was aware of something else, of the disconcerting way in which Rose had watched not only the destruction of a possession she must surely have cherished but the possibility of a terrible accident. She had simply not moved but sat silent, staring into the fire. With the touch of morbidity that had grown on me of late, I thought there was some difference in her mouth, an ugly droop at the corner as if an invisible hand were dragging it down, quite altering its expression, or perhaps I was seeing it in a different way.

And there was another thing, an impression so irrational that at the time I dismissed it as merely proof of my being overwrought, a curious fancy that she had dropped the screen into the fire *on purpose*.

Then there was the incident of Blanche's kittens, three squirming pink-faced creatures secreted by their mother in a warm corner of the coachhouse. Their arrival was fraught as usual with conflicting elements of delight and pain. Father had decreed with Binnie's full support that there were to be no more cats, there being three already besides Blanche. The kittens must be drowned.

Usually these ghastly executions were performed by Nancy's father who simply spirited the kittens away to a silent end. But Kirkup had gone to his brother's funeral and would be away for a few days. By the time he came back the kittens would have grown too endearing to destroy.

"I can't do it, Miss Ellen, that's flat," said Nancy. "I can kill a chicken which there's some reason for, seein' as we have to eat, but kittens—no."

In this we were unanimous. Binnie declared that it was quite beyond her. Lucy retired to our bedroom and shut the door.

But it was not beyond Rose. With a totally unexpected firmness she marched into the coachhouse with a bucket of water, swept aside the wretched, spitting Blanche with her skirt, and one by one held down the tiny struggling things until their feeble movements ceased.

Spellbound, I watched, recognizing in her something I had not seen there before, a fierce impulse that curved her hands in those strong, purposeful movements and lengthened her face so that all its softness was gone.

"They're dead," she said, and her face changed. She gave a long shudder, staring down at the limp bodies with unbelief, with loathing. Her teeth chattered. She raised her eyes and looked at me but as if I were miles away. "I had to do it," she said. "It had to be done."

"Yes, Mamma, of course."

She wiped her shaking hands on her handkerchief and went indoors, closely followed by Blanche, who from that time rarely left her side but accompanied her from room to room like a familiar spirit.

I dug a grave at the top of the orchard and gingerly laid the kittens to rest.

It was no doubt the defection of Blanche that marked a decline in the relationship between Lucy and our stepmother, which had so far been a pleasant one—though Lucy's first infatuation had long since died.

The first hostility between them was shown by Rose. It stemmed from an incident as inoffensive as could be—a letter from Alec which was passed as usual from hand to hand before being folded and put away in the black tin box where Binnie kept her valuables. The regiment had been moved to Cairo.

"They're talking about sending British troops to relieve

[117]

Gordon in Khartoum," Alec had written, "and a good job too. It's time Mr. Gladstone got a move on if you ask me."

To speak of Mr. Gladstone like that was almost sacrilege— and more than enough to revive all Binnie's fears.

"It isn't even as if he would be fighting Christians," she said, unaware of any irony.

For the first time I remember feeling a touch of apprehension in the thought that Gordon needed to be relieved. Surely he was invulnerable. Had he not outfaced whole regiments of Russians in the Crimea, armed with nothing more than a cane? And if he were in danger, what of Alec?

But Alec wrote cheerfully and we were intrigued at the thought of him riding a camel.

"I often think of Miss Ellen and Miss Lucy," he had written, "and those recitations, especially that one about the schooner *Hesperus*. . . ."

The mere reference was enough to revive Lucy's histrionic ambitions.

"It's ages since we had charades, Ellen. Let's do one this very night," and drawing herself up with an air of superb command she proclaimed in her shrill, clear voice, "I have you in the hollow of my hand. You see I *know* your secret."

A crash sent us both running to the foot of the stairs where Rose lay, white-faced, in a cascade of frilled petticoats. She had evidently caught her foot and fallen down the last two or three stairs.

I helped her up, shaken but unhurt. She sat down heavily on the oak chest and leaned her head against the wall.

"Did something startle you, Mamma?"

"I heard Lucy call out. It threw me off my balance."

"It was only a line from a play, one that Alec taught me. I shouldn't have shouted out like that."

"Alec?"

"Binnie's Alec. He saw a play in Stanesfield and he taught me that line. Would you like your smelling salts?"

Rose moistened her lips and shook her head.

"I'll sit here for a while."

"I'm sorry, Mamma."

"Are you?" Rose sat forward suddenly. In spite of her shaking there was anger in her voice. "Are you? Are you?" She repeated the words in a hard, threatening tone. Her eyes were green and brilliant. Lucy clutched my hand. It seemed like the onset of the hysteria that had so frightened us. But this time the emotion was more purposeful. Before I could intervene, Rose had pulled Lucy toward her and given her a stinging slap across the face.

Lucy shivered and gave a great gasp. I saw a curious glitter in her eyes as if she had momentarily lost her senses. Then to my amazement she said quite calmly, "I shall write and tell Father, of course."

We went out together into the garden, leaving Rose on the oak chest, silent.

The slap, though undeserved, was no great matter. We had both felt the impact of Binnie's palm when we were small.

"She must be missing Father," I said soothingly. "After all we must remember she is his wife."

"I do try to remember but sometimes I don't quite know what she is."

We both knew that a façade, carefully maintained by many an act of service or restraint on our part had fallen: but there could be no lasting breach between ourselves and

Rose, living together, mutually dependent as we were. So that the sky had cleared before the affair of the cowslip wine loomed up like a thundercloud to darken it again.

I have mentioned Rose's penchant for exploring cupboards. One day she gave her attention to a recess halfway up the cellar stairs—no more than a stone cavity where bottles of homemade wine were stored. Not surprisingly Binnie had found no time for winemaking during the past year. Some of the wine was much older than even the previous year's vintage. Moreover it was the custom for country housewives to exchange bottles of wine as gifts. By the time Rose had taken out all the bottles they stood on the cellar steps in a fine confusion, many of them unlabeled.

"I believe Binnie usually keeps the oldest on the bottom shelf," I ventured, trying to remember whether the rhubarb had been behind the potato and parsnip. "This is elderberry, I think."

"Does no one drink this wine?" Rose asked.

"Not often. Father never does. Sometimes Binnie gives it to her own visitors—and Alec rather likes the cowslip."

"This?" She picked up the pale golden bottle and calling to Nancy to fetch a corkscrew and glasses, took it up to the parlor, leaving Lucy and me to put the rest away.

It was an oppressively warm afternoon, one of many in that mainly sultry summer. When we went upstairs, Rose was sipping a glass of wine in a leisurely, genteel manner.

"It does look nice. I'm dreadfully thirsty." Lucy pushed back her thick hair and sat down with her elbows on the table. "Do you think I could have some?"

Rose poured out two glasses. I found the wine faintly pleasant but sweet and cloying and after one or two sips drank no more. Lucy swallowed hers at a gulp and asked for another glass.

"I shouldn't have any more," I warned her, and taking my book, went out into the garden.

Some little time elapsed before my attention was distracted by the sound of Lucy's voice, always high-pitched, now raised to a peculiar tone, a kind of wail. Rushing into the parlor, I found her flushed and incoherent, hiccupping and giggling over a pool of spilt wine on the plush tablecloth.

"She's tipsy," I exclaimed. "Mamma! How could you let her?"

Rose's response was to pour out another glass of wine for herself.

"It's very pleasant," she said, and looking at poor Lucy she burst into a loud fit of laughter, peal after peal, showing her red tongue and white, even teeth. For the first time I found the very shapeliness of her mouth repellent. Even in my anger I remember feeling that there was no humor in her laughter. Like so many of her mannerisms it had a mechanical quality, unmotivated by any warmth of feeling.

With the help of an irate Binnie and Nancy I put Lucy to bed. An attack of sickness left her white and weak and presently she fell asleep.

Feeling unable to face Rose for a while, I went back to the garden, but through the open window I heard the conclusion of an interview between her and Binnie.

". . . wouldn't like to hear of this, the care he takes of them. How could you let her, ma'am, knowing how delicate she is?"

I heard Rose say something about a storm in a teacup.

"There's no call to make a joke of it," Binnie said. "Tea would have been a different matter."

"How was I to know that she would drink glass after glass?"

"But surely you know it's because of her state. Parched with thirst. They're always like that. If you haven't seen it before, I have. But then you knew her mother. I only hope and trust she hasn't come to any harm, poor little soul."

I remember how the unspoken fear that was always with me in the dark, leapt out into the sunny garden and became horrifyingly explicit.

"Oh God!" I thought. "If Lucy dies, let me die too," and looking down, I saw my hands white and waxen as if they were already dead.

The sun had gone when Lucy woke. Our room was dim and cool.

"Oh Ellen, what shall I do? What will Father say? Suppose Miss Southern hears of it. Nancy will be sure to tell. You know I was *drunk*."

"No. One doesn't say 'drunk' about a young girl. You couldn't help it. You were just a little tipsy. It went to your head."

"I didn't know it could happen with cowslip wine. She didn't tell me. She laughed and encouraged me." Lucy struggled to sit up, pale as the pillow. "She's supposed to show us how to behave. I don't believe she's a good influence. I'm beginning to hate her."

"Hush. You mustn't say that. You'll soon forget about it."

"I dream about her sometimes," Lucy broke in. "Coming out of the dark and bending over me. Oh, Ellen."

Once acknowledged, Lucy's ill-health became startlingly obvious. Throughout that long, airless summer the watch I had always kept over her sharpened into an agonized care. I watched her from her first waking, pallid and exhausted after a restless night, through the languor of the morning to the renewed fever of evening.

"It's too low-lying for her here," Binnie would say. "Take her up the hill where the air's not so heavy and there's more sun."

Lucy would set off quite gaily but there were very few days when she was strong enough to climb the hill. More often than not she would stop, breathless, at the turning into Plum Lane on the excuse of gathering groundsel for Pip, her canary.

"It's so warm, Ellen. Shall we sit here for a while?"

I can picture her still, pushing back her hat with the blue ribbons, among the tall grasses and pale meadow-sweet under the elders heavy with bloom. She seemed suddenly to have grown taller. Her cheeks had lost their childish roundness. Once, noticing the new sharpness of her nose and chin, I thought with a pang of fear that she looked almost . . . not old, that was impossible, but not young either—as though she had already been drawn into that limbo of invalidism where young and old alike lose their identity and become merely the sick.

As the day wore on she always became more talkative, full of plans, how we would alter our dresses, make a cosy corner like the one in Sylvia's *Home Journal,* learn to cook really well before Father came home. Her color would rise so that when Nancy brought in the tea, her cheeks were pink, her eyes bright and she looked so well that my spirits rose too. By bedtime she was too much excited to sleep but would fall at last into a troubled doze. Once she woke, moaning and shivering. I slept at that time almost as lightly as she and was immediately awake to say reassuringly, "You're quite safe. What was it that frightened you?"

"I thought she was coming along the landing—with something in her hand. She was there at the door."

Involuntarily I turned my head. Across the dark room it was just possible to see the thicker darkness of the door. It was closed. I could hear nothing but the murmur of water below the window and the occasional creak of floorboards as the old house turned in its sleep.

"Hush. There's no one there. Go to sleep."

Sometimes Binnie's possets and herbal teas and cooling drinks seemed to take effect and for a few days Lucy would be almost her old self.

"If we can keep her free from colds through the winter," Binnie said, "your father'll perhaps be able to arrange a sea voyage for her. That's said to be a good thing for the likes of her. And for all we know, once she's past her sixteenth birthday she may take a turn for the better."

Summer declined into a damp autumn with white mists shutting us in for much of the morning and evening. I tried to calculate how long it would be before Father came home. The clippers were generally back before the middle of December, sometimes three or four weeks earlier, but certainly in time for the January wool sales. Fortunately a spell of sharper weather late in the year had a reviving effect upon Lucy. The twelfth of December—it is not a date I am likely to forget—was a day of intense cold.

With a touch of her old energy, Lucy had got out her wools and needlecase, intending to start on a Berlin-work footstool like one of Miss Southern's which she had admired. She had laid her materials on the hearthrug to arrange the colors. Rose lay yawning on the sofa as she scanned the newspaper.

I was still standing at the window and thinking that it was more than time to abandon the drawing room for the cosy parlor downstairs when I saw a man on the bridge looking up at me. For one rapturous moment I thought of Father but before the wave of joy had ebbed, I recognized Mr. Southern. He was standing quite still. Presently, despite the cold, he took off his hat and smoothed his hair with his hand. Then he took out a handkerchief and wiped his lips. His face was almost as white as the linen.

He turned and walked to the gate, over the footbridge, up the flagged path. I heard him open the front door without knocking and cross the hall. I heard his foot on the stairs, heard it with a sense of disaster so absolute that I could only stand like a marble image, bracing myself to face him when he opened the door. It was at me that he was looking, to me that he came.

"Ellen. I have news for you. Bad news."

"About Father?"

He drew me to the window-seat. Without a word Lucy came to my side. It was as though we had always known what would happen and knew now what to do. We faced him together.

"Is *Miranda* missing?" asked Lucy, her voice high and steady.

He shook his head.

"Lost—with all hands."

Then there was no hope. An immense darkness unrolled itself like a web of sable cloth, shrouding the ceiling, the cold air, the winter sky; and yet surely Father was there in the room. I looked round—at his chair—out of the window at the frost-bleached pasture—feeling him everywhere, expecting him to touch my hand, more real than Mr. Southern, far more real than Rose, of whom I remember nothing but a noisy outburst of hysterical weeping.

"I'm deeply sorry, Mrs. Westerdale," Mr. Southern kept on saying. "If there is anything at all that I can do . . ."

Her wailing brought Binnie upstairs, and it was Binnie who mercifully coaxed her away with promises of vinaigrettes and brandy.

But I could only feel the irrelevance of Rose as if she were a character from another play who had stumbled on to the scene by mistake.

"The Company wrote to me. Doughty wrote to me himself," Mr. Southern was saying gently. *"Miranda* was sighted south of the Horn. She had been spoken the night before by a ship twenty-five days out from Christchurch. Then the *Langley Queen* sighted her. There was a great deal of ice about. A few minutes later there was a terrific squall. The skipper of the *Langley Queen* was hard put to it to save his own ship. He never saw *Miranda* again. The weather lasted three days . . ." He broke off, felt in his pocket and with an effort went on, "And there's another letter, from one of your father's friends. Some one called Golightly . . ."

Old Golightly. I took the letter, hearing Father's voice, irritable, patronizing, seeing the careful penmanship, the kind, laborious phrases only dimly as if the chilling mist had come into the very room.

". . . My respectful sympathy to the young ladies . . . a good friend . . . fine seaman . . . never knew his equal as a navigator . . . knew his ship and the condition of his gear down to the last inch of rope. It was always his way to hold on to all sail in dirty weather, but he never drove his ship beyond the limits of sound seamanship and consideration for his crew . . . a master-rigger, or the clipper could never have carried her royals in heavy weather round the Horn as she did more than once . . ."

Then he had held on just too long, for all his flair and courage to be beaten at last. There were some things that winds and tides could not permit.

> "Down came the storm and smote amain
> The vessel in her strength."

Like news of an old disaster the trite lines came into my mind. I heard them through the roar of wind and thresh of waters, gray and pitiless and endless, so that they seemed to cover the earth.

Even then I do not think we believed it. But after Mr. Southern had gone and we went up to our room, Lucy read old Golightly's letter right through to the end.

"I never thought they would have cause to ring the bell at Lloyds for my old friend Westerdale," he had concluded.

"They rang the bell," Lucy said, and somehow then we knew that it was true. Together we threw ourselves on the bed and wept—for Father, for the lovely lost *Miranda*, for the terrible sadness of the world.

Chapter Twelve

I t was Mr. Southern who insisted that everything should go on as usual. At first he called every morning, usually before Rose came down, and I am sure it was he who encouraged Binnie to serve meals as regularly as ever and to see that Lucy and I carried out our daily occupations so that we kept a small sense of purpose though at times the very meaning of life seemed gone forever.

We had always relied on him in Father's absence. Now he became—apart from Binnie—the one constantly reassuring presence in our changed world. We knew better than to look for comfort to Rose, whose moods alternated between noisy outbursts of grief and long spells of settled gloom. Like clinging plants seeking support, we turned instinctively to Mr. Southern. Though neither relative nor guardian, he contrived to fulfil the roles of both, and somehow with his help we pieced together the fragments of our shattered lives.

Characteristically Lucy was the one who made the most strenuous efforts. With her usual tendency to overdo things, she even persisted in finishing the slippers she had been working for Father's Christmas present.

"Please leave them," I begged, finding her drooping miserably over the work. "I don't believe you should do it. It's morbid."

"I must do something. It isn't as though we could even have a funeral."

I knew how she felt. He had been dead long before we knew of it. The only form of expression left to us was our deep mourning. Rose had hers made at Ebury's; a black dress entirely covered with crepe, with a black lawn collar and cuffs and a widow's cap with weepers. Lucy and I had bombazine dresses quickly made by the village dressmaker.

"You're still growing," Rose said. "It isn't worth going to more expense."

Our sense of decorum was satisfied, but the mournful spread of black skirts about the dim rooms, the sunless days of midwinter, the early twilight, the endless quiet evenings in the little parlor all worked upon the nerves so that I for one often felt as if the walls were closing in and pressing me down into a deep well of gloom.

It was natural perhaps that I should seize upon any brief opportunity of escape that was offered. All the same, I blame myself for what happened to Lucy. Since she was rarely well enough to go out of doors and certainly could not manage the walk to Saxelby, lessons had gradually been discontinued and I realize now that she must have been confined to the house and the unrelieved company of Rose for almost the entire autumn and winter.

I, on the other hand, had continued to walk to the Southerns several times a week, if only to borrow books and practice my French and music, and now Miss Southern and her brother encouraged me to visit them as often as I liked. Often when the weather was dry, Mr. Southern and I went for long walks together. It was not only the exercise and fresh air that helped me: we talked endlessly about Father, touching often on the deeper issues of life, death and immortality—which now for the first time I tried, gropingly, achingly, to interpret.

Each day Mr. Southern devised some small object for our walk. Once he took me into the church to look at the Jacobean pulpit and told me how as a little boy he had gazed at it all through every sermon—and how it had inspired him to take up his own work.

"I never took my eyes off it," he said, tracing with his hand the outline of the ancient carving, black and smooth with age, and I remembered what Father had said about the intensity of feeling, amounting almost to fanaticism, in Oliver's nature. "And yet," he went on with the quiet humor that often lightened his conversation now, "it did no harm to my devotions. I absorbed the doctrine indirectly, soaking it up unconsciously as other people respond to the carving and stained glass."

One morning as we walked along the field path from Cross Gap, we talked about Lucy. Her frequent colds and persistent cough had led to a gradual loss of strength but there had been no crisis in her condition and there had seemed no urgent need to call in the doctor. But when Mr. Southern confessed to me that he had been disturbed by her appearance that morning, my whole being awoke at once into a tumult of anxiety. Feeling that I had neglected her, I could scarcely wait to be at her side and I was wondering how, without being impolite, I could curtail our walk, when to my relief it began to rain, and we were obliged to turn back.

The shower soon turned to a stinging downpour. I left Mr. Southern at the stile at the top of our lane and ran down the hill, my hands full of the yellow aconites we had gathered together, my head bent against the rain. Something caught my eye as I passed the twin-boled elm tree halfway down the lane—something black. Turning, I recognized to my astonishment the figure of Lucy. I say "figure" because to my first horrified glance that is how she appeared, a small black form devoid of personality, almost of life, as she crouched shrinking between the two boles of the tree.

"Lucy! Whatever are you doing out here in the rain?"

She was wearing neither hat nor jacket, only a shawl pulled over her head, and the bands of cheap crepe on her dress, already soaked with rain, were spotted with leprous patches of white. She was terribly pale, petrified almost with cold, and there was a blankness in her eyes as if she scarcely knew where she was.

"Get up. You must come home at once."

We were not usually demonstrative, but now—dropping the flowers—I put my arms round her and held her close.

"What happened? What were you doing?"

She stirred and seemed to revive a little.

"I was waiting for you."

"Here? With only a shawl? But why?"

"I couldn't stand it any longer. Being in the house—with Mamma."

I drew her to her feet, wiped her face with my handkerchief and rubbed her cold hands. Together we stepped over the scattered gold of the aconites into the lane, and taking her by the arm, I set off as briskly as possible for home.

The movement and my company restored her to something like herself.

"I thought you would never come. I didn't think it would rain but anything seemed better than being shut up down there."

"You've been too much indoors. I shouldn't have left you."

"It's Mamma, Ellen." Her voice was beginning to rise. There was a strained, almost a strangled note in it, as if in spite of her cold wet state she was still holding out against—panic.

"What has she done?"

"Nothing. Nothing really. You know she never *does* anything. But sometimes I just can't bear it. I can't breathe when she's near me. Now that she's dressed up as a widow. . . ."

"Dressed up? Whatever do you mean? She *is* a widow."

I glanced sideways at Lucy. She looked confused.

"I know. But she seems so—unavoidable."

There was indeed something pervasive in Rose's personality. She could never be ignored. But at least if I had been there, I told myself guiltily, the effect she had on Lucy would have been diluted.

"I won't leave you again. Why don't you go into another room? Nancy can light a fire in the little study. We must have the chimney swept. Would you like that?"

She nodded vaguely.

"Yes. But Mamma likes me to be with her. She doesn't care to be alone."

"Does she talk?"

"Not very much. She taps—on the chair arms—for ages sometimes. Then she goes to the window and taps on the panes, as if she wanted to get out. Sometimes quite loudly. I can't work or read—or think of anything else except her. It's as though—as though she devoured me, Ellen." She brought out the colorful word with a hint of her old love of drama. "It's like being smothered alive."

"I do wish she would find something to do," I said desperately. "Why can't she sew or read like other people? She doesn't like piquet or whist and even *she* can't play solitaire forever."

All this time I was hurrying Lucy down the hill and when she said, "I wonder what she writes," I came to an abrupt halt, breathless with exertion and astonishment. In fact it crossed my mind that Lucy must be feverish.

"Writes?"

"In her room. Sometimes she goes to her room and locks the door—and writes."

I must confess that it had come to be a relief when Rose withdrew, as she often did, to her room. I had always thought that she employed herself in going through her clothes and arranging her hair and toilet.

"I saw her one morning—from the orchard," Lucy said. "She was sitting at the table, writing."

"Perhaps she keeps a diary," I said, though nothing could be less likely and I had never known her to write a letter in all the time she had been at the Mill. But I was more concerned just then with the thought that Lucy's escape from the house this morning had not been the first of its kind.

"It may be a secret journal," Lucy said, recovering a little, though she spoke through clenched teeth and was shuddering with cold. "How *dull* it must be! Whatever it is, she doesn't like any one to know about it. After I watched her from the orchard, I went indoors and crept upstairs—to our room. . . ."

The word disturbed me. When had Lucy been in the habit of creeping about the house?

". . . and Mamma opened her door to call to Nancy to bring more coal. When she saw me she slammed it shut again."

"Never mind about her now. I'm going to put you to bed and give you a hot drink."

I felt in my bones that the crisis we had so far avoided was upon us now, and sure enough by the time we had got Lucy to bed, her ashen pallor had given way to the burning crimson of fever. During the night she could find no resting place for her head, complained that her limbs ached, and at times she was quite incoherent.

I told Binnie what Mr. Southern had said.

"I'm relieved to hear it," she said. "Whether the doctor should have been fetched before or not, we shall have to have him now and that's certain."

The next morning—it was cold and foggy, I remember, I heard her knock on Rose's door and open it without waiting for more than a perfunctory second or two.

"It's about Miss Lucy, Ma'am . . ." "I think the doctor should be sent for and should have been long ago. I've said it before and I'll say it again . . ."

Rose's reply was inaudible, murmured from the pillow.

"I'm sending Nancy now, Ma'am."

For once Rose was sufficiently roused to come along to our room. I was giving Lucy her breakfast of bread and milk but she seemed hardly aware of either me or the bowl as she lay propped up on the pillow, staring almost vacantly at the white wall.

Neither of us was prepared for the sudden appearance of Rose in the doorway, still in a peignoir, with her hair down. My hand shook so that I spilt milk on the counterpane. Lucy's head came round with a jerk and she shrank back against the pillows.

Rose came between us and bent over the bed.

"Are you ill? I hope you aren't going to bring me more worry and trouble."

We were used to the petulant manner, but now Lucy seemed quite unnerved, looking at her blankly, her neck and mouth stiff as if she were inwardly shuddering.

"Oh well, I suppose you must have the doctor." Rose shrugged, walked round the room, casually glancing at the toilet things on the chest, peeped at herself in one of the shell-framed looking-glasses and sauntered out.

"Ellen, if I'm going to be ill, don't let her come to me. Please. Promise you won't let her."

The fog persisted all day. It was afternoon when I heard the doctor's gig coming down the lane. I took him into the parlor where Rose was sitting as usual by the fire. Dr. Wareham had the reputation of taking a lively interest in people, sometimes more unkindly interpreted as a love of gossip. I saw his quick observation of Rose and felt sorry that she was not looking her best. In fact, I realized all at once that she

[135]

had a slightly neglected look. Her cheeks were blotched from the fire; her hair was loose. A few stitches had come undone below the arm-pit in the body of her old black mourning dress.

Dr. Wareham was on his way to visit another patient at Cross Gap and asked at once to be taken upstairs. As he held open the door, Rose did not stir but Binnie followed us upstairs and discreetly stood by the door while he made his examination.

Even in the short time she had been alone Lucy seemed to have grown worse. There was a wildness in her look that frightened me. She was a favorite with the doctor but now she had no smile for him, seemed hardly to know him.

"I don't like this," he said afterwards in a low voice on the landing. "She has a high temperature and her general physique is poor. Is there any breathlessness? Does she complain of a pain in her side?"

He had with him the materials for a cooling medicine to be taken at once.

"I'll call on my way back from Cross Gap. But I'll tell you plainly, Ellen, when she recovers a little, you must get her away from this picturesque deathtrap, at least for a while. I told your father the same thing when your mother—but there, I won't say more. You've been through a sad time, my dear, and we must do our best. Oh, and another thing. Cut off some of Lucy's hair. I'll speak to your stepmother."

He went back to the parlor to take a hasty glass of wine before driving off.

Lucy woke from a restless doze as I went to the chest and took a pair of scissors from my work-box. "Dr. Wareham says you must have a little of your hair cut off."

She nodded listlessly but when I went over to the bed, she looked distressed.

"You won't do it now?"

"He said you would feel better. It's so heavy for you when you aren't well. Sit up a little."

I took a thick, fair curl in my left hand. It was beautiful hair, strong, shining, vigorous—so that by contrast Lucy herself looked sadly wasted and therein, I knew, lay the danger, the very reason for cutting it off.

"Let me see it." With a faint revival of girlish vanity she twisted her head. "It does seem a shame."

Again I gripped the curl, again my heart failed me. Just then the parlor door opened; the doctor was leaving. Glad of the excuse, I ran downstairs to see him out. When he had gone, I went into the parlor, still holding the scissors.

"The doctor says Lucy must have some of her hair cut off. I don't quite know how to do it."

"I'll do it." Rose jumped up in one of her rare moods of animation. She seemed stimulated by the doctor's visit and had taken the opportunity, I noticed, of changing her dress while he was upstairs. "I've a better pair of scissors in my room. Besides, I know how to do it so that it will look quite nice."

Pleased and grateful, I followed her and waited while she rummaged in her drawers and came quickly along the landing. As I opened the door Lucy sat up, startled by the small commotion, her eyes dazed with fever—to see Rose bearing down upon her, smiling, intent, with the bright scissors in her hand. Even to me—and I was on my feet—she seemed, from the top of her black cap to the hem of her black dress, suddenly overpowering, like a tall dark column in the low room.

[137]

"I'm going to cut your hair." She laughed as if the whole thing were a delightful joke.

But her words were drowned by a piercing scream as Lucy threw herself across to the other side of the bed in a desperate attempt to escape. Foiled by the bedclothes, she screamed again and again, tearing at the tangled sheets as if she was mad with fear.

Binnie and Nancy came running upstairs as I tried to hold her but she struggled and fought, beating me with her hands, her eyes glassy with terror.

"She doesn't know me," I cried, horrified.

"Out of the way, ma'am." Binnie bundled Rose unceremoniously out of the room. "God grant she may not be going into a brain fever. There now, my lovey, there now . . ."

I shall never forget that night. When I drew the bedroom curtains the fog had thickened, cutting off everything but the steep pasture. For once even the flow of the river was muffled almost to silence, but if it had roared like thunder I would not have heard it. I heard nothing but Lucy's demented screams. It was as if all the unrest, anxiety and grief of the past year had quickened to a climax, combining with the hallucinatory power of fever to conjure up nightmare figures, or rather one figure. It was Rose who dominated her delirium, Rose who took on ever-changing shapes: a tree, a falling chimney, a dark rock, a tall press . . .

"It makes you wonder . . ." Nancy had come into the room to replenish the fire and stood listening with a sort of horrified relish. "It makes you wonder what she's done to her—the Missis, I mean." Then, encouraged no doubt by the abnormality of the situation—"I mean to say, like that time when she tried to push her in the fire. . . ."

I came to myself with a start.

"What are you saying, Nancy? You forget yourself." Then, seeing her heavy-eyed with weariness and recalling that she had stayed up all night, I checked myself.

"It's only delirium and Lucy is very ill. Go and lie down on the sofa in the kitchen, Nancy, and have some sleep."

Not until after midnight did Dr. Wareham grope his way to the door, leaving the care of his horse to Kirkup. I could see that he was disturbed by the change in Lucy. A stronger draught put her to sleep at last and he stayed by her side till morning.

It was still dark when we went down to the kitchen where a fire had been kept burning all night. I had lingered to bathe my face and brush my hair and came in to hear Dr. Wareham say: "The child is afraid of her. I take it there is no actual unkindness?"

Binnie hesitated.

"It's more—ignoring them. Not knowing they're there. Not knowing that anyone's there, except herself. If that's un-kindness . . ."

"Some mental disturbance, do you think?"

"There's something, sir. Something I can't put my finger on."

"Come along, Ellen." The doctor turned to me. "Drink a cup of hot tea and then lie down for a while. Lucy will sleep for some hours now. But we must get her away from here for a complete change. Have you a relative you could go to?"

Since the first suggestion that Lucy should go away, I had considered the possibility of writing to Aunt Lumley, our only other surviving relative on our mother's side. Though we had not been in touch with her since Mother's death, she had after all given a home to Mother when she was a girl and had been fond of her.

"The climate of the Isle of Wight should suit Lucy as well as any," Dr. Wareham said when I broached the idea. "A change would do you both good. It might be advisable to write at once."

"A change of air?" Rose sat up when I told her, looking surprisingly alert and interested. "Perhaps that would be a good thing." But when I tentatively suggested that she might write to Aunt Lumley, all the brightness faded from her face.

"Or shall I write myself," I ventured, when she made no offer.

"Yes. You had better write. I was never a favorite with Aunt Lumley, and you are good at putting things tactfully."

It took me an hour to write the letter. I had just sealed it when Mr. Southern called and undertook to post it for me. The whole village already knew of Lucy's illness. He had brought a jar of calves'-foot jelly from Miss Southern as well as an affectionate message and offers of help. He was still there when Lucy awoke, almost too feeble to speak. But at least she knew me. When the doctor called in the afternoon, he declared himself fairly well satisfied.

"But she will need very careful nursing and absolute quiet. The least excitement would be dangerous. Frankly, I doubt if she would survive a second attack like this last one. I suggest that you and Mrs. Binnock look after her between you, Ellen. But take care of your own health. I'll look in again tomorrow."

He and Mr. Southern left together. I heard them talking in the hall as the doctor put on his ulster and I waited on the landing until they had gone, too tired to speak to them again and perhaps delay their departure.

"It's an odd situation," the doctor said. "What do you make of her? Poor Westerdale seems to have made a blunder."

"Yes."

Mr. Southern's terse monosyllable was enough for the doctor, who went on, "There's quite a lot of talk in the village. Of course I don't pay any attention to servants' gossip and all that nonsense of old Solomon's about a white cat and the evil eye. But there's no smoke without fire. To put it at its most rational, she's scarcely a helpful influence for those two girls, cooped up here alone with her. What about the purse-strings? Do you know?"

"She's his widow."

"Yes. Perhaps things have worked out better for her than anyone else."

Though at that time I was far too much absorbed in Lucy's condition to pay attention to anything else, I was aware of the doctor's implications and later they were to recur more forcefully to my mind. Mr. Southern had already spoken to me about our financial position but I was too ignorant to understand his concern.

It would be some time, apparently, before Father's estate could be wound up and our exact position known; but according to Mr. Southern, Father's investments had done well; he was a shrewd speculator and had used his opportunities as a sea captain to gain an insight into foreign markets. A considerable sum, for instance, had been invested in South American minerals, others in Australian and New Zealand wool. Most of the sum of £10,000 from his father remained intact. Mr. Southern knew all this because until a year ago he would have been executor of Father's will and co-trustee with Mr.

Petersby, the Stanesfield lawyer, if Father should die before Lucy and I married or came of age.

"But your father changed his will when he married, making your stepmother executrix. Fortunately her co-trustee and executor is still Petersby."

When Mr. Southern said this, I did not see the significance of the word "fortunately."

However, Father had confided in him the terms of his new will; a pecuniary legacy to Rose, the remainder of the estate to be divided, one half to be held in trust for Lucy and me until our marriage or majority. In the other half which would revert to us on her death, Rose was to have a life interest. She would also, so long as we were minors, have the handling of the interest accruing from Lucy's money and mine to use for our maintenance and education.

"Until you come of age, you will be dependent on your stepmother. You won't be able to touch your money, unless you marry."

Beyond an involuntary distaste which I was in no mood to analyze, I felt little interest. We had always lived in comfort, though simply, needing little money to spend, if any. Besides, having lost Father, I regarded any other deprivation as so slight as to be negligible.

But in the following days for the first time I was to feel the need of ready money and not only to buy delicacies for Lucy. Once, in some embarrassment, Binnie mentioned that though Quarter Day was long past, she had not been paid and Nancy's wages were two weeks in arrears.

"It doesn't matter so much for me, but Nancy needs her money. This didn't happen when Mr. Southern had the handling of things. And Shaw threw out a hint about last month's bill when I was ordering the meat on Tuesday. If you could just mention it."

Binnie had worries enough of her own. The newspapers were full of the battle at the wells of Abu Klea, in which a thousand Ansar had been killed, but not without the loss of eighteen British officers and one hundred and fifty men killed or wounded. There had been no news of Alec since November when we had heard that his regiment was to form part of Wolseley's force to relieve Khartoum.

Of course I mentioned the matter of the wages. Rose frowned and looked offended but she went upstairs with her bunch of keys and returned with the money.

Aunt Lumley must have replied almost by return of post. Feeling that she was our last hope and that if she failed us I would lose heart altogether, I nervously tore open the envelope. She had, it seemed, a grudge.

"I simply cannot understand your Cousin Rose, or stepmother as I should call her. So many things have happened in the family without a scribe of the pen from her to tell me about them, her own kith and kin. As for your father's death, I am deeply sorry, my dear Ellen. He was a good, kind man and his loss is a grievous blow to you all."

Then came the shock of disappointment.

"Lucy may certainly come to me if the journey can be managed safely and the sooner the better, as was the case with her mother. Someone will have to bring her and she can look on this as her home until her health is secure. Had you been alone I would have taken you both but as things have fallen out, your place is with Rose. It would not be right for you both

[143]

to leave her alone. There has been too much of that in her life it seems to me and I am wondering if she has got into a low state."

It had never occurred to me that Lucy and I might be parted, especially now. For days I had scarcely stirred from her side. There was a strange seclusion in our room, the door curtained to shut out every sound from the house, the window closed because Lucy could not bear even the murmur of the river. Between us Binnie and I had nursed her back to life and sanity, but the passive creature whom I fed and washed and propped up with pillows seemed little more than the ghost of my sister—so docile and helpless that I could not let her go. Either we both went or Lucy must remain. But a moment's thought showed me the folly of this. Somehow the parting must be faced and the journey arranged.

After a little hesitation I went to Rose.

"It would be much better for you both to go," she said, having read the letter without any sign of offence at Aunt Lumley's remarks.

"But I can't possibly go since she hasn't asked me," I said and after a pause gathered courage to ask, "Will you take her, Mamma?"

"I? Why, it's quite out of the question. Binnie can take her. In any case it's the wrong time of the year to move an invalid. She must wait for the warmer weather."

There was a good deal of truth in this. All the same I knew that left to Rose, Lucy's journey would be indefinitely postponed. To my surprise, Dr. Wareham favored Lucy's going at once, winter as it was.

I was so entirely without experience, never having traveled

farther than Stanesfield, that there seemed no alternative to asking Binnie to go. However I decided first to consult the Southerns and once again it was they who came to the rescue. Miss Southern, it seemed, had long contemplated seeking a change of climate to recruit her health. Ventnor would suit her admirably and Mr. Southern would not only arrange the journey but would himself escort Lucy and his sister. They would travel by easy stages; he would reserve a compartment in each train. It remained only to prepare Lucy's clothes and extract from Rose sufficient money to cover the expenses and give Lucy a suitable sum for pin money.

It may have been the almost daily presence of Mr. Southern at the Mill that affected Rose with a sufficient sense of urgency to make her more reasonable than she might otherwise have been. She made a special trip to the bank in Stanesfield and gave me twenty pounds. I insisted on giving Mr. Southern six pounds for Lucy's expenses; the rest I gave to Lucy, except for one sovereign which after a little thought I kept for myself, feeling that some day I might have need of it.

Since all Lucy's dresses were too short for her, I was obliged to alter some of my own and have them dyed for her. In seeing that she had the best of our united stock of gloves, stockings and underwear, I left myself sadly depleted, but there was no sacrifice in this. It was as though my own future stretched no further than the day of Lucy's departure.

Lucy and I were to be driven into Stanesfield to stay two nights with Sarah's mother who let apartments, so that Lucy could rest before the long journey. When Mr. Southern had carried her out to the carriage and Nancy had followed with shawls and foot-warmers, cologne and brandy, I found Binnie in the kitchen, crying bitterly.

"Why, Binnie. You didn't cry even when Alec went away."

"Take no notice of me, love. It's all just got on top of me."
Then she burst out, "She seems so changed."

I could only agree miserably. It was not just the wasting,
the pallor, the cropped hair that gave Lucy the look of a shorn
lamb. These I had grown used to during the long hours in the
sickroom. But there were other changes. She never mentioned
Father now—nor Rose. It was as if she had reverted to that
earlier time which only she and I and Binnie had shared. All
the old brightness of spirit had faded, as if, I found myself
thinking, the real Lucy had already slipped away.

"Goodbye, Miss Lucy. It's a good thing one of you at least
is going out of harm's way," said Nancy cryptically as she gave
a final twitch to the rugs.

Rose waved from the window. I saw Blanche leap on to her
shoulder as we drove away, leaving her in possession.

Chapter Thirteen

A cold drizzle drove me to the sheltering doorway of the King's Head to wait for Babbitt the carrier. Mercifully, perhaps, my sensations at that moment were purely physical. Not even Lucy's sudden, anguished, "Ellen, what will you do?" as the carriage doors were slammed had really distracted me. All my strength seemed directed to the endurance of a strange soreness in my left side, as if part of my body had been torn away. I felt it as I stood there in the doorway, my left shoulder dragged down as though I were deformed.

And all the time a ragged newsboy was calling: "Murder of General Gordon in Khartoum. Gordon murdered . . ."

Melancholy as the croak of a raven, the cry seemed to usher in a new era in which the ramparts of security were tumbling and the impossible could happen.

It was bitterly cold too. It dawned on me that I had forgotten my muff—or lost it somewhere; that my last year's jacket, dyed black, was scarcely thick enough to keep out the February damp; that the cotton gloves Nancy had got for me at the village shop were already worn thin at the fingertips.

It was market day in Stanesfield. From the cattle pens nearby in Mart Street came a forlorn lowing and bleating. In similar mood a streetsinger warbled a mournful ballad, moving inch by inch over the cobbles with a pale-faced toddler at her side.

Normally, with Lucy for company, even in the rain I might have enjoyed the booths with their bright display of flowered crockery and hand-woven baskets, the gingerbread stall, the cheap-jack selling watches and jewellery. But business was slack. The weather had discouraged the usual cheerful shoppers, especially the young ladies from the farms and country houses who would have interested me most. I caught sight of Solomon haggling over cotton pillowcases at the corner of the square and shrank further into the doorway, hoping he would not see me.

The cattle sales were coming to an end, judging by the group of leather-gaitered farmers who began to drift toward the ordinary across the square or the more attractive King's Head, where the kitchens were sending out the warm smell of roast beef and boiled pudding.

It was then that I saw Mark Aylward riding under the arch to the hotel yard. He had seen me too and dismounted quickly, threw the reins to an ostler and came to speak to me.

"Miss Ellen. Good morning. How are you?"

At first I could only stammer a greeting and stand tongue-tied; too tired and cold, too much surprised at seeing him again so unexpectedly to have anything to say.

"You are alone?"

I saw his first look of pleased recognition change to one of concern. "Is no one with you?"

Haltingly I explained. My quite unfamiliar feeling of shame at having to resort to the common carrier was intensified by a swift impression that Mark Aylward's appearance had changed for the better. In those first moments I was not aware in detail of his well-cut jacket and breeches, shining boots, his well-groomed bay mare, only that his whole appearance was now in harmony with his voice and manners and that he was far more in command of the situation than I.

"It's much too cold for you here in this draughty place. Let me take you inside and order something for you—some hot tea."

"But Babbitt—I mustn't miss him. It's almost twelve."

"You can wait for him as well inside. Hi!" He hailed a bare-foot urchin who was crouching, blue with cold, over the vent where warm air rose from the kitchen. "Can you watch out for Babbitt the carrier for me?"

"Yessir."

"There's a threepenny piece for you—and there'll be another if you tell him to wait for the young lady . . ."

The kindness, the ease with which he took my carpetbag and ushered me into the low sitting room, the welcome warmth stealing into my hands and feet as I sipped the tea together had the unfortunate effect of reviving my feelings. In a sudden wave of loneliness and misery, I felt the tears flowing down my cheeks. Ashamed, I bowed my head over the teacup, aware of his look of concern, unhappily conscious too of the figure I cut in my cheap bombazine with its baggy gathers and graceless folds and my cheap gloves.

"Miss Ellen, I can see that you are in mourning. I'm afraid you are in trouble. It's surely not your . . ."

"My father."

"I'm very sorry."

With an effort I forced down the lump that was choking me. ("Men cannot stand weeping women," Father had often said.) Except for a farmer's wife sitting comfortably over a tray of tea, we were alone in the room but I was determined not to embarrass him by crying.

"Since we had the news about Father in December, Lucy has been very ill. I have just seen her off to the Isle of Wight —for a long stay."

"You couldn't go with her?"

"No. We have kind friends who have taken her."

"Then you are not alone at the Mill? You have some relative?"

"My stepmother."

"I see. I didn't know."

"And Binnie is still with us."

We were together only as long as it took to drink the tea. When I had recovered myself, I looked at him with less awkwardness and now saw how well he looked. His face had filled out; the pinched look had quite gone. Little of the Wild Boy remained except the candor and kindness, the sense of understanding he imparted, as if we had always known each other, almost as if my problems were his.

[150]

"You are well," I said.

"Well? Oh, rather. You didn't come to watch the children on May day."

"No." I had forgotten about it. "That was the day Father went away." The recollection diverted me from the thought that Mark had gone as usual and had missed seeing us there. "I think you look happy too, happier than you used to," I ventured.

Our meetings were always so unconventional that I could speak frankly despite the slightness of our acquaintance.

"Yes. I am happier. Things have taken a turn for the better with me. I have been very fortunate. Grandfather and I were leading a wild, bachelor sort of existence but now, well, that's over. . . ."

The antics of the urchin at the window drew our attention to Babbitt's arrival. I had time only to thank him and say goodbye.

"I wish . . ." He had taken my hand. His eyes were serious. "I should like . . . if there is anything . . ."

In the little flurry of mounting and taking my bag, I gave him no time to finish, but as Babbitt threaded his way between a dray and a gig and then waited for a score of nervous sheep to pass, I saw Mark joined by an older man with thick white hair, who came out of the lawyer's office in the square. Together they crossed to a toy-seller's stall. I watched Mark looking appraisingly at the drums and wooden horses. After some hesitation, but with the whole-hearted interest he gave to everything, he settled in favor of a Dutch doll and tucked it under his arm with an utter lack of embarrassment that made me smile.

Cushioned by the various packages and sheltered from the

rain by the canvas cover, I contrived gradually to feel a little less unhappy. Temperamental as all carriers seemed to be, Babbitt happened to be in one of his better moods and occasionally called out a remark over his shoulder.

As we crawled up the long hill and out on to the open road, the rain eased off. There was nothing more colorful than a flight of black and white lapwings to brighten the landscape of dark moors and gray stone walls, but a freshness in the upland air seemed to bring a faint illusion of spring.

At last I dared to think ahead. I consoled myself with thoughts of my books, of writing letters, of necessary sewing and comfortable chats in the kitchen with Binnie; and soon Mr. Southern would be home again, so that though I never expected to be happy again, instinctively I found what comfort I could.

"I'll take you down to the Mill if you like," said Babbitt when at last we came in sight of the cross-roads, "and no extra charge. You've had a long cold ride and you're not looking too clever. And no wonder by all I hear."

"No, thank you, Mr. Babbitt. I'll get down at the cross-roads and walk. I can cut across the pasture."

"Suit yourself. There's no accountin' for women's ways. The last passenger I had for the Mill changed her mind and got down in the middle of the road. Walking a couple of miles with a heavy bag isn't my idea . . ."

That would be Rose. I remembered her dusty dress and shoes, her weariness, her evident reluctance to face the new life she had launched herself upon. At the recollection, my heart sank as I recognized in myself a similar shrinking.

I paid Babbitt and stood for a moment by the signpost as he drove off along the ridge. The canvas-covered cart might have been venturing into wild Indian country, so little did I know of those rolling heather-clad slopes.

"Kindlehope," declared the signpost, pointing up the valley to where the hills seemed to float apart under a rift of turquoise sky; and although I knew from Mr. Southern that 'hope' meant only 'heap,' the name augured well. Some day I would go there. The thought of the tiny adventure pleased me.

Looking down over the pasture, I saw the Mill framed in its bare-branched copses and tilted fields. And after all I avoided the short-cut and went soberly down the lane, half-inclined to delay my arrival, yet longing for the warmth of the kitchen fire and Binnie's company.

In the steep lane I lost sight of the Mill, but by the time I had slithered down the rutted surface to the very bottom it had played its familiar conjuring trick of appearing suddenly at the water's edge. After the tingling freshness of the moors above, it was like going down into a deep well—or a prison.

Then I saw a figure standing at the gate. It was Binnie, dressed in her outdoor clothes—her jet-trimmed cape and feathered bonnet, her best black dress and boots.

"Binnie! Have you been along to the village?"

She did not answer. I noticed something unusual in her face and manner. She did not smile, did not seem to notice me. Her eyes were hard. A small frown creased her brows.

"Is something wrong? Oh Binnie, is it Alec?"

Mechanically she fumbled in her pocket.

"He's been wounded," she said bluntly. "There's a letter here from some officer. It came yesterday. In the foot. It isn't serious, seemingly."

I skimmed through the letter. After the battle of Abu

Klea Alec had been taken on to Metemma and was to be shipped down the Nile to a base hospital at Dongola.

"Poor Alec! But we mustn't worry too much. He's alive and he'll get better. Perhaps they'll send him home."

I broke off, struck once again by the strangeness of her manner. Why was she standing at the gate, wearing her Sunday best in the middle of the week?

"It's in God's hands," she said in the same mechanical way. "And at least he'll be away from those murdering heathens."

"Then, is there something else, Binnie?"

"I'm going, that's all."

"Going where?"

"Going away. I'm leaving. I only waited till you came back or I'd have gone before."

The bald statements seemed wrung from her as if the one idea had seized upon her mind to the exclusion of every other.

"But you can't go. You have nowhere to go. This is your home. You and Alec live here."

Her face softened into a look of passionate regret. I knew that she was suffering intensely.

"It's on account of Alec. The things she said about him—and him lying wounded in the desert or worse. I can't stay now."

"Mamma? What did she say?"

The story came jerking out: the tiresome business of the silver bonbon dish again.

"I made up my mind to have a good look for it to take my mind off other things. And I'd no sooner mentioned it than she flares up, 'Why pretend to look for it?' she says. 'You know who's taken it. And he's far enough away by this time.'"

"She didn't mean Alec? She couldn't."

[154]

"That's what she meant all right and him as honest as the day and not here to defend himself on account of fighting for his country. 'I've got the rest of the silver under lock and key,' she says, 'and it won't happen again.'"

High words had been exchanged, Binnie hotly defending her son and going no doubt beyond defence.

"There were plenty of things I had to say to her and thought I might as well take the chance of saying, things she didn't like. 'Take your belongings,' she says, 'and a quarter's wages and go. Neither you nor your son shall set foot in this house again.'"

"But it's impossible. How can we go on without you?"

"That I don't know, Miss Ellen." (When had she ever called me Miss?) "It's as if the earth had opened under my feet. And what's to become of you I don't know."

"Me?"

"But the Southerns will look after you and some day—perhaps it won't be too long—when you have a place of your own . . ."

Her words meant nothing to me. I scarcely listened.

"Where are you going now?"

"I'm going to the Mortons' for the night. Not another hour will I spend under that roof with her. Reg Morton'll come for my things in the morning."

"Shan't I see you again, Binnie?"

Appalled as I was at her plight, I could not help feeling her indifference to mine. Famine or earthquake could not have shaken my existence more than the loss of the homely, loving influence I had known all my life.

"Someday perhaps." The unfamiliar hardness seemed to have returned. "But there's no coming back while she's here."

A dismal pride kept me from saying more.

"Goodbye then, Binnie."

We embraced but there was no tenderness in her kiss. I watched her toil up the hill toward Saxelby, her best boots a little uncomfortable—a plump, middle-aged woman—a stranger. Then I went over the footbridge, across the courtyard and into the kitchen.

The fire was out. For the first time in my life I saw the huge grate black and cold in the daytime.

Chapter Fourteen

I stood at the foot of the stairs, listening. The house was utterly still, the rooms above so silent that I dared to imagine that Rose had gone too. The feeling passed almost before I had time to recognize it as one of hope.

After a while I went slowly upstairs, pausing to hear the creak of each tread die away. It was absurd to feel like an intruder in my own home, yet on the landing I hesitated.

"Mamma! Are you there?"

Unexpectedly the door of my own bedroom opened. Rose stood there, unsmiling.

"You're back at last. I was looking round to see if she had taken anything else. I've put all the silver and valuables in the hall press and locked it. It was asking for trouble to leave everything unlocked."

I suppose it was typical of her self-absorption that she should assume I knew what she was talking about. Fleetingly I saw it as a danger signal, but I was more conscious of the change in her. Her voice was harder, more assertive. I could almost have imagined that she was taller. Certainly she filled the door of my room—her face a pallid triangle between the black lappets of her cap. It needed an effort of courage to face her—as I must. There was so much to say, if only I had felt less cold, less tired and hungry.

"Please don't speak about Binnie like that. Her honesty is beyond question. This was her home and Alec's. We had a duty to her after all the years she has looked after us, and especially now, with Alec wounded . . ."

It seemed to be someone else speaking. The tone, the phrases were not mine but Father's. To me they expressed the whole world of difference between his outlook and hers but I felt that they lacked weight, that I was incapable of piercing her extraordinary insensitivity.

"You cannot imagine that Binnie or Alec would rob us. They gave us far more than we can ever repay."

I moved toward my room, and Rose—to my relief—stepped aside.

"She made herself very comfortable here at your father's expense but she shan't do it at mine. When a servant overreaches herself, it's time for her to go. She can be replaced."

Leaning wearily against the bedpost, I tried to find words to explain that servants of Binnie's caliber were not to be found in a district like ours; that Binnie had been recompensed for her small wage of thirty pounds a year only by the security of a settled home.

Then I caught sight of the birdcage in the window. The seed-tray and waterpot were empty. Lucy's canary lay at the bottom of the cage, dead.

"Oh Pip! I forgot you. We all forgot you."

I felt the small neglect as part of a larger betrayal. It was as if all the sickening details of illness and death which had preyed on my imagination in the past weeks were drearily epitomized in the pale ruffled feathers—the appealing claws—the fixed eyes. Looking at the bird I could see only Lucy.

"Couldn't you have remembered him? For Lucy's sake."

Rose had come back into the room.

"What does it matter now? She won't be coming back. You may as well face it." She opened the cage and took hold of Pip without a qualm. "It's dead. There's no use moping about it."

Pushing open the casement with a jerk, she threw the bird out. Too light to travel far, it fell in a distortion of wings and claws at the river's edge. Without another word she went away.

I watched the brown current lap about the stones, rocking Pip gently to and fro.

"I shall be here forever," I thought. "Everyone has gone—Mother, Father, Lucy, Binnie, Alec—except me—and Rose."

The river would go on flowing under the bridge and over the weir, dark under the trees and bright in the open sunlight where it curved out of sight, and every day I would watch the foam flakes drift away and the ripples change until at last I grew old.

Unless . . . The rhythmic wash of water on stone was

soothing after all. It would rock Pip in a cool brown cradle until he ceased completely to be. Slowly there stole over me a feeling of envy, even of longing for that ultimate and lasting quiet. Drowning, they said, was an easy death, especially farther along the river where the water deepened. It would need just a step, a final yielding. . . .

When in a little while I went downstairs, it was with a prisoner's faint hope of reprieve. I raked out the kitchen fire; relaid and lit it; hooked on the kettle. It was Nancy's afternoon off, I dimly recalled, but it would not have surprised me if she too had been spirited away in the universal holocaust.

If Lucy and I had ever been in doubt as to our social status, there was no doubt about it now, I reflected, as I tried to scrub coal dust from my hands at the slate sink before setting out bread and cheese and cold meat. Then, realizing that when Binnie left, she had taken the dear, exasperating Miss Pritts with her—that they too were gone—I felt, absurd as it was—a tiny additional loss.

To my relief Nancy did materialize as usual the next morning. She had gone to Greater Saxelby on her day off and had known nothing of Binnie's dismissal until she passed Mortons' farm on the way home. The whole village, it seemed, was agog at the news.

"She'll get no one from these parts to come," Nancy said flatly when I tentatively mentioned engaging another servant, "the way she's treated Mrs. Binnock. Neither as maid, cook, housekeeper nor nothing else. I said to Mary Shaw, 'For Miss Ellen's sake I'll stop, at least for a while, living so near. But I wouldn't sleep in, not for anything.'"

Clearly she had said it to the whole village and much more besides, but she did consent for an increase of five shillings a week to take on the cooking. I was determined that she should have her wages regularly and made a practice from then on of going to Rose with a list of expenses every Friday morning and waiting patiently until she gave me the money.

As for the daily chores I threw myself into them with a desperate sense that if I worked hard enough, time would pass and I would grow old more quickly. I also made a highly unorthodox and one-sided arrangement with the Almighty that if I worked my fingers to the bone, He would let Lucy live. My only excuse for this primitive code of morality is that it did keep me from utter despair.

"I hear Mr. Southern's back," Nancy said one morning, and I scarcely had time to savor the pleasure and relief before he called. Rose was still in her room.

"Oh Mr. Southern," I cried as he came into the parlor. "Oh, Mr. Southern, you've come back at last."

I had longed for his return but only now—seeing his tall figure in the room—did I realize how much I had missed him. It was irrational perhaps, but I felt a sudden conviction that he was there to protect me—that he had always been there to protect me. From what? Until now I could not have answered, but now there flashed into my mind quite simply the word "Rose." The thought—it was less than a thought—was momentary; but I remember thinking with a sort of strange, sad triumph that here was the one person Rose could never take away from me.

The warmth of my greeting evidently pleased him. He smiled and took both my hands.

"You're pleased to see me, Ellen?"

"Oh yes, indeed. How is Lucy? Is she up? Does she sleep? Is she taking food?"

[161]

When he had satisfied me that she was at least no worse I had many more questions to ask, about Miss Southern and Aunt Lumley.

"My sister has taken very pleasant rooms at Ventnor, not too far away for her to walk over often to see Lucy. Your aunt was good enough to say that she would always be welcome. She sent kind messages to you. But it was not only on that account that I called. I have something to say to you."

But he walked over to the window and it was after a little hesitation that he said, "I heard of course that Mrs. Binnock had left. You must miss her. You have been working hard, I see."

Abruptly he came back, took my work-roughened hand and stroked it gently.

"It grieves me to see you looking thin and tired. You are not happy, Ellen?"

My eyes filled. Of course I was not happy.

"But I'm not really unhappy—apart from Father and Lucy. The days pass quickly."

"Have you thought of the future? Do you want always to live like this?"

Though I had tried to face the prospect, the word "always" frightened me.

"Let me give you a better life, Ellen, a home such as you deserve."

In a flash I saw Lucy and myself in one of Mr. Southern's cottages—happy—alone. I looked up eagerly.

"You would like that?" He sat down beside me. "You are too young, I know, and if things had been different, I would have waited even at the risk of losing you. But I love you, Ellen. To me you are the most precious being in the whole world. The interest of all my life is centered upon you. Seeing you grow more lovely every day—knowing what you must endure from your . . . but I won't speak of that. You could give me happiness such as I have never known if you would be my wife."

Numb with astonishment, filled with a sort of perturbation, a sense that it was not fitting for a man like Mr. Southern to entrust his life and happiness to me, an ignorant girl, I was still aware of his absolute sincerity. I had grown to value his friendship more than anything in my life, had known that he found pleasure in my company—but that he should love me . . . Here was a circumstance so far removed from anything I had thought of as probable, or even possible, that the ability to grasp it, much less to understand all that it implied, seemed altogether beyond me.

"We are such old friends, Ellen. I remember when you were a little thing and I found you on the hearth rug with your head buried in a cushion because you were afraid of the Vikings. Do you remember what you said?"

I shook my head, marveling at the tenderness in his eyes and voice.

"You said, 'It isn't those two I'm afraid of. It's the other two inside the glass, because I can never see them properly.'"

"Yes," I cried, "and you took them down and said, 'Look, they've all gone, all four of them.'" And I almost added, "You were quite young then to bother about a foolish little girl," but I checked myself in time and he went on, "It seems to me that I remember every word you ever said, Ellen, as well as every look, every gesture. I have watched you grow from a baby to a girl, from a girl to a young woman. And I have persuaded myself, perhaps because I wanted to believe it—

though I can scarcely hope that you feel as I do—that there is a special bond between us. A harmony. . . ."

I nodded. It was true. My thinking was attuned to his. He was my authority. His judgments were mine.

"But it is far more than that." He was looking down at me with an expression so unguarded, so totally loving, that I saw him transformed, and softened. "You are so beautiful that waiting for you has been a kind of anguish."

I believed him, of course, but I did not understand. Had we not enjoyed those hours together, walking and talking? Where then had been the anguish? And as if in proof of the sympathy between us he said, "We have walked together in the lanes and fields where I have walked with your father. Every stick and stone of this countryside is infused for me with memories of him. And yet in spite of that loss, they are dearer to me than ever now for your sake. For me you are part of everything I see, everywhere I go. . . ."

That I could almost understand, for he had taught me to love the woods and hills as he did.

"You are so young, Ellen. I had schooled myself to wait, forever if necessary, knowing that I shall never love anyone else, but our lives have changed. Do you know when I first hoped that the long waiting might soon be over?" He took out a pocketbook and opening it delicately—his craftsman's fingers trembling a little—showed me the carefully preserved petals of a white rose. Dried to flakes, they crumbled and fell in a shower on the carpet. "I kept it," he said ruefully, "as a talisman."

I do not know if I loved him then but I longed to love him, knowing how much he wanted it.

"I am much older than you," he was saying, "but it would

be a good marriage, Ellen. Your father would give us his blessing if he were here now."

"Father knew?"

He nodded. It was almost as if Father had come into the room, which seemed lighter though the morning was gray. It was true. He would have hated my cheap dress, my work-worn hands. Of course he would have wanted me to turn to his closest friend for comfort and protection. And all the time there persisted in my mind the delightful picture of Lucy and me in that sunny parlor. I saw the geraniums in the window, the sun on Lucy's hair, the two of us sewing and talking—hardly realizing that it was something very like Miss Southern's parlor that I saw, with Miss Southern herself vaguely in the background and Mr. Southern, coming in occasionally from his workshop; as though marriage would be no more than a permanent extension of those tranquil lesson times.

He must have seen the look of dreamy happiness such thoughts aroused. Bending his head, he kissed my hand with a reverence that touched my heart.

"Promise me you'll think of it, Ellen. Will you?"

The pleading note, the eager look were new. Still amazed beyond expression I said, "Yes, I will think of it, I promise."

When he had gone I thought of it so profoundly, remained so utterly lost in contemplation of it, that the morning passed without my moving from the sofa. I wondered if God had sent Mr. Southern as a means of rescue, for there seemed no other; and he was such a good man that there could be no irreverence in seeing him as an instrument of Providence.

"The Southerns will look after you," Binnie had said. Had she guessed that Mr. Southern was—in love with me? I said the words to myself incredulously. Then, remembering his conversation with Father on the terrace, I strove to realize that it was I, Ellen Westerdale, of whom he had been speaking. Though it remained beyond all belief, the very fact that he had told Father about it, gave a kind of authenticity to Mr. Southern's love.

"Father," I whispered in an agony of longing to reach him, "please tell me what to do." And as a sort of acceptance slowly grew upon me, the very hope of escape made my present life seem intolerable. In contrast to that bright imaginary parlor the Mill seemed crumbling, decaying—dead. I knew that there was dust in the corners of the silent rooms; mildew on the books; a film of damp on the furniture, no matter how often I rubbed it. I knew that eventually Nancy would leave, tired of spending long hours alone in the shadow-haunted kitchen; that new servants would not come; that the house was becoming a focus of local gossip; and on a deeper, more instinctive level I knew that Rose's constant companionship was bad for me, though as yet I could not have said why this should be so.

For the next few days I saw nothing of Mr. Southern. If it was his intention to let me grow used to the idea of marrying him, he was successful. I thought constantly of it—and of him —and with no impulse to reject his offer; rather with a growing sense that I would accept it. And I felt happier than I had done for months.

One morning, wakened by birds singing, I ran downstairs to throw open the front door, persuading myself that it was spring. Something lay on the quarry-tiled porch, a large brown paper parcel with a neatly printed label: "Miss Ellen Westerdale, Saxelby Mill."

At first I wondered if it had come by post the day before but Leish would surely have brought it to the kitchen door in the usual hope of a cup of tea. Besides, it bore no postmark and had obviously been delivered by hand at some extraordinarily early hour: it was not yet seven. I opened it in my room, to find inside many layers of tissue paper, a dress.

To this day I remember the pleasure I felt as I held it against me in front of the looking-glass. How can I describe it, the most beautiful dress I had ever had? Black, of course, but of the softest cashmere with a plastron of shining satin on the bodice and a velvet edging to the high neck. The overskirt was looped up at the sides with velvet bows: two bands of velvet encircled the skirt. I pored over it, the buttons, the balayeuse, the tucks. Every exquisite stitch had been put in by hand.

I tore off my old morning skirt and blouse and drew the soft, satin-lined bodice over my head, did up the satin-covered buttons, shook out the skirt. The fit was amazingly good.

Transformed, I saw Miss Ellen Westerdale of Saxelby, a creature whom I had thought never to see again, and took such delight in her appearance that I gave no thought to where the dress had come from, accepting it like fairy gold for itself, without question.

I arranged my hair and, forgetting all awkwardness, all restraint, glided—yes, glided—along to Rose's room.

"Mamma! May I come in? I want to show you. Look! A dress!"

Sweeping in without invitation, I found her at the dressing table.

"On the doorstep. Can you believe it? For me. Isn't it beautiful?" At her long mirror I stopped, enthralled by my own elegance. "May I have some of your glycerine and cucumber for my hands? There's no crêpe but it's three months now. Do you think I might begin to wear it at once?"

"Was there a card?" she asked as she handed me the jar.

"No. Nothing." I was still too much absorbed in the gift to speculate on the identity of the giver.

"It isn't difficult to guess who sent it."

Something in her tone pierced my mood of elation.

"I suppose he just couldn't wait."

"He?"

"Your friend. Oliver Southern. I hadn't realized, I must confess, that you were so intimate—yet—though it has been plain enough what he wanted."

Without fully understanding her implication, I felt myself turning red. I put the jar of glycerine back on the table.

"You must keep him at a distance. Have you spent any time alone with him?"

"We talked in the parlor the other day. He asked me to marry him, Mamma."

"Marry! He ought to be ashamed of himself. A man of his age talking to a girl like you of marriage. Do you understand what it means? As for the dress, surely you must have guessed."

"I thought perhaps Aunt Lumley . . . or Miss Southern."

Indeed I hardly knew what I had thought. Now I realized that Aunt Lumley or Miss Southern would have sent the present openly.

"Respectable girls do not accept presents of clothes from men," said Rose bluntly. "Go and take it off. Upon my word, these holy, righteous men are positively the worst when it comes to young girls. Has he said anything improper to you?"

I could not answer. Humiliated beyond words, I went and took off the dress. I had made a fool of myself. Nothing that Rose said could diminish my respect for Mr. Southern. Yet the crude, knowledgeable way in which she had spoken about him presented his image to me in a different light. He was a man, it seemed, and men were different from gentlemen.

The rest of the morning I spent in wretched indecision, unable to read, weary of every kind of occupation. My fidgets were only the outward sign of a deeper uncertainty. For the first time I had begun to think of marriage in connection with Mr. Southern himself. He would be my husband. To him my closest and most intimate affection would be due. But even then ignorance obscured from me the details of that duty.

That afternoon he called and was shown into the drawing room. Usually he confined his visits to the morning, avoiding Rose whenever possible. In her presence he was always stiff and constrained.

Hearing his voice I was suddenly embarrassed and fled to one of the attics like a naughty child unable to face him. All the same when ten minutes had passed, I crept out on to the stairs. From below came the sound of raised voices. Rose was shouting hysterically. I scarcely recognized the other voice— loud and furiously angry—as Mr. Southern's.

"When have you ever considered the welfare of these girls?" he demanded. "What care did you take of Lucy? If Jonathan could know how you neglected her . . ."

I could not make out Rose's reply but I heard my own name and Mr. Southern went on, "I fully understand that it is to your advantage to keep Ellen unmarried," and then he said something about Petersby the lawyer.

"You've said what you came to say," Rose shouted, "and

now you can go. You are not welcome here. I know very well that you hang about here in the mornings in the hope of seeing Ellen alone. You should be ashamed of yourself. But Ellen cannot marry without my consent. It is my duty to protect her from . . ."

How could she speak to Mr. Southern like that, as though he were a follower of one of the servants? Even then I was conscious of something false, in her voice and turn of phrase, in contrast to Mr. Southern's deadly sincerity. Burning with shame, I was on the point of retreating to the attic, never, I felt, to come down again, when she added, "In future please keep away. I will not have you in my house."

"My house, I believe," said Mr. Southern. He sounded quite calm again and his tone was like ice. "You have not forgotten, I dare say that this is in fact, my house. It so happens that Jonathan's lease expires in September and I have not the least intention of extending it. In fact you are here on suffrance. For Ellen's sake I shall not disturb you before September but you had better look around you, Madam."

He must have had the last word. I heard the front door close and his footsteps on the flagged path. I sat down on the attic stairs, wishing quite simply that I could die. If Rose refused to let me marry Mr. Southern, I must remain, bound to her for three and a half interminable years until I came of age. Having dreamed of escape, I could not face what seemed an eternity of living with Rose. Moreover if she withheld her consent, Mr. Southern would refuse to renew the lease and my bondage to Rose would also mean exile from the Mill. Where could we go, Rose and I, to make a new life together? A life, I drearily foresaw, in which Mr. Southern would have no part.

[170]

If I could have overcome the terrible inertia that kept me motionless on the dark stairs, I dare say I should have run out of the house, along the lane to Saxelby, and thrown myself into his arms, begging him not to mind the things Rose had said, beseeching him not to leave me. But I continued to sit there until my hands and feet were numb with cold and at last I could no longer resist the lure of the drawing-room fire.

As I passed her room, Rose was standing at the window. She was still fuming, even deliberately fostering her resentment. I knew it by the way she was jerking her shoulders and tapping her foot on the floor.

"He's been here," she said without turning round, "your friend, Oliver Southern, and I've sent him packing." Then when I said nothing, she went on, "I hope you aren't going to sulk. You should be grateful to me. But then you don't know what I've saved you from. You don't know what marriage means. I'll tell you, shall I? Come here."

I went and stood beside her. Together we looked out at the water falling white as lace over the weir, and without looking at me, she told me what marriage would mean. Plainly, crudely, minutely, she told me. Rose had no conversational gifts, no refinement of thought or speech. In all the time we had lived together, she had said nothing striking or memorable. But that short speech by the window is burned into my memory and will remain there, I believe, forever.

What had been vague, romantic conjecture became abruptly specific—and nauseating. The images she conjured up awoke in me a shuddering disgust of fear that extended to all men, even Father. My first impulse was to rush from the room where he and Rose had been together. I believe I left her in the middle of a sentence and stumbled along the landing to the dismal refuge of my own room.

From my window I watched the dusk gather and deepen, the darkness pale again as a full moon rose. At last unable to stay indoors any longer I drew a shawl over my head and walked up the hill. At first the moonlit pasture, the smell of earth, the aromatic scent of fir trees soothed my spirit, and I walked quickly with the sensation of rising into a freer, wider air.

But halfway up the hill I heard voices. Two people were coming along Plum Lane. I stepped into the shelter of the hedge to let them pass, recognizing Daisy Marshall, the girl who had been last year's May Queen and a boy from Saxelby. Closely intertwined, deep in conversation, they came slowly down.

"I don't believe it," said the boy. "It isn't commonsense."

"It's true, I'm telling you," Daisy spoke with a wholly enjoyable relish. "Where she came from, there's no knowing, but bad luck was what she brought. Not fit to be in these parts, the likes of her, and shouldn't be let. The butcher's wife at Saxelby, Mrs. Shaw, she told my mother . . ."

They were evidently talking about that stranger of long ago, the woman from Chantry Cottage. It had been Mary Shaw's great-grandmother, I recalled, who had first laid hands on the woman, "sitting in her ladder-backed chair, still in her white apron." The phrases recurred like the lines of a ballad. In fact the story was already firmly embedded in the folklore of Saxelby and here—appropriately enough in the very lane where the woman had last been seen—here it was filtering down to another generation; and losing nothing in the process.

Indeed on Daisy's lips it seemed to be taking on quite a new form.

"There was a young girl living there," she was saying, "and she gave her something to drink. Nearly sent her out of her mind, she did; and cut all her hair off, every inch. They had to get her away quick or she would have died. There it is now." Daisy stopped dead. "I wouldn't go past it on a night like this—not for love or money."

"I don't know about money," said the boy, "but for love give me Plum Lane any time."

They kissed lingeringly and went slowly back up the hill.

When it dawned on me that this was not after all a revised version of the old story but an entirely new chapter of village history, that it was no longer Chantry Cottage that frightened passersby at night but our very own Mill—my first impulse was one of angry repudiation. But it quickly gave way to a feeling of shame and disgust at the whole rigmarole, as at the clinging touch of cobwebs in a dark room.

Yet how striking the coincidence! In each generation a strange woman; a young girl frightened out of her wits, and this was how it must have started—the witch hunt—with whispers in the dark, distortions, lying rumors, until some resolute character took up, so to speak, the first stone. The memory confronted me of Mary Shaw's steady judicial gaze, her reference to Holy Writ. Was she really a replica of her formidable great-grandmother, as Mr. Southern had said?

And there had been someone else to avenge—another victim. What was it that had happened to Mary's great-grandmother's sister, who should have been her great-great-aunt? Lost in the intricacies of kinship, I turned to go home, though momentarily the word had lost its meaning. As I came

out of the shade of trees on to the bridge, the Mill confronted
me with startling suddenness. For a few seconds its aspect
was unfamiliar. Under the distorting effect of moonlight it
looked larger, as if it had moved forward. I had not noticed
until now how crookedly the near chimney pointed upward.
The front windows were unlit but as I turned my head, one
of the oriels winked into prominence like an eye opening and
shutting. To a stranger coming upon the Mill in its present
mood there might well seem to be a sinister mischief in the air.

And the air itself was cold. Feeling as if the whole world
were falling apart to reveal a canker in the heart of things, I
wanted now only to be safe indoors. I had almost reached
the gate when a voice spoke from the shadow of the chestnut.

"Ellen! Did I startle you?"

I was not really afraid. It could only be Mr. Southern. As
he came up to me I smelt the rough tweed of his jacket.

It reminded me of Father.

"Mr. Southern," I burst out. "Thank you for the lovely dress.
It was kind of you but I can't take it. Mamma says I shouldn't
accept it."

"The dress! What dress?"

"Then it wasn't you?" Before I could grasp the fact he went
on.

"I know nothing about a dress, though if I had thought it
would make you happier, I would have given you all the
dresses you wanted." He seemed agitated. "Ellen, I have been
waiting here in the hope of seeing you. Do you know that I
come here every evening, longing to see you? Have you
thought about what I said to you?"

"Yes, of course, but . . ."

Why did I hesitate? There was nothing now to keep us

[174]

apart. Rose had misjudged him as she misjudged everything.

"What is this woman to us?" he demanded. "I shall not let her spoil our lives. She has done enough harm already. I warn you, Ellen—" Had it been anyone else I should have been alarmed by the wildness in the way he spoke—"she will take everything you have to give. I knew it from the first. I tried to warn your father. She is a bad influence. She ought never to have come here."

We were face to face. Without turning, I felt the Mill behind me, dark and obscurely hostile now as it had never been before.

"She has forced me into a situation I have always wanted to avoid. You know that she won't give her consent—but that can be overcome. There are ways. I shall see Petersby—and I may be able to bring pressure upon her personally. There is something in her life—something amiss, I am certain of it. Believe me, Ellen, I shall not pity her."

His face was pale in the moonlight. Awed by his intensity, I drew away and saw behind him the tree shadows reaching across the lane like hands, clutching and unfulfilled. For the first time in my life I wished he would go away and leave me to myself.

"Now that I have spoken, now that you know I love you, to wait for three years would be torture to me, Ellen." I thought his manner strange, his whole person altered. "Come to me at once, now. I cannot wait any longer."

With a kind of moaning sound that terrified me, he took me in his arms, holding me close, and kissed me with such a thrusting violence, so complete a forgetfulness of both himself and me that it was as though someone else, or something else, had manifested itself, a savage thing which had nothing to do with either of us—something intent only upon its own gratification. All that I had admired and liked in him, his protective gentleness, his thought for me, his calm self-command, vanished in that close, demanding embrace. I found it utterly repellent.

The primitive challenge aroused in me a primitive response. I struggled and kicked and fought, beating his face with my fists until at last he let me go.

"Forgive me." He was as white-faced and shaken as I. "Forgive me, Ellen. I have waited so long. You must marry me or I cannot bear it."

"No. No. Never. I would hate it, hate it, hate it."

Shivering with revulsion, I dragged myself to the gate, longing only for the sanctuary of my own room. In the hall I saw at first only the floor, checkered with moonlight and dark shadows. Then something brought me to a halt, terrified: the tall figure of a woman in a white apron, standing at the foot of the stairs.

I closed my eyes—and when I dared to look again, it was to see, with no feeling of relief, that it was Rose. She stepped forward, a shaft of moonlight making a white tabard on her black dress. She must have seen my loose hair, my disordered dress. I think she said something but I did not hear. I felt her watching me as I stumbled up to my room and shut the door behind me.

Chapter Fifteen

The next day I heard from Nancy that Mr. Southern had gone away again. Weeks lengthened into a month without a sign or word from him. It was not long before, perversely, I came to miss him, at first only fleetingly when I had nothing to read or when I passed some place where we had been together, but gradually the faint prick of regret deepened into a prolonged heartache as I recognized the loss of the dearest friend I had ever known, and as I came dimly to understand how much more than friendship he had offered me.

Though the pictures Rose had thrust into my imagination were to remain, as time went by they receded and their application to Mr. Southern became less direct. Sunshine soon restored to the Mill its normal aspect, and in the same way the passionate man of that encounter by the gate faded, to be replaced by the more familiar image of the man he had been before. Having no other companion I saw him everywhere, heard his voice, longed daily for his advice. More than once I went into the church and sat looking at the oak pulpit, thinking of him and wishing that I had been less callow and ignorant in the way I had treated him. I suffered too from a numbing bewilderment, having thought naively that only death could take away a friend.

Then as time went on, my longing for a reconciliation gave way to a morbid dread of his sudden return, a nervous fear that I would do something foolish and hurt him again.

Both Aunt Lumley and Miss Southern had written to me but their carefully worded references to Lucy as being "no worse" or "as well as can be expected" served only to make me feel more acutely my distance from them all. From Lucy herself I had only a line scrawled on the end of Aunt Lumley's letter: "Oh Ellen, the lovely, lovely sea," and though this did little to relieve my anxiety, it helped more than anything else to restore to me a sense of her living presence.

From Binnie I heard nothing, only as the days grew longer there were rumors in the village that Alec would probably be home toward the end of April.

My entire world had shrunk to the dimensions of the Mill with Rose as my sole companion: from the moment she came downstairs (though this was not often before noon), at our perfunctory meals when we faced each other across the round table in the parlor, to the welcome hour when I took my candle and bade her goodnight.

[178]

I had not been mistaken in thinking she had changed; or rather the dominant aspects of her personality had intensified so that once or twice I found myself remembering with amazement the passive, will-less creature she had been when she first came. I missed the little touches of wry humor, the half-smiling pout and almost deprecatory shrug which had once charmed me. Now, without the fear of any critical presence but my own, she seemed to have grown more confident. Lucy's description of her as noticeable was more than ever apt. Thrown together as we were, it would have been impossible not to be mutually involved in a score of tiny incidents each day; yet we never reached that state of intimacy where I could take her for granted. Her tall figure, her voice, her face seemed to occupy all my consciousness. I was forever watching her, waiting for the rustle of her dress, wondering where she was. Sometimes in the long evenings as I carried trays up and downstairs, I would come upon her in a doorway or at the stairhead just out of range of the candlelight. Once, with a can of hot water in my hand, I stopped abruptly for fear of bumping into her, to find that it was only the long shadow of the oak press—when all at once her step behind me set my heart thumping.

Even then I recognized my preoccupation with Rose as unwholesome, but it was some time before I realized that whereas once she had been an outsider in my world, now the position was reversed: the Mill had become her domain. Looking back, I seem to see a shrinking of my whole personality.

Small wonder that I fell prey to unhealthy fancies; that the rambling passages and unused rooms developed a life of their own. Sometimes in the evenings, when chill airs rose from the river and crept into the house, it seemed as if something else, some influence more dominant even than Rose's, had moved in with them.

In such a secluded existence the most trifling event became momentous, so that an encounter I had one day on the Stanesfield road inevitably took on the quality of high drama, though at the time I could not know the effect it would have on all our lives.

It was a bright afternoon in March, a day of high white clouds and a stinging wind that sent me almost running up the hill. My walks were usually in this direction, toward the crossroads. I did not examine the reasons for my growing reluctance to walk into Saxelby nor did I admit to myself that the name "Kindlehope" on the signpost was beginning to exert an increasingly romantic appeal. Since the day I had watched Babbitt driving away, the moorland road had intrigued me. Childishly I imagined myself escaping to a more open country where the sky was always brighter, a fantasy which I would have been ashamed to put into words.

I had reached the high road and stood breathless, clutching my hat and wondering whether to turn left into the teeth of the wind, when I saw about a quarter of a mile away someone riding at a steady trot from the direction of Stanesfield.

Immediately I thought of Mr. Southern and wished the earth would swallow me up. The last thing I wanted was to meet him here—and now. I looked round desperately for some means of escape.

With some thought of retreating into Plum Lane, I turned back down the hill. But the rider had obviously seen me. He had put his horse to a canter and was rapidly overtaking me. A swift backward glance assured me that it was at least

IMAGES OF ROSE

not Mr. Southern, but an altogether heavier man, broad-shouldered and wearing a wide-brimmed soft hat.

I now felt a touch of nervousness. It was unusual to meet a stranger in that remote spot. The nearest dwelling was the Mill—or the Pellows' cottage midway along Plum Lane. Half inclined to throw dignity to the winds and make a run for it, I had settled my hat and gathered up my skirts when the stranger called out, put on a burst of speed and caught up with me.

"Excuse me, Miss."

Looking up into a fresh-colored face, flushed with air and exercise, I forgot my nervousness. He had taken off his hat and was holding it with an almost excessive courtesy, considering the sharp tang of the March breeze. He looked like a middle-aged farmer in his comfortable tweed jacket and loosely cut breeches, but his boots and leggings were well polished—his linen was fresh and clean.

"Could you by any chance direct me to Saxelby Mill?"

"Yes, indeed." My instant impression that he was a farmer made me add, "but it isn't a mill now, you know, and hasn't been for at least a hundred years."

"It isn't the Mill I want, Miss." He laughed so pleasantly that I smiled, noticing that although the hair of his temples and moustache was threaded with gray, his expression was unexpectedly youthful. His eyes—they were blue and candid—had an eager light, which matched the buoyancy in his voice and manner. "It's a person I want to see—a lady. Perhaps you'll know the name. It's Miss Rose Warden."

In spite of himself, he smiled as he spoke, looking away across the valley as if he could scarcely restrain himself within the bounds of an ordinary conversation.

"Of course I know her. I live at the Mill. Miss Warden—except that she isn't Miss Warden now. She's my stepmother, Mrs. Westerdale."

I looked up at him with the gratified feeling one has in helping a stranger.

The effect on him was breathtaking. One moment his eyes were bright with interest, his cheeks suffused with color. The next he was deathly pale. All the color had drained from his face, leaving it yellowish-brown like parchment. In a few seconds I saw him twenty years older.

"I'm afraid you're ill."

Involuntarily I put up my hand as he positively swayed in the saddle, though there was little I could have done, little that anyone could have done. It was spiritual comfort he needed. He looked like a man who had felt the whole current of his life change.

"You're quite certain?" He moistened his lips. He seemed to have shrunk—sitting with his shoulders bowed as if flinching from the possibility of a second blow. "You're quite certain? I beg your pardon, but you see I've come a long way. There couldn't be some mistake? I meant the Miss Warden who used to live at Appleby End."

"There's no mistake," I said. "Will you not call and see her? The Mill is just down there. My stepmother is at home."

But his expression had changed again. His whole countenance had darkened.

"No." He clapped his hat on his head.

"Let me give her a message. Your name . . ."

"No, by God. There's no message. I've got nothing to say to her. Nothing in the world."

His voice broke and I saw his eyes hard and gray before

he dug his heels into his mount and plunged recklessly down the hill.

"But it seems a shame," I called after him, "when you've come so far . . ."

A gust of wind carried my words away. The curving lane had already taken him out of sight between the high hedges. I heard his horse's hooves going rapidly down, over the bridge and up the incline toward Saxelby as he passed the Mill without drawing rein.

Distressed and saddened by the incident, I hurried home and found Rose sitting at the parlor table, laying out cards for a game of solitaire.

"I met a man," I began breathlessly, "riding from Stanesfield. He asked for you."

She jumped to her feet in a hurry, spilling the cards on the floor.

"Who? Who is it?"

Her face was alight with interest.

"I don't know. He's gone." I told her what had happened. "It was someone who very much wanted to see you. He seemed quite—broken down."

Rose stooped to pick up the cards. Her hands trembled.

"What was he like?"

I described him. "Do you know who it would be?"

"Oh—I don't know. At any rate it's too late. He's gone, you said?"

She was clearly agitated as she plumped down in her chair again and leaned on the table, her head in her hands. I had gone down on my knees to help to pick up the cards and now, still kneeling, I looked up with a sudden longing to reach her.

"Do you not feel sometimes that you would like to talk about Appleby End, now that it's all so far in the past? We knew

[183]

about your . . . unhappy love affair. Now that we're alone together . . ."

Surely I could speak about it now. It simply did not occur to me that having married Father, she could retain even a trace of the old romantic attachment. When she did not answer, I blundered on. "When we knew that you were coming, I thought it would be like Appleby End here, all the same things to do and talk about."

As I spoke, the old forgotten dreams revived, dreams of a more gracious way of life which had once seemed almost to be reborn at the Mill. If only we could talk, she and I, about Mother and Aunt Ann, recapturing something of that distant idyll, then surely from the surviving fragments of the past we could make a new life together.

I stopped, discouraged by her silence. Then at last she raised her head. Without looking at me she said,

"Will you never understand? You talk about samplers and mulberry trees and honeysuckle as if life were no more than a pretty picture. Do you know what it can really be like? Appleby End." She spat out the words with loathing. "Appleby End is nothing to me except that I hate the very name. I hate everything about it. I detest the thought of it. It means nothing to me, nothing, nothing."

This time there was no hysteria. She was speaking the cold truth. As her last words died away, "Nothing, nothing . . ." the room was very quiet, as if all the life of the house had died away, as if the whole world had been reduced to a meaningless void. It was almost a relief when in answer to some mysterious inner prompting, Blanche sprang on to the table and faced me, looking twice her normal size, her eyes blazing.

I felt a pang of loneliness. Everyone had gone from me, all the good and loving influences of my life. Only those childhood memories survived to remind me of a warmth and sweetness I had once known, of a faint familiar perfume, the crooning of a lullaby: memories that were fading rapidly every day.

And now were they too to forsake me altogether? Had my mother's tales been hollow lies? There never was a magical place called Appleby End. Those two girls? One had been shallow, heartless, empty; the other a sentimental dupe. Feeling the languor and pain of it, I wondered if this was the final loss that would break my heart.

Wanting only to escape from the house, I went out and along the river path to where the current ran swift between overhanging alders, then broadened into a deep pool. This was Fuller's Reach, where Mary Shaw's kinswoman—I remembered now—had been found drowned. I stood on a projecting tussock of grass and thought of her.

"There was no reason," Mary had said. Only the evil eye of an older woman, someone who perhaps without seeking them, had become the instrument of powers stronger than herself. And after all she would not need to do very much—only to impart a sudden revelation of the world as empty, void of meaning and purpose.

"Nothing, I tell you, nothing." I heard the words; saw the tall figure inclined, the mouth drawn down at the corner as if by an unseen hand. Had she not already frightened Lucy out of her senses, bending over her with the scissors?

But that was Rose.

Confused, I leaned my aching head against a tree and watched the water stealing away. It needed no more than a step, a moment's surrender.

It was the thought of Lucy that saved me. So long as she lived, I must live too, dragging out my days at the Mill, without hope now of rescue. Reluctantly I went home.

Chapter Sixteen

My heart did not break; but for the next few days I suffered from feverish headaches and lassitude and was not well enough to leave my room. I slept fitfully and was troubled by haunting dreams, of still water and floating white faces and the loud mewing of cats.

Rose seemed to have become a little more active. I would hear her moving about the south room until quite late at night. When I came downstairs, it was to find that she had left off her crepe and seemed to be taking a renewed interest in her appearance and clothes.

She also resumed her occasional trips into Stanesfield.

Though she never discussed them, I presumed that she must visit the solicitor, Mr. Petersby, or go to the bank to draw out money as it was obviously unwise to keep large sums in the house. But she never told me what she did on those days she spent in town and never suggested that I should go with her. For my part I looked forward to them unashamedly as holidays when I could make little excursions on my own, taking a picnic and a book.

I remember one such day about a month after my meeting with the farmer, if such he was. Rose had been driven off by Reg Morton in the pony trap, wearing her sealskin jacket for the cool drive over the moors. But our sheltered garden was warm and sunny, the orchard white with pear blossom.

Taking a book and cushions, I went through the rose garden to my favorite nook where the last three steps led down to the pebbly foreshore. For once I was in no mood for reading. The soft air, the scent of gorse, the hour of leisure all stirred in me, vague dreams, half memory, half longing. I missed Lucy so deeply that my mind had somehow fashioned its own defences, carrying me back to an earlier period of my life when there had been no problems or pain.

Leaning against the sun-warmed stones, I pictured myself as a little girl again, Lucy no more than a fair-haired child beside me, an extension of myself, as I sat with my cheek against my mother's skirts, knowing, far below the level of conscious thought, a security that need not be questioned.

In spring and summer the garden was a place of continual movement, the flutter of blackbirds, the sudden whirring flight of our own white doves, the occasional blue flash of a kingfisher. When I started awake after a brief doze, memory and dream had fused to create a strong impression of someone ac-

[187]

tually there, near me in the garden. What was it that had wakened me? Something more, surely, than the rustle of birds or the tiny splash of a water-rat close at hand.

I sat up, half convinced that someone had been there, listening for the brush of a skirt or the more distant crunch of footsteps on the bridge.

There was no one to be seen in the garden, on the bridge or in the pasture over the stream. But my mood had changed. I thought of that last unexpected meeting with the stranger who had asked for Rose. He had seemed to me a good man, almost defenceless in his sincerity. There must be some good quality in Rose to arouse the love—as I supposed it must be—of such a man; and for that matter of Father. Mother too had loved her.

I considered the enigma of my stepmother, seeking to reconcile the earlier Rose with the woman I now knew. When had my attitude toward her begun to change? With the bright clarity of pictures in a stereoscope, certain scenes revived, taking on a vividness they had lacked at the time of enactment; and I saw them as if they had been slotted in the stereoscope in reverse order: Rose on the sofa talking to Miss Southern—and I watching her intently, feeling that there was something wrong: Rose on her bed, screaming in hysteria: Rose standing on the bridge.

Involuntarily I glanced toward it. There was no one there now, no one anywhere: Nancy had gone home an hour ago. Then equally vivid, I saw Rose's letter lying on the brass tray in the hall. I almost smelt again the cool damp of stone walls as we came in out of the sun.

But—here was the incongruity—the letter had touched me. It had aroused in me some indefinable concern, and it had been concern for Rose, as though a cry for help—no, rather a wistful sigh—had been breathed from the smudged paper. Yet once Rose had appeared in the flesh, among all the complicated feelings she had aroused, I had felt no similar concern—not on her behalf, beyond an ignorant and unformed wonder that anyone could be so tired, so indifferent. I had found her fascinating but never appealing, never wistful.

Had not my first misgivings, if that was the word, been roused by the letter? What was it she had said? "Everything coming to an end and perhaps that would be for the best." Something about "painful decisions." I tried to remember what quality it was in the letter that had impressed me.

By this time I was on my feet. Without any definite purpose beyond finding the letter and rereading it in the light of my later feelings about my stepmother, I went into the house. But search as I might I could not find it, neither in my lettercase nor in any of the drawers in my room. On the day it arrived, I recalled, we had changed the mattresses and prepared the south room for Rose. Could I have put it into one of the drawers there and in the bustle of her arrival have forgotten it?

Rose still kept some of her things in her old room though she slept in Mother's, and since we were so sadly short of servants, it was vaguely understood that she kept her own rooms tidy and that Nancy periodically gave them a thorough cleaning.

It was a shock to find the door of the south room locked. I stood for a moment with my hand on the latch, staring down in disbelief at the empty keyhole with a sense of outrage, even anger. I already knew Rose's passion for locking cupboards— and Father's secretaire. Had she extended her ridiculous suspicion of Binnie to Nancy—and to me? It was intolerable.

All the indignation in the world would not unlock the door; but it occurred to me that she might have overlooked the other means of access to the south room. I therefore marched down the front stairs to the kitchen level and up the back stairs to the narrow landing where the door of the old dressing room opened outward.

No. She had not locked that. Groping my way across the tiny, windowless apartment, little more than a closet, I turned the handle of the door into the bedroom. It too was locked. There was something so disproportionate, so irrational in these unnecessary precautions that even in my anger at the implied insult, I felt another kind of disquiet. Standing among the cob-webbed portmanteaux and dress-baskets, I saw in the looking-glass of a pointed toilet table—with detachment, as if they belonged to someone else—a pale face, brows anxiously arched above troubled eyes, the face of an intruder.

As I turned to go, my skirt caught a pile of objects on the floor. Something fell with a crash. I was nervous enough to be quite startled. It was a gilt picture frame, one of half a dozen stacked in a corner beside a pile of vellum-bound books. I sat down on the dress-basket and looked at them, recognizing them as those we had helped Rose to unpack. The frames were of various sizes but they had all something in common. They were empty.

All except one. At the bottom of the pile lay the wooden-framed sketch of Appleby End over which I had pored with such earnest interest. The sketch remained but it was unrec-ognizable—every inch of it obliterated by the glass which had been pounded as with a hammer into small particles and ground into the sketch. One or two fragments tinkled to the floor as I dropped the picture with a shudder, appalled by the frenzy of hatred and renunciation which must have driven my stepmother to destroy these innocent relics of her past. Why had she brought them if she hated them so much?

The April evening was drawing in but I continued to sit there, lost in thought. The word "ordeal" came back into my mind. It seemed to me that something more than the frustrated life of an unmarried daughter caring for an invalid father must have produced the state of senseless violence which led her to deface the sketch and burn—as I supposed—the family likenesses. And with the same stereoscopic sharpness as before, I saw the gilt-edged water-lilies and ivory silk of that exquisite handscreen withering in the heart of the fire.

I think it must have been then that I began gradually to move into the state of mind associated with nightmare, when the normal standards of behavior no longer apply and the safeguards of reason are sickeningly absent. What I had felt in my stepmother from the beginning was a kind of irresponsibility. She was not governed by the rules and obligations that ordered the lives of other people. "Is there some mental disturbance?" It had been Dr. Wareham who put the question. Had he noticed other symptoms besides the secrecy, the indifference to others, the touches of violence?

Entombed there in the very middle of the house, I must have missed the sound of the trap. The first thing I heard was Rose's tread on the landing. Shocked into wariness, I got up quickly. The creak of the basket sounded deafeningly loud.

She would go either to her own bedroom or to the south room. I waited breathless, as if my life depended on the decision until I heard the key thrust into the lock of the south room. In a sudden panic lest she should throw open the door of the closet and confront me, I stole out on to the back landing, gently pushed the door shut and waited, listening. I heard the bedroom door open, the floorboards creak, the turn of a smaller key in a drawer, the drawer opened and closed; other small movements in the room. Then she returned to the landing and locked the door behind her.

I went quietly down the backstairs, through the kitchen and up to the hall. It was here that I was suddenly aware, as once before under the distorting effect of moonlight, of a change in the house. For one thing since Rose's return it seemed unaccountably more silent. As the familiar damp airs of evening rose from the river, the unlit hall and stairs felt cold as a tomb: and the cold and silence combined with my uneasy thoughts to produce the impression that something was different, or rather that something was waiting there—a presence, pervasive . . . and unwelcome.

"What exactly is evil?"

The memory of Lucy's shrill voice revived me a little like the faint scent of a breeze blowing over sunny pastures on a May morning.

"I don't know." That was Mark's husky voice. "The absence of everything good, I suppose, so that the other sort of things take over. . . ."

And then the white-faced lamb had leapt into the air where the children had been dancing.

Could there ever be an absence of everything good? Even though everyone else had gone away and only I was left to stop the other sort of thing from taking over.

All at once I experienced a sort of revelation. It was not enough to be patient and good—to wait and hope for some improvement in my lot. In some way I must act. If there were evil influences about, I must dispel them, I alone. (I smile now at my vast presumption.) Without having the faintest conception of how this was to be done, I felt, astonishingly, an increase of strength: I felt my body thin and purposeful like an active instrument.

It was in this frame of mind that I came into the drawing room and saw Rose with the knife in her hand.

Chapter Seventeen

For years it had hung on the wall above the secretaire—a Burmese dagger with a curved blade of finely tempered steel, yet another of Father's unsuitable gifts. He had brought it home for Mr. Southern who had promptly refused to accept it.

"Come now, Oliver, you're surely not superstitious." Father had obviously been taken aback.

"Where that thing is concerned, yes, if you like," said Mr. Southern plainly.

"But it's a magnificent piece of craftsmanship," Father protested.

"No doubt. But it's also a villainous weapon and if you take my advice, you'll lock it up where it can do no harm."

Father had compromised by turning it into an ornament, suspended from a hook by its leather thong, but he had never ceased to warn us not to touch it and it literally never had been touched so that the intricately chased silver handle was black with tarnish.

Rose's hands in contrast looked more than usually white and slim. I stopped dead on the threshold, watching her. She held the dagger in upturned palms. I saw the fingers of her right hand close on the shaft before she raised it slightly, slowly pointing the blade down. There was something deliberate in her movements, or rather, deliberating, as though she were considering the weight and thrusting power of the blade. It was unusual to see in Rose such concentration. Unusual, and to me at that moment, intolerable.

I stepped forward, and the start she gave shook the elegant little secretaire and set the filigree handles swaying. Her lips parted, she began to speak, but I paid no attention.

"It must have fallen off the hook," I said, seeing swiftly that the hook was as firm as ever, the thong unbroken. "It's a dangerous thing. Father told us never to touch it."

I did not look at her face as she turned toward me but in what seemed the most decisive action of my life I laid my hand on hers.

"I'll take it, Mamma," I said firmly, "and put it away."

I felt a momentary resistance before she released her hold. Her fingers were stiff and white.

"You're cold," I said. "I'll make you a hot drink."

"Yes." She gave a long trembling sigh. "I'm frozen almost to death—and so tired. I believe I'll go straight to bed."

I ran downstairs and out to the back of the house, where I threw the dagger into the weed-choked water by the rotting

[195]

remains of the old mill wheel. Then I took her the mulled wine she liked and found her already in her nightdress, brushing her hair.

I on the contrary felt so wakeful that I could scarcely imagine ever sleeping again. In fact it was as though I had just awakened from an entranced sleep into a new kind of consciousness.

I sat down by the kitchen fire, in Binnie's chair, and rocked abstractedly, my entire energy directed inward to the swiftly changing memories, impressions, half-formed conclusions which composed the unconscious harvest of months and years: nearly two years in fact, since the day of Rose's coming. I could still feel her cold fingers yielding to mine as she let go of the knife. That slow recoil had been a turning point. It had liberated me from the suffocating sense of being bound to Rose. Whereas I had accepted her as a child accepts the inexplicable burdens imposed by the adult world, now I was able to see her with more detachment, if such a word could ever be used of our relationship. From now on my thoughts of her would be rational and sensible.

At first they were. It was because I was lonely and tired that I had harbored superstitious fancies. Rose, I could now see, had done nothing actively wrong. She could no more help her faults of personality than I could my own. The suddenly blank look, the refusal to talk about her own home, her apparent revulsion from any reminders of her past, these I now accepted simply as evidence that she was secretive by nature. Why the secrecy should extend to the locking of doors in our own house, I could by no means fathom, unless the habit of secrecy had indeed turned her brain. It was only necessary to understand her difficulties, I arrogantly told myself, to be able to deal with them in a practical, helpful way.

For the first time I began to think of Appleby End, not as a scene in a fairy tale, but as an actual place. I tried to envisage Rose's life there in its practical details. There must have been servants. She never spoke of them—or anything. Had they been dismissed—years ago—even before Uncle Adam's death?

Somehow there came into my mind the vision of a silent house, tenanted only by the old man—and Rose; a place of cobwebs and the stale smells of a neglected sickroom. Binnie and I had tried so hard to keep Lucy's room sweet and whole-some, fumigating it daily with a shovel of burning coals and lavender. Try as I might, I could not imagine Rose doing that for Uncle Adam. What had she done for him?

Or *to* him? For she was not always passive. There had been that time with Solomon. I remembered too her hands, strong and purposeful, holding the kittens. "I had to do it," she had said, suddenly sickened at the sight of death.

So step by step I came at last to the question that affected me more directly.

What had she been going to do with the Burmese dagger?

The Dutch clock whirred and struck twelve. I came to my-self to find the fire sunk to a dull glow, night pressing dark on the uncurtained window, unbroken silence in the rooms above.

In spite of my new-found firmness I was too nervous to go upstairs. It was all I could do to light a candle and climb the wooden steps to Binnie's old room, where I crept between the blankets in my petticoat, comforted a little by the homely smell from the apple room and memories of Binnie and Alec.

[197]

Chapter Eighteen

I woke to hear Nancy singing in the kitchen. Daylight restored my common sense, but even without the somber thoughts I had allowed myself to entertain the night before, there was sufficient abnormality in my situation to try the nerves. Once or twice I felt an impulse to ask Rose outright why she found it necessary to lock the south room, but after her crude way of speaking about Binnie and the silver, I shrank from any repetition of such a scene, and the very wildness of my suspicions made me hesitate to confirm them.

Amid all the uncertainty and loneliness of that dismal time, one resolution supported me. Having imagined Appleby End gone to wrack and ruin, I was determined that the same thing should not happen at the Mill. Sooner than that, I would work myself to skin and bone, and my days were spent in such a vortex of cleaning and polishing, with such relentless applications of beeswax and turpentine, that even Nancy protested.

"It's bad enough you doing one servant's work, Miss Ellen, let alone two or three."

I was wearing one of Binnie's old aprons and a mob cap one morning when Leish came with the letters. Rose had made one of her rare descents to the kitchen to ask him, if he was going on to the village, to order Morton's trap to take her into Stanesfield the next day.

"I hear Alec Binnock's coming back," Leish said. "He'll be arriving in Stanesfield on the eleven o'clock train tomorrow morning they say. Two letters for you, Miss Ellen."

I took them eagerly, recognizing Aunt Lumley's writing and, with a tremor, Mr. Southern's.

"Would you like a cup of tea and something to eat?" I asked mechanically, and was a trifle surprised when he declined.

"No, thank you, Miss. I'll be getting along to Saxelby." He paused, until the sweep of Rose's dress on the stairs died away. "My, things change, don't they."

He had stumped away across the courtyard before I realized what he had said. I was bracing myself to open Mr. Southern's letter, knowing that anything he wrote must be painful to read. Then after all I opened Aunt Lumley's first and quickly forgot everything else.

Lucy's progress had been slow. Reading between the lines—and Aunt Lumley had done her best to be cheerful—I concluded desperately that there had been virtually no progress at all. The cough persisted and the fever at night. She had no appetite or energy.

[199]

"But fortunately," Aunt Lumley wrote, "an opportunity has arisen for a second opinion. Sir Maxwell Keyne is coming to Ventnor to see a patient and I have written to ask him to see Lucy too. . . . We must find out whether the lungs are affected. Perhaps he will be able to suggest new treatment. . . ."

The letter seemed to offer a ray of hope, yet almost at once the anxiety that never left me sharpened into a more acute fear. Sir Maxwell's reputation was so high that I should have been reassured, but I quickly saw that if he failed to do anything for Lucy, there would be no hope left.

Almost with indifference now I opened Mr. Southern's letter. The address was not Ventnor as I had expected but The Angel, Athelby.

My dear Ellen,

In writing to you I have no intention of raising again that matter between us which has caused so much pain to us both. To me it has been more than pain. I have felt since I last saw you a remorse so bitter that I cannot forgive myself. Perhaps some day you will be able to forgive me, knowing that I have loved you all your life, that I care for your welfare more than anything in the world.

It has occurred to me that in coming away from Saxelby I have left you friendless. Should you be in need of help at any time, you can reach me through the County Bank in Stanesfield. Do not hesitate to consult Petersby if you need advice. He is my friend and was your father's, as well as co-trustee of the estate.

You will not think me intrusive in alluding to money matters, I know. Before leaving Saxelby I heard rumors of irregularity in your stepmother's handling of her affairs. If you should be worried about unpaid bills, go to Petersby, who may be trusted to use his influence with your stepmother.

Do not, without consulting him, consent to any changes in your circumstances or sign anything whatsoever at your stepmother's instigation or indeed take any important step that your present situation might seem to impel you to . . .

"How pale you look, Miss Ellen." Nancy found me standing by the fire, lost in thought. "And on a lovely May morning. Now why don't you let me make you a nice cup of tea—and then go and see the May Walk like you used to."

"You're kind to me, Nancy. Perhaps I will."

"Somebody needs to be, I'm sure. You go and make yourself tidy."

On an impulse I dropped Mr. Southern's letter into the fire and the envelope after it, watching the paper turn yellow and curl at the edges. Just before it quickened into flame, I caught sight of the postmark. Whatever was Mr. Southern doing at Appleby End?

Rose was coming out of her room as I went upstairs.

"I've had a letter from Mr. Southern," I began, too much intrigued to maintain my usual reserve in speaking of him. "Isn't it strange? It was posted . . ."

"He is my enemy," she said.

The words were melodramatic. Yet she spoke with none of her usual affectation so that my instinctive, "Oh no, not Mr. Southern. He couldn't be an enemy to anyone," carried no conviction. I knew that she was right. At the same time I longed for his advice, his wisdom, even, at last, for his physical presence.

"He won't renew the lease," she went on. "I don't know where we shall go."

"I'm sure he will. Mr. Southern would never turn us out of the house."

[201]

"He will turn me out if he can."

As always she impressed me. This time it was the oracular simplicity of her manner that held me hypnotized, until I remembered the letter in my hand and said slowly,

"I was going to tell you. It was posted at Appleby End. I wonder what he's doing there?"

She stood stock still, tall and rigid, with the light behind her so that I could not see her face.

"Appleby End."

I had not heard her say it like that before, not with that sad cadence. In her beautiful voice it had the finality of a closing line.

She wandered into the drawing room, played a few chords on the piano, drifted into the opening bars of a song and then broke off. A vision confronted me of Rose and myself, homeless, detached from the rest of mankind, wandering about the face of the earth forever. But the notion was too improbable to be entertained. The sun was high, the birds were singing, I hurried to change my dress.

When I set out for Cross Gap, Rose was taking one of her walks. Seeing her pace restlessly to and fro on the bridge, I realized for the first time that she was waiting—that she had always been waiting. But for what—or for whom—I could not imagine.

Chapter Nineteen

Nothing was changed in Plum Lane since that May morning two years ago. The same sky-reflecting pools filled the deep ruts: the same May-scented hawthorns crowded the hedgerows: perhaps even the same chaffinch fluttered ahead. On my left the meadows already lay deep in purple clover and yellow vetches; the stone-edged border by the Pellows' cottage bloomed bright again with wallflowers and pink daisies.

But if the whole world had changed, I could not have felt more keenly the difference between then and now. Every step reminded me of Lucy, running ahead in her white stockings with the scarlet clocks, looking like an agitated chicken, flapping her linen bag at the Pellows' gander, her voice shrill and excited. "Hurry! They've started."

Neither the soft spring morning nor the prospect of seeing the children and the garlands was any longer sufficiently attractive to make the outing worthwhile. Though I would have blushed to admit it, it was something else that drew me to Cross Gap.

On the steep slope about the village I heard the church clock strike twelve. The children had scattered, some to the cottages, some to the bridle paths leading to the more distant farms, their white pinafores and sunbonnets sprinkled like beads on the open hills. I scanned the village green, the street, the dry-stone walls climbing to the sky, and far away, where a thin track curved up through green bracken to the edge of the heather, I saw someone striding away.

I was too late. My eyes watered and not only with the strain of looking. There seemed no point in going down, though I had thought of buying soap and candles at the village shop. Instead I cut across the hillside between the gorse bushes and out into the lane which connected the village with the high road.

I had had enough of Plum Lane with its mournful echoes of a happier day. It would be a change to walk back along the more open road along the ridge. There was just a chance that Babbitt might go by on his way to Stanesfield. I would not refuse the offer of a lift. Disappointment had brought with it an unfamiliar lassitude. Besides I had worked hard before setting out. Then I remembered that yesterday, Thursday, had been his day for Cross Gap. On Mondays, Wednesdays and Fridays he plied between the Moorcock and Stanesfield.

No matter. He had served only as an excuse. In fact I pre-

ferred the wider views from this upland road with its wild
sweep of cloud and heather. After the half-light of the low-
lying Mill, I felt, tired as I was, a reviving sense of freedom.
A curlew hurled a shower of liquid notes into the empty air.
I threw back my head to gaze after it into the limitless sky,
until earth and sky together seemed to wheel around me.

"Miss. Miss."

A voice speaking apparently from my feet almost threw me
off my balance.

On the right a rough tangle of bramble and elder bushes
marked the upper boundary of the field which sloped away
from the road to Plum Lane below. Looking dizzily down, I
saw a face peering out at me through a gap in the bushes.

"Cissie," I said. "What are you doing there?" Through the
branches I saw a red-tiled roof, a scatter of white geese and
two tethered goats. This must be the top of the Pellows' half-
acre of rough pasture.

For a moment, the face did not move. It looked oddly dis-
embodied, thrust between the elder stumps and twisted to look
up at me like the face of a curious sheep. Then it vanished
and presently Cissie emerged from an opening a few yards
along the road.

"I know who you are," she said.

Could she still be wearing the ancient Dolly Warden dress?
I had an impression of faded chintz, crumpled but clean—a
pale face, not so much silly as vague, as if Cissie had lost her
way long ago and remained permanently astray, light eyes in
a slightly trembling head.

"Of course you know me, Cissie," I said gently.

"You're Miss Ellen Westerdale." She brought out the syl-
lables carefully with the pride of a child repeating a well-

[205]

learned lesson: an old child, innocent but worn. "Mother says, 'You watch for Miss Ellen when she comes back and ask her . . .'"

She hesitated, already confused.

"You saw me then, going along the lane?"

Cissie nodded and remembered.

"Ask her, Mother says, will she come in and have a drink of goat's milk."

"And you waited for me?"

"Yes. There." She pointed diagonally across the pasture to a point overlooking the lane, "And here."

She took my hand, clutching it firmly, and led me through the bushes.

"There."

On the lower side a deep, rain-washed hollow undercut the hedge so that the roots curved out of the earth to form a sunken gallery.

"You can see the road from here," I observed, "without anyone seeing you."

"Yes." She pulled me toward the gap where I had first seen her. "I see . . ." She became eager. "I see folks going along the road."

"There aren't many people to see, are there, Cissie?"

"Sometimes it's just folks or carts. But once," she tugged at my hand and drew me nearer to the gap, "once I see a lady sitting there."

Bending my head slightly, I looked through the curving stems and twigs and saw sunlight on the stones of the wall opposite, where a spring gushed from a brown drain pipe to flow between fronds of new green bracken.

"A lady sitting there. What was she doing?"

[206]

Here I experienced that curious sensation, common enough but always mysterious, of having held this conversation before.

"She was crying."

Cissie nodded until I thought she would never stop.

"Who was the lady?"

"I dunno who she was but she was a lady."

"How did you know she was a lady?"

"She was dressed," Cissie made an unexpectedly graceful movement of her hands toward her own bunchy skirt, hesitated, then went on triumphantly, "with a veil on her face. And she pushed her handkerchief under the veil because she was crying—fit to break her heart, she was."

The very simplicity of Cissie's story gave it a peculiar touch of drama. There was something arresting in the picture of a lady crying there in the empty landscape as if to cry were an activity to be pursued for its own sake.

"Was there no one else there?"

Cissie shook her head.

"Where had she come from?"

"I dunno but she had a bag—a big bag—and she was tired."

At once the incident emerged with startling clarity from the realm of poesy into the world of sober fact.

"When did you see the lady, Cissie?"

Cissie's pale blue gaze wandered. She tugged at my hand.

"And Mother says 'Ask Miss Ellen . . .'"

"Was it yesterday you saw the lady?"

She shook her head.

"Yesterday were the day for doin' the front step."

"Was it a long time ago?"

"Yes. And Mother says . . ."

"Was it a fine sunny day or was it raining?"

"It weren't rainin'. The larks were up."

A bright day with larks singing and a lady weeping.

"Thank you for waiting for me, Cissie. Tell your mother I said, 'Thank you very much and I'll come for the goat's milk another day.'"

With difficulty I withdrew my hand and climbed back into the road.

"Goodbye." I waved as to a child. How could I ever have been afraid of this poor, lost creature?

"I know you. You're Miss Ellen Westerdale," she called.

Fearing that the whole incident was about to be re-enacted, I began to walk firmly away. Cissie came out on to the green-sward.

"You live at the Mill."

"Yes," I called over my shoulder.

"You shouldn't live there."

I stopped. She came a few steps after me, her arm raised, her finger pointing crookedly.

"Why not?"

"Because it's an unlucky place. It'll bring you bad luck."

"That's a wicked thing to say. You mustn't say such things. Who told you it was an unlucky place?"

She looked sideways at me, plucking at her fantastic skirt with its long-faded flowers and limp panniers.

"That woman at the Mill is a bad'un and it's a shame," she said, again as if repeating a lesson.

"If you say that again, I shall never come and drink the goat's milk. Do you hear?"

Whether the threat had any effect on her I could not tell but as I walked away again, she called out, "You should have a sprig of rowan and a bit of iron about you, Miss Ellen Westerdale. . . ."

Quite shaken out of my apathy, I walked on at a rare pace. It should have been easy to dismiss Cissie's fantastic warnings as a figment of her poor, addled imagination. But she had obviously been repeating local gossip of a particularly unpleasant sort. It revived in me something of the bewilderment and disgust I had felt when listening to Daisy Marshall, as if the familiar landmarks of my life had shifted and regrouped themselves in a new and more menacing form.

The bad luck I mournfully acknowledged; and after all had not I myself thought evil of Rose? Ashamed of having sunk to the level of ignorant country folk, I resolved to rid my mind of any critical judgment of her, particularly as I now felt that I understood and could deal with her. As for the notion that I might be in any personal danger, it was quite absurd. Besides, to the many images of Rose there had been added a new one: of Rose sitting on the sun-flecked grass with larks singing, and crying as if her heart would break. How sad her life had been! To have escaped one set of trials, to have found the hope of fresh happiness and to have it snatched away in a few short months! In my grief at Father's death, I had been almost indifferent to hers.

By the time I came in sight of the cross-roads, I was determined to make a new beginning in our relationship. Surely we could adapt our lives to a new pattern and be comfortable together.

But the sight of the signpost pointing to Kindlehope brought fresh misgivings. What had Rose been doing on the Kindlehope road that day she came? Had she lost her way? Hardly had I formulated the question, when the little finger-post saying "Saxelby Mill" pointed to the shady tunnel of Mill Lane. The letters though worn were quite legible and it was only in high summer that the finger-post itself was swallowed up in a tangle of traveler's joy. Coming from the Moorcock on foot and on a day like this, she could not have missed the turning. And why, if she hated Appleby End so much, had she wept so bitterly on leaving it?

All at once I felt mentally exhausted. The sheer complexity of her personality and the distracting effect of my everchanging attitude toward her oppressed me so that I could actually have fallen to the ground, as under the weight of a heavy burden. Dragging myself as far as the cross-roads, I sank down on the grass and leaned back against the signpost with my eyes closed.

Larks were singing now. I took off my hat and felt the cool moorland breeze in my hair. Behind me the white road marched with Roman directness to Stanesfield; to my right the Kindlehope road ran along the ridge above the deep valley into a waste of grass, boulder and heather.

I thought of a woman—a lady, a stranger—coming from Stanesfield, carrying a bag. At the cross-roads she would look down at the Mill. Some fugitive idea teased my mind. There was something I had forgotten. But even then, how far, how very far I was from suspecting the truth!

Opening my eyes, I too looked down at the Mill. For the hundredth time its beauty ravished my heart as it had done Father's. A touch of perfection, an inevitable rightness in the relation of its tiles and gables, the way the blue smoke rose, the stone roof dipped, the garden wall surrendered to the river. Yet it occurred to me that a stranger might feel in that very perfection too inviolate a quality. It allured but did not welcome; a place complete in itself.

From here I could not see the water but I saw the top of the trees, the footbridge and leaning on the handrail, my step-mother.

At once I felt in the harmony of the scene a discordant note. "You do understand why I wanted it?" Father had said, speaking of the Mill. *"You* understand." Rose had not understood. She had never liked the place, had never belonged. Perhaps it was as well that we should go away, she a prisoner released, I an exile from a Paradise whose beauty was now more than half pain.

I got up. Rose was still there, half hidden by the mountain ash which sprawled over the bridge and down to the water. Had she forgotten that the handrail was loose? She seemed to be leaning on it quite heavily and looking down into the now stagnant water of the old Mill race.

"Mamma! Be careful."

Thin as a reed in the wide air, my voice died away, useless. I saw her stand upright and swing herself back, then lean forward, pushing on the rail. Even in my panic I recognized the idle wilfulness of her behavior. But I was already running full tilt down the field.

As I reached the gate, through the shrouding branches I heard the creak of straining wood and saw her, tilted at a perilous angle over the water, holding on to a branch bent like a bow.

With a bound I was at her side and had laid hold of her arm. I cannot tell how it was: the whip of the branch as it sprang back; a flurry of new leaves and tangling skirts; the splintering of rotten wood. Most vividly I remember the terror of falling. Father was there and Binnie. I saw a flash of white wings and heard Lucy say quite clearly, "There's an angel in the orchard, Ellen."

Above me I saw the face of Rose, watching me intently as the green water closed over me.

[211]

Chapter Twenty

The angel's wings transformed themselves into Nancy's white apron, limp now and gray with slime from the weed-mantled stream.

"She's coming round, thank God." Dazed and sick as I was, I recognized the relief in Nancy's voice. "Lie still, Miss Ellen. You'll feel better in a minute."

A paralyzing weakness made even my eyelids feel as heavy as lead. I closed them again thankfully.

"You alright, Nancy?" That was Kirkup's voice.

"Oh, I'm alright. Just a bit wet. She wasn't in the water above a minute. I was just peggin' out the teacloths and saw the two of them on the bridge."

"And Missis you said . . ."

"She pushed her in, as sure as I'm sittin' here. What I mean is, suppose I hadn't been about?"

I opened my eyes and tried to protest.

"No . . . No . . ."

"The wickedness, eh? Funny I should be there every time she's tried it."

"You mean when she pushed Miss Lucy into the fire?"

"That—and when she went for her with the scissors," she went on. "Frightenin' one of them out of her mind and tryin' to drown the other. Funny how it all fits."

"Like yon other, you mean?"

"Two of a kind, if you ask me. It's gone far enough."

Again I tried to protest, but the words died feebly away. Lying there too weak to speak or move, I had the impression that the order of things had somehow changed and that the crux of the change lay in Nancy. With my shoulders cradled between her wide lap, my head supported by her strong arms —bare to the elbow and cool still from the water—I was conscious of her as the source of a more than physical power. It seemed to flow from her like an intensification of my own weakness. It was there too in her slow voice.

"She's gone too far this time. There'll be others besides me that'll say so."

Her tone was implacable.

"Hush up!" said Kirkup. "She'll hear you."

I was aware of a dark column on my left. I lay in its shadow. The stones were hard: my head ached. But presently when the feeling of nausea passed, I struggled to sit up.

"Where is Mamma?"

[213]

"She's over there." The dark column wavered. "Standing over by the wall—like a statue."

Even in my confused state I was struck by that inflexible note in Nancy's voice.

"White as a sheet herself, isn't she?" said Kirkup.

"And needs to be," said Nancy grimly.

"She didn't . . ." I knew that it was important to say this. "Nancy, I fell in."

"That's as may be."

The dark column moved again and Rose stood beside me.

"Ellen, you're feeling better?"

Far above me a pale disc floated, disintegrated and reconstructed itself as Rose's face—white indeed—and agitated. I contrived to smile but the smile relapsed in a shiver.

"It's cold."

Kirkup carried me upstairs and Nancy put me to bed where I instantly fell asleep. When I awoke, Rose was sitting by the bed. That, I remember, surprised me.

"Do you feel better?"

"Yes." I sat up experimentally. "I'm quite better, I believe."

"I'm so thankful. Ellen, you know it was an accident?"

"Of course, Mamma."

It was Rose who brought tea and held the cup to my lips for the first heartening sip. But I was quite well enough to take it in my hand and sit up.

"You know," I said, "one couldn't drown in the old stream. It isn't very deep, only dreadfully dirty."

"But you hit your head and went under."

"It does ache a little."

"Ellen." She leaned forward and said again, "You do know it was an accident? Nancy said . . ."

"I remember now. The branch sprang back and I over-balanced."

"You know I wouldn't harm you like that?"

For once she seemed shaken out of her indifference. Several times during the afternoon she came to me with food and drink, a napkin soaked in cologne, an extra pillow. The mishap had not been serious but I felt exhausted and content to lie in bed, watching the daylight fade. It was, as always, very quiet except for the doves cooing outside the window and the placid river sounds, but I knew from the absence of even the usual clatter of pots and pans that Nancy was not in the kitchen.

When she brought me a tray at about six o'clock, she seemed a little breathless.

"I'm a bit behind today. Father asked me to give him a hand holding the rail while he mended the bridge. Then I had to run along to the village and it's put me back."

I could tell from the hurried way in which she slapped down the tray so that the milk spilt, that her mind was far from her work. She had doubtless spent the afternoon gossiping. The story of my fall into the water would be well known in the village by this time, with who knows what embellishments.

"Nancy," I called her back as she scurried out. "I want it clearly understood that I fell into the water because the handrail was loose. Your father has been asked a dozen times to repair it and to lop the tree."

"He's doin' it now, Miss, Father is."

She stood facing me, a broad-shouldered, deep-chested country girl, as familiar to me as the furniture in the room or the pictures on the wall. But now as if a lay figure had moved, I seemed to be seeing her for the first time as a person in her own right, and again I was struck by the impression she gave of forceful energy. Especially my eyes were drawn to her bare, muscular forearms. I must have seen them often enough in the kitchen lifting the heavy iron saucepans as lightly as toys, or pressing vigorously on the board as she cleaned the knives, but now for some obscure reason they worried me.

"It's a very good thing the accident was no worse," I forced myself to say gravely and was annoyed to hear my voice quiver.

"Yes, Miss, I'm sure."

She spoke quite without the deference I was used to and although I could not doubt that she wished me well, her affirmation seemed so vehement as to sound almost like a threat.

She withdrew but the mischief was already done. I got up, bathed my face and went out into the courtyard. Half an hour later I was sitting listlessly on the stone bench in the last of the sun when a boy from Morton's farm came whistling through the gate. Seeing me he stopped whistling and hesitated, his lips still pursed, his eyes fixed upon me as if I were an object of wonder.

"Did you want to see me?"

"Er, I dunno." Then he blurted out, "Mester Morton sent me to say 'e won't be bringin' no pony and trap tomorrow— nor 'e won't be bringin' them no more. 'e says for all 'e cares, she can crawl into Stanesfield on 'er 'ands and knees."

"That will do," I said. The parlor window stood open. Could Rose have heard? "You can tell Mr. Morton that you gave me the message."

He took himself off but with a touch of insolence in the way he swaggered, whistling, to the gate. I had the feeling that he was hanging about in the road outside.

Just then Rose came out of the house and we walked over

[216]

to look at the half-repaired handrail. Kirkup had lopped the mountain ash savagely, leaving only a mutilated trunk and one or two branches. His tools lay on the bridge.

Rose stood looking down at the thick, green-mantled water.

"If I had wanted to harm anyone," she said suddenly, "it would have been myself. I had been thinking—if only I dared—how peaceful it would be."

"You mustn't say that."

"I wouldn't have dared to do it. But I stood here for a long time, wishing I could."

For the first time she spoke from the heart. At last I was listening to the real woman who had eluded me for so long. That puzzling gap between her words and gestures on the one hand and the essential inner spirit on the other no longer existed. The very change in her taught me that my instinct had been a true one. The falseness had existed. I had not imagined it.

But I forgot it in my pity for her.

"You must have been very unhappy." Then as she said nothing, I blundered on: "It's a sad time just now. There doesn't seem much to be happy about, but perhaps if you remember better times . . ."

"What is there to remember?"

"But surely you were happy with Father. *He* was happy. I never knew him as happy as when you were married. He loved you."

She stared at me as if thunderstruck. Then to my astonishment she burst into tears. It was the last thing I expected, to see her standing there in the evening sunshine with tears streaming down her cheeks, her sides heaving with sobs.

"Oh, Ellen, I have done wrong," she blurted out at last,

[217]

snivelling and dabbing at the tears with the back of her hand like a child. "I have done something terribly wrong. Sometimes I think . . ."

She broke off, startled. I heard it too: the scurry of feet in the road outside, the slither of hob-nailed boots. We both swung round to see a swarm of village boys at the gate. One had already climbed up it and was sitting astride the top rung. Two others were mounting the gateposts. Then came the rattle of stones. One of them landed at my feet. The boy on the gate shouted something. The rest took up the words, whatever they were—in a taunting chant.

The patter of stones became a continuous bombardment. Panic-stricken, we ran to the house, as one well-aimed flint sent the glass of the kitchen window tinkling to the ground. It was a relief to hear Kirkup come tramping down through the orchard.

"Get away, you young scamps," he shouted but another volley of stones had thundered to the back door before the boys, still chanting, fled up the hill. I heard Kirkup muttering as he went out into the lane and shook his fist after them.

If the demonstration was directed against Rose, it was successful. She was plainly terrified and so was I. We went into the parlor and sat down shakily at the table.

"I wonder if we should close the shutters," I said.

"Do you think they will come back?"

"I don't know. Perhaps we should send Nancy or Kirkup for Constable Lauder." It occurred to me that Nancy was once again absent. "Or I could go myself."

"Oh no. Nothing like that. Don't leave me alone here."

The sun had gone; the courtyard lay in shadow. From the river crept the familiar mist of evening, damp and cool. It

[218]

stole into the room, quietly occupying the house, so that I felt again the strange, separate life of the Mill, bound as it was to the river in a conspiracy of water and stone.

"Do you remember," Rose was rigid at the table, her hands clasped on the red cloth so that the knuckles showed white, "that story about the woman?"

"What woman?" I said, knowing very well.

"The woman they drove out of the village. The woman at Chantry Cottage."

"Yes, of course I remember but . . ."

"It could happen to me."

"But that was ages ago. . . ."

"They'll do it to me." She was looking at me with a directness I had never known, and she spoke with such conviction that I was shaken.

"But they're all dead, those people, or else they're old, like Nancy's grandmother." I paused. Uneasily that old memory revived, the memory of Nancy's story, told in the Hallowe'en firelight, bringing with it the damp scent of an autumn evening, a flurry of wind, the shuffle of feet, the clatter of iron pan-lids and fire-tongs. And with the terror of those hurtling stones upon me, it was hard to bring into my voice a suitable note of common sense. "Such things don't happen now. Besides they don't know you," I went on lamely.

"They didn't know her either, the woman at Chantry Cottage. They didn't even know her name but they hated her." She spoke still with the same childlike simplicity. "And they hate me. You heard what Nancy said—and Mortons' boy."

The rest of the room had receded into twilight. My vision extended no further than Rose's pale face and clenched hand.

[219]

It was easy to let reality slip away, to feel the century turn back to that earlier time.

I saw how my falling into the water would be interpreted in the village: as the second scene in the re-enactment of that other woman's drama. But for me the interest had already moved to the third scene—the last. Rose had only put into words what I myself had subconsciously feared from the moment I had come round and heard Nancy speaking. All my distaste for the old story of the witch hunt revived in a wave of pity for the outcast woman and dread of her pursuers. Only now the cast had been altered with Rose in the central role.

The blow on the head had, as Binnie would have said, knocked some sense into me. I could now see Rose as she really was, a troubled human being whom I desperately wanted to help. Yet the possibility that the women of Saxelby might take the law into their own hands again almost reduced me to a state of panic. I had wild thoughts of hurrying Rose to the farthest attic and bolting the door.

With a determined effort to restore a normal atmosphere, I closed the shutters and lit the lamp.

"Where's Nancy?" Rose asked.

I opened the door and listened.

"She must have gone home. I shall have to speak to her tomorrow. She's taking advantage."

"I did mean to go to Stanesfield tomorrow," Rose said, "to draw money from the Bank. But now, if Morton won't send the trap . . ." She hesitated. "If anything happened there would be—no means of getting away."

The next day would be Saturday. I knew that if Nancy were not paid, in her present mood she would more than likely give notice. Besides, I told myself that it would be good for Rose to have a change of scene. She had got herself into a nervous state, I thought, trying to be sensible.

"If you can make an early start, you could ride into Stanes-field with Babbitt. He goes past the cross-roads at about eight on a Saturday morning." I tried to calculate his mysterious and complicated movements and found that my head ached still with a dull, throbbing pain. "Then he comes back as far as the Moorcock at about two, goes back to town and then comes back to Cross Gap in the evening."

Drawn together as we had never been before, we sat talking nervously until bedtime, more isolated than if the Mill had been under siege. We settled that she would buy a few things in town so that there would be no need for me to go to the village.

She must have been up at cockcrow. When I came down, I found her already in the hall in her hat and gloves, with a bag containing two dresses to be altered at Ebury's.

"I'll come up the hill with you."

I opened the door, letting in the scent of wallflowers and the fresh river smell. Rose shivered.

"It will be cool driving over the moors. Perhaps I should take a heavier wrap after all."

She ran upstairs and came down with her sealskin jacket. We walked up the pasture, making the lambs skip and bound.

"We used to say that when you could tread on seven daisies with one foot, it must be spring," I said.

She laughed and tried it.

"There."

A cool wind blew across the open moor, stroking the long grasses at the base of the signpost. Rose put on her jacket, an incongruously elegant figure in that wild place. We had only a little while to wait before Babbitt's cart crawled into sight along the Kindlehope road.

"I'll come and meet you this evening," I offered, thinking that it was not safe for her to walk down alone with a large sum of money, and again not acknowledging to myself that impulse to protect her from other dangers, not to be named.

"If you like."

"But if I'm not there, come down through the pasture, not the lane."

Babbitt was almost here. Idly I put my hand on the signpost, hearing the breeze sigh in the cross pieces, and glancing down into the wind-combed grass, I saw a small point of brightness like a drop of dew: a large drop—and it was yellow. I stooped and picked up a gold trinket—an earring cut in the shape of a pendant rose. The wire had worn thin and snapped.

Babbitt had drawn to a standstill and got down to take Rose's bag and help her up. Still electrified by my discovery, I looked at her in a daze.

"I'm going, Ellen."

She was standing on the step, ready to take her seat under the tarpaulin cover.

"See what I've found," I called triumphantly. "I didn't even know you'd lost it."

She stepped down again to look at the earring lying in my palm.

"It's pretty," she said, "but it isn't mine."

"Ready, Mum?"

Suddenly she stooped and kissed me. It was the first spontaneous caress I ever had from her. Her eyes, looking down at me, were softly gray like the morning sky.

[222]

I watched the wagon draw steadily away along the white road until it was no more than a wavering point in the distance, until it was gone.

I knew at last that she was not my cousin Rose.

Chapter Twenty-one

I knew it with absolute certainty; and it seemed now that I must always have known. There was no need to compare the earring in my hand with the pair in my drawer. I knew every curve and groove of the roses. On this one the wire had worn thin and broken off a little nearer to the end than on Mother's.

All the same I went blindly down the hill and up to my room, to sit in a trance on the window-seat with the three identical earrings in my hand, trying to unravel the tangled events of the last two years, but in a dull, stupefied way as if I were recovering from a long illness, so that I failed to make the obvious connections, failed utterly to detach my stepmother from the role she had played since the disastrous moment when Lucy had rushed to her on the bridge, shrieking a welcome.

More than ever her presence filled the house. At every creak of the old timbers I looked up, expecting to see her in the doorway. When at last I went along the landing, it was to feel her everywhere.

Yet I knew with the same conviction that she had gone for good. She had made her escape in time. The door of the south room stood open, revealing the secret of why it had ever been locked. Trunks and boxes, baskets and bags were packed and corded, ready for despatch. She had been preparing steadily for flight. How would she have contrived it, I wondered, if at the end panic had not driven her away; if at the last minute her means of transport had not failed? As it was she had gone off meanly in the carrier's wagon with only what she could cram into a handbag and her sealskin coat. To the end she had lied to me about taking the dresses to Ebury's.

Her bunch of keys, discarded on the chest of drawers, convinced me that I was right: she would not be coming back. In a leather writing-case I found sheets of paper covered with nothing else but the name "Rose Warden," endlessly repeated until at last it changed to "Rose Westerdale," written over and over again. The dressing-table drawers were empty. Mother's silver toilet things had gone from the west room. Father's tortoise-shell and silver paperknife, his gold-mounted ink stand, his pearl-handled reading glass were missing from his secretaire. The hall press too was empty. She had kept it locked to conceal what was no longer there. I could only suppose that she had taken the silver bit by bit to Stanesfield and sold it, beginning with Mother's bonbon dish. I remembered her in the shade of the apple tree, smiling up at Father, her eyes soft and luminous under the brim of that enchanting hat. . . .

It was long, long before I understood it all, before all the inconsistencies of the past two years resolved themselves into a clear pattern; before I realized fully her dilemma, her enforced silences, her savage rejection of every vestige of the life at Appleby End that she had never known, her growing dread of discovery. In my first bewilderment I grasped only the one bitter fact—that while we had been living in earnest, for her it had been a masquerade. While I had longed for, had blunderingly tried to establish a true and sympathetic relationship with her—she had been concerned only to cheat and deceive, waiting for the same capricious fate that had brought her, to contrive her escape.

And yet I could not hate her. False, shallow, selfish—I had known that she was so almost from the start, but to me she had also been fascinating, beautiful, and in the last twenty-four hours I had understood that she was wretchedly unhappy. And when I cried, my throat swelling, my heart aching—it was because she had not loved me as I could, in spite of everything, have loved her.

I fell on my knees by the bed and hid my face in the counterpane, feeling the slow stirring of a deeper anguish. If it had not been for her, Father might have been alive here at the Mill. I thought of Lucy, neglected, pining with grief; Mr. Southern, lost to me; Binnie trudging stonily away up the hill; and somewhere, on a different level of consciousness there awoke, only to die, another thought, like the first shifting stone before an avalanche.

From an immense distance I heard Nancy call.

"Are you there, Miss Ellen? Is it alright if I go now?"

She came up to the landing.

"Are you sure you'll be alright, Miss, till Missis comes back?"

I went to the door.

"Yes, perfectly. I'll walk up to meet Babbitt later on."

How still the house was when Nancy too had gone! Weak and famished as I was, I could not eat the food she had left on the parlor table but wandered like a wraith through the empty rooms. In the drawing room a glimpse of my face in the mirror startled me so that I felt the prick of perspiration. Yet I saw nothing. I might have been invisible, my entire being diminished to vanishing point. How could it be that I existed when everyone else had gone?

Suddenly the silent rooms were too much to bear. I went out through the garden and along the river path, stooping under the alder boughs until their sheltering leaves enclosed me; but even then the movement of my dress in the water made me nervously aware of the absence of any other living thing and drove me away from the river and up the hill.

I cannot tell why I waited, knowing that it was useless. My stepmother would not come back. Perhaps it was the need for absolute confirmation that kept me there by the cross-roads for two hours and more before Babbitt lumbered into view.

"She wasn't there," he said tersely when he had pulled up. "I waited the best part of half an hour."

I could only nod, standing there like a wayside image. There were no other passengers. He pushed back his hat and took out his pipe.

"She your stepmother? I've heard tell of her." He began to

fill his pipe ruminatively. "I've heard a lot about her. She wasn't what I expected."

"But you had seen her before, Mr. Babbitt."

"Never laid eyes on her in my life. I don't know how she's to get back from Stanesfield without she hires a cab and that'll cost her sixpence a mile. Ay, wicked what they charge."

The wagon was a quarter of a mile away before I realized that he had gone. Shock had so stupefied me that it no more occurred to me then to wonder where she would go than to wonder where she had come from in the first place. Again that other thought stirred in my mind, that unformulated question. I knew that it was immensely important and at once in my weariness I forgot it. There were so many things I must think about.

Somehow I found myself in the west room. The sight of the unmade bed, the littered toilet table, and washstand revived me. Relieved at knowing what to do, I stripped off and folded the sheets, straightened the bed, carried away the dirty water, wiped the marble top and replenished the ewer; dusted and rubbed the furniture till it gleamed; shook out the bed curtains, found a fresh white counterpane. All this I did unthinkingly, soothed by the familiar actions, and when the room was clean and shining again, I quietly closed the door on it.

The unquiet spirit of my stepmother still haunted the Mill but imperceptibly it had changed, transformed now, to a frightened ghost. To my surprise I realized that she had been afraid all the time, not only of discovery but of the place itself; of the low rooms and murmuring water; the enfolding trees, the watchful hills. Like a creature out of her element she had been afraid of the simple society into which she had stumbled. To her the local people had never become individuals, only a close-knit organism, hostile and unyielding as the landscape itself in some of its moods.

The evening was overcast and still. I wandered out into the lane and climbed the hill toward Saxelby. Away from the trees the air felt fresher. To the west as always the sky brightened behind a broken pile of silver-edged clouds. But I turned and stared along the road, fixing my eyes on the point where it curved and vanished to join the village street, and listened with an intensity that only relaxed into a fit of shivering.

Suppose she had been right. This was the way they would come, red-faced, arms bared to the elbow, sending angry spurts of dust from their thick boots, filling the quiet lane with the din of their fire-irons and saucepan lids—as their grandmothers had done.

And who could blame them? Surely there had been something strange, something inexplicable in my stepmother's coming. The hills, the clouds hung motionless, charged with the question: *who was she?* Impossible not to feel that she had emanated from the very stones and trees to stand upon the bridge, casting a dark shadow on our lives. Who could blame them if in their ignorance and superstition they came again?

I remembered that implacable note in Nancy's voice when she said, "It's gone far enough"—some quality that had penetrated even Rose's insensitivity, except that she was not Rose, and not, after all, so insensitive. She had been terrified by the shower of stones and the boys shouting.

Straining my ears, I listened. I think I must, just then, have been feverish. I had eaten nothing all day and I could still feel the throbbing pain and soreness where I had struck my head— long, long ago in falling. My childish dislike of that steep tunnel of houses at Saxelby seemed now to take on the authority of a premonition, warning me that they would certainly come again; so that I actually expected to see at the narrowing of the lane the first of a moving tide of heads and to hear the distant shuffle of feet; and it would be I who would have to face them because I was the only one left.

Alone in the electric stillness, I waited for a sign. One silver-edged cloud had turned to black, swollen to a height that dwarfed the hills, and towered above the western end of the valley. Half a mile away Saxelby Crag brooded over its green slopes like a giant toad. Far away, slender as a rush against a steel-gray sky—persistent, significant—stood the signpost. I waited—for the rumble of thunder, a single jag of forked lightning, a sudden whirlwind. But there was nothing, only the rattle of a loose stone at my feet. The lane was empty.

But the sign did come and I believe that it was heaven sent. It took the form of a young woman with a basket coming along the field path from Cross Gap. She stopped to wait for a little boy who straggled behind, took his hand and came steadily on toward the stile.

I moved aside to let her pass. It was Mary Shaw, her face serious as ever under her stiff-brimmed hat. Her basket was full to overflowing with primroses, pale and soft as silk.

"How pretty they are!" I said, seeing them as feminine faces: golden-eyed and meek.

"Ay, there's naught as pretty and there's more than ever this year. Edward, give the lady some flowers."

The child thrust his hand into the basket and held out a fistful of primroses, then retreated behind his mother's skirt, overcome by the ordeal. Mary smiled and picked him up.

"I think we s'll have rain," she said.

I pressed the cool petals to my face as I watched her walk away toward the village, taking with her all my fears. From time to time the little boy dropped over her shoulder a crumpled primrose or two to mark their passing; and I thought how beautiful it was to see them—and how timeless a picture— of a woman with a basket on her arm and a child on her hip, walking safely home. Certainly there were some things that did not change, that must never change.

I felt the cool touch of rain on my face. By the time I reached the gate it was falling heavily, sweet spring rain shining between the orchard trees in a deluge of pink and white blossom.

In the twilit hall I turned the key and bolted the door; in the dark kitchen I slid the bolt and closed the shutters across the broken pane. To my surprise I could scarcely climb the two flights of stairs to my room, but at last I lay down between the sheets with a relief that was more than physical as I gave myself up to the darkness and stillness, hearing the eternal murmur of the river below, no longer caring how it had all come about.

And there were some things I would never have known, if an Ansar sword had deviated in its downward curve by as little as a fraction of an inch . . .

I woke in the darkness to hear footsteps coming down the hill from Stanesfield, muffled on the wet road. The gate opened. A man's feet in heavy boots crossed the courtyard— limping. I waited to hear a knock but the caller moved round to the east end of the house. There came the light patter of stones on my window; a familiar voice.

"Miss Ellen."

In a moment I had opened the casement and leaned out.

"Alec! It can't be. Dear Alec!"

[231]

He was no more than a dark form below, a face looking up.

"I'm on my way to see Mother at Greater Saxelby. Thought I'd just call in on the way but it's later than I expected. I'm slower these days."

"Your bad foot! You shouldn't have walked so far."

"Only from the cross-roads. And I'll stay the night at Mortons'."

"But—will you be lame, Alec?"

"Well, I've got my discharge. I'll never walk right again but it don't trouble me much—and it's good to be back for good."

"Things have changed here too, Alec."

"They have that. It was a terrible blow hearing about the Captain, Miss Ellen—and Mother being turned away."

"I haven't heard from Binnie. Naturally she was vexed and hurt."

"She was that. Broken-hearted. I haven't heard all but after what the Captain did for me I don't intend to desert you and Miss Lucy. You find a different way of looking at things out there in the desert and I reckon there's nothing here that can't be sorted out with a word or two in the right place."

We were almost whispering. He did not guess that I was alone. It did not occur to me to mention it. Besides this was not the time.

"I'll be back. Just couldn't pass the old place without a word. Goodnight, Miss Ellen."

"Goodnight, Alec."

He moved away.

"How is Sarah?"

"Right as rain."

"You're going to be married?"

"Soon as I get fixed up with a job of work. I'm thinking of

trying the cutlery trade. I've had about enough of the other sort of steel. By the way, a funny thing. Sarah met me at Stanesfield station this morning. When we came out there was old Babbitt just pulling up. Who do you think got down? Dressed to kill in one of them sealskin jackets and a fancy hat. 'Look who's there,' Sarah says. We both recognized her."

"Who was it?"

"The Lady from Locarno. Don't suppose you remember but Miss Lucy would. That actress we saw the night before I went away. Regular down-and-outs they were. Sarah's mother wouldn't have them in her place. But any way there she was large as life and handsomer than ever. She must have stayed on in these parts."

"Where did she go?"

"Into the station. Off to London, I shouldn't wonder. Well, goodnight, Miss Ellen. Pleasant dreams."

I closed the window and turned back into the dark room. A penniless actress. How obvious now: the voice, the style, the gestures, the staged hysteria, convincing enough to deceive a pair of guileless ignoramuses who had never even seen a play; the outwardness, the laughter that could be turned on at will. And she had been hungry, homeless, desperate. I understood now her determination to be rid of Binnie before Alec, the only one likely to recognize her, should come back. How narrowly she had missed him! Chance, which had saved her two years ago, had saved her again.

But I never really believed it. So intimately, so painfully, so hauntingly had she entwined herself with the most sensitive fibers of my being that for me she could have no identity before she strayed into my life, and no identity after.

And after all Cousin Rose had not come. We had never

really believed that she would. That ethereal figure had remained forever in the wings. Strange that we had not heard of her death, for dead she must be.

"Everything seems to be coming to an end and after all that would be for the best. Another life . . ."

She had simply faded away, never entirely real. Unless she had actually directed in her will that my father should be informed of her death, there would be no one to let us know. We had not after all been so very closely related.

Falling at last into the twilight state before sleep, I consigned her to oblivion. But sweetly, insistently, the old dream of Appleby End reshaped itself: the two fair-haired girls in the honeysuckle bower came quietly back as if they had never gone away.

Tomorrow I would go to Lucy.

Chapter Twenty-two

Ellen! Come here quickly. I want you."

I woke to the sound of Lucy's voice. Happiness possessed me—a happiness so intense that the room seemed full of light. The illusion of Lucy's presence was so vivid that I had actually slipped out of bed and gone to the window before the dream faded, leaving a dull sense of loss.

I pushed open the casement and leaned out, feeling the cool air on my face, hearing the ecstasy of birdsong, remembering . . .

"There's a person up there by the crossroads."

Suspended between sleep and waking as Lucy had been

then, I could not tell when the revelation came. She had not been dreaming. On that other May morning, so long ago it now seemed, there really had been a person up there, a lady in gray, kneeling beside the signpost.

At last the question which had hovered in my mind the day before defined itself, and with such force that it might have been written in stark black letters in the air before me. Who could have dropped the earring if not Cousin Rose herself? And Babbitt's passenger, who had asked for the Mill and then, inexplicably got down a mile or two away—who could she have been but Cousin Rose? After all the years of delay she had come as far as the cross-roads only to repent even then; to linger up there on the moors all night; to disappear, leaving no trace apart from the drop of gold in the grass. Why could she not face the Mill? And yet the strangeness of her presence there at dawn was no more remarkable than the profound mystery of her absence ever since. Where was she now?

Fumbling with buttons, hooks and tapes, I dragged on my clothes and went out into the garden as though enlightenment would come with the wider view of hills and pasture and the white stretch of moorland road beyond. A pale mist still lay on the river, rising here and there to leave a boulder blurred in outline and crowned with a shining wreath of white; and my thoughts hovered between certainty and surmise, doubt and fear, as the mist parted and thinned to deepen again elsewhere.

By this time I was convinced that Lucy had actually seen a woman up there, a woman at the end of her resources with no hope left but to say her prayers, and that the woman had been Cousin Rose. My brief mood of happiness had faded into bewilderment, deepening into an anxious concern.

[236]

She must have traveled with Babbitt on the Tuesday. It had been at dawn on Wednesday, May first, when Lucy saw her; and later in the day my stepmother had arrived. The afternoon had been well advanced when she came, the sunlight long and low. Lucy had been swinging on the rail of the footbridge, I had been sitting by the breach in the wall of the old herb garden.

I sat down now in my old place among the springing ferns and rosemary, letting the months and years roll back, seeing nothing. I sat so still that a thrush alighted almost at my feet and began to batter the snailshell in its beak against a stone, with a single-minded energy that roused me at last; and instantly, miraculously—I saw amid the small cascade of broken masonry, almost as if the wilful beak had pointed it out—the hagstone.

I picked it up and pressed it to my cheek, then held it tenderly in my hand so that I saw an arc of my line of life through the magic circle, and cradled it there as if I loved it. Certainly the feeling it aroused was one of love. It was like the return of something more than a friend.

At once, with relief, I knew what I must do. Events had overwhelmed me so that I could no longer act alone. I had neither the strength nor the experience nor the resource to deal with the mystery of Cousin Rose's disappearance. Even to guess what might have become of her made me tremble and feel sick.

I felt too, dimly, that someone should be told about my stepmother. Yesterday there had been no one. Mr. Southern alone could have helped and advised. Had he been near I would have gone to him, overcoming my embarrassment. Indeed I had come to feel bitterly ashamed of the shabby and childish way I had treated him.

But now with the hagstone in my hand I could think only of Mark. He was my friend. I never doubted it. I could tell him everything, ask his advice. My confidence in his understanding brought an exhilarating warmth to banish the weary sensations of grief and shock and restore me to something like a normal state of mind.

I went firmly into the kitchen and being by this time almost giddy from lack of food, made a good breakfast of bread, honey and milk. Then I found an old kit bag of Father's—easier to carry than a basket or carpet-bag—and put into it some bread, cold meat, a napkin, the old horn cup, a shawl and a spare pair of stockings. I hesitated as to whether to take my stepmother's waterproof cape but decided that it was too heavy. It was still early when I unbolted the back door, locked it on the outside and left the key on a bench in the old coach house, with a note for Nancy asking her to feed the cats and poultry while I was away.

Then with the slack of the kit bag tied with cord so that I could carry it either over my shoulder or in my hand, and my one sovereign in my pocket, I set off up the hill.

At first the welcome exercise, the stirring life of birds, the long-absent sense of adventure were all invigorating. Turning from the deep lane into the high road brought, as always, a feeling of release. Below on my right the meadows were already ankle-deep in grass. Sheep and lambs were grazing on the rough pasture at the roadside. They served as company.

It was not until I reached the clump of elders and bramble at the summit of the Pellows' field that I felt a touch of misgiving. Perhaps it was foolish to sit down and rest on the very spot where Cissie had seen the lady; but a flat stone in the shelter of the wall made a seat and I filled my cup at the spring which gurgled from a brown spout in the hillside.

For of course it must have been Cousin Rose who sat here weeping in the May sunshine with the larks singing, within half an hour's walk of her friends. Had she too seen the flutter of that faded chintz gown or the pale segment of a watchful, crazy face? A sudden fear that Cissie might be watching now from her hiding-place behind the elders sent me hurrying away.

It was these thoughts that changed the nature of my journey. At first it had been a perfectly straightforward expedition in search of Mark. According to Binnie he lived "over Kindle-hope way" which I knew lay at some indefinite (possibly considerable) distance beyond Cross Gap. It was only a question of walking far enough, of being able to walk far enough. I had not realized how unusually tired I was.

But now the road was haunted for me by the woman with the bag who had walked this same way two years ago. Or had there been two women? I stopped, confused, to shift the kit bag from right hand to left and for a fantastic moment or two yielded to the delusion that my stepmother was there with me, strolling along the stone causeway in the middle of the road; and there was someone else on the other side whom I could not see; until the phantoms vanished and I was looking down on the gray roofs of Cross Gap, the level green by the river, the squat tower, from which came the thin beat of the bidding bell.

I had forgotten that it was Sunday but my consciousness of behaving in a manner most unsuitable for the Sabbath was outweighed by a sudden longing to be among people—to hear them talk. Besides, the green by the river had pleasant associations. I reached the wooden bench as the children were going into Sunday School and watched until the door closed on the last straggler.

It was surprisingly difficult to get up again. Miss Blewett the schoolmistress was coming out of her gate with a prayer book in her mittened hand as I went slowly by.

"A pleasant morning," she said. "We haven't seen you in Cross Gap for some time."

Surprised that she should remember me, I made some vague reply and hesitated. It seemed churlish to go on without the chat she so obviously intended. She was an alert little woman with bright brown eyes. They were fixed on me with some curiosity.

"I did come to see the May Walk on Friday, but I was too late."

"You are coming to the service?"

"No. I'm . . . just walking."

"There's nothing like fresh air and exercise," declared Miss Blewett heartily while her bright eyes explored my face and clothes and rested for a few seconds on the kit bag. "But we mustn't overdo it, must we?"

I managed to smile and move on, regretting the wooden seat in the sun. Several heads turned as I walked along the village street. At the end where the lane curved up again to rejoin the road, I looked back, half reluctant to begin the climb. By the school gate Miss Blewett was talking to the Rector. They were both looking after me.

It had not occurred to me that there was anything eccentric in my solitary outing; but now I saw that it might well seem a little odd to be walking away out of the village to nothing—so far as I knew, for I had never been further than the village shop—but open moors. I was reminded of the difficulty, in fact, the impossibility of doing anything in a district such as ours without arousing interest. For the people of Cross Gap a solitary female would stand out like a landmark and be remembered, no doubt for a long time.

For two years?

Halfway up the hill I came to the last cottage, sending half a dozen hens in a panic across the lane. A cat sunned itself on the windowsill. A baby wrapped in blankets slept in a wooden box in the porch, where an old woman was peeling potatoes.

I stopped and asked the way to Kindlehope.

"You keep on up this 'ere lane till you come to 't high road and then you go on up 't valley. But it's a powerful long way."

I fancied a quality of permanence in her as she sat there with a potato in one twisted brown hand and a knife in the other, as though she had been placidly peeling potatoes for hundreds of years. By contrast there seemed something fantastic, almost insane in the idea of a person wandering across the moors to Kindlehope.

"It's very quiet here," I said, looking down at the sleeping baby—with envy.

"Ay."

"You don't see many people passing by?"

"Not more'n a two-three, except on a Market day."

"Do you remember seeing some one going by, quite a long time ago—two years ago?" I felt the absurdity of the question. "A woman with a bag?"

"You mean a pedlar woman?"

"No, no. A lady in gray, wearing a veil."

"You wouldn't see a lady on 'er own with a bag. Not 'ere. Where'd she be goin'? Nay, there's nought but village folk and mebbe a tramp or two and not many nor them, for there's no Work'us on this side Saxelby. Have you come far?"

"No. Not far."

I nodded vaguely toward the village and went on, feeling her eyes upon me until I rounded the bend.

Leaving the lane, I turned westward. The sky had changed. Huge galleons of white cloud moved above the hills, filling the landscape with changing shapes. Up here where the gaze foundered in distances of blue and green, it was easy to feel close to Father and I leaned forward over a stone wall, watching the cloud shadows and breathing in the thin air with the sensation of sailing over a wide sea.

Or perhaps I was a little light-headed. I unwrapped the parcel of food but could scarcely swallow the bread and meat. The sight of the road rising endlessly ahead reminded me of how short a distance I had come though it was long past midday. Yet the strange feebleness in my limbs kept me sitting there until my hands and feet were numb with cold. Detachedly, without fear or interest, I wondered what it would be like to lie down and die by the wayside. It was a restful idea; until I was struck with a self-pitying notion of the pathos of it: to die in a ditch and lie there undiscovered—for years.

Through my apathy there stole a newer, deadlier chill. The moors had darkened. Only an occasional boulder, a barely moving sheep punctuated the somber waste. The strange pleading notes of a golden plover filled the void for a moment, then left it silent. A sense of awe, of limitless melancholy, almost overwhelmed me. I was saved from despair by nothing more than a dim feeling of responsibility to an unknown woman; and the longing, more insistent than ever, to find Mark Aylward and share the burden with him.

[242]

I got to my feet and went on. The road narrowed, turning slightly to the north and climbing away from the river which tumbled in yellow foam far below between shelving rocks. The air freshened. A grayness in the sky threatened rain. Without the sun I had no means of knowing the time beyond an impression that it was well on in the afternoon.

From the top of the next rise, I told myself, I would see Kindlehope. Not knowing whether to expect a cluster of roofs or a scattered hamlet, a spire or a farm, I toiled doggedly on. But at the top the road turned westward again and went mercilessly along a hillside bare of any sign of habitation.

But not entirely empty. Far away, a pinpoint in the distance, I saw a moving figure. Instantly the prospect changed. The human world reimposed itself. A burst of energy set me walking more briskly than I had done all day. A hopeful spirit whispered that it might even be—Mark. The very thought warmed my cheeks and chilled hands.

I had walked for several minutes before this illusion died. The approaching figure took shape as that of an older man, thick-set, slow-moving, filling the narrow white road. There was no avoiding him. On the right a few yards of rough grass soon yielded to springing heather too short to offer a hiding place. On the left a slope of bracken and boulder fell steeply to the river. We would soon be face to face.

I walked more slowly but my pace was quicker than his. He seemed scarcely to be moving. In fact he had stopped and was standing in the middle of the road as if he had taken root there, and no wonder with that huge bundle on his back.

"Solomon."

At first he did not recognize me. He seemed not to feel any interest such as the sight of a fellow traveller in that lonely

[243]

spot had aroused in me. His heavy face had a mottled look; the skin was loose; his beard long untrimmed; his thick hands with their dirty fingernails hung stiffly at his sides as if the very impulse to move had gone.

The thought occurred to me that if he were to fall, he would roll unresistingly down the slope into the churning river and lie there forever like another gray slab of millstone grit.

"Solomon. Don't you remember me?"

My voice brought a faint stirring of recognition into his glazed eyes.

"Yes, yes. I know you, Miss. But I can't exactly say . . ."

"You're very tired. Will you not take off your pack for a while and rest? Look. You could sit here out of the wind."

A heather-circled hollow in the hillside made a natural shelter. I drew him into it.

"Nay. If I take the pack off, I'll never get it on again in this world."

But he leaned against the sandy bank and closed his eyes.

"Would you like something to eat? I have some bread and meat."

"Nay. I've got something better than that." He winked with a faint revival of the old puckish humor, and heaving up his hand as if it were a heavy tool, fumbled in his coat and brought out a pocket flask. A mouthful of spirit revived him wonderfully. At once his little eyes brightened with curiosity.

"Miss Ellen. You've come a long way from the Mill all by yourself. Where might you be off to?"

"I'm going to Kindlehope."

"Walking all the way? You'll have friends there likely."

"Oh yes," I said confidently in the hope of discouraging further questions. "It can't be far now."

[244]

"Seven miles. Mebbe more. It's a mite late in the day for you to be going all that way on your own. It's not right for you to be wandering on these moors at any time let alone when it gets dark. I wonder she lets you—your stepmother." In spite of his subdued state there was something vindictive in the way he spoke about her, and he eyed me speculatively from head to foot until I grew uneasy.

"I thought you'd have had a husband by now to keep you at home. Hadn't you better turn back with me?"

His company was the last thing I wanted. I looked along the valley and saw the horizon blurred in a gray haze of cloud. I felt the first moist breath of rain on my face. Seven miles! As far again as I had already walked with such toilsome effort.

"You're not wanting to go back to the Mill then?" he persisted. "Things aren't the same there. . . ."

"I'm visiting friends at Kindlehope," I said firmly, realizing the folly of trying to present this ill-considered expedition into the hills as a social call, and I took a determined step or two as if to leave him.

With an effort he pushed himself away from the sheltering bank and settled his pack; but he swayed dizzily and put out a hand for support.

"Are you going all the way to Cross Gap?"

"Nay," he said when he had recovered himself, "and it's not so far when you know the tracks. But I'll be stopping the night down there—at Jennie Armstrong's."

I had not noticed the cottage on the other side of the river, a tumbledown place with stone roof-tiles, rough as the natural rock. A thread of path through the bracken seemed to lead to a narrow bridge over the stream.

"Are you sure you can walk so far? Would you like me to

come with you?" It seemed wrong to leave him, a sick old man, bent under the weight of his pack and dwarfed by the great sweep of hills behind him. Far below the river swirled between dark rocks in a flurry of yellow foam. I watched a pair of crows rise from the spring-green turf to flap and wheel above our heads, dark and hostile as the whole desolate scene.

"There's no call for that, Miss . . . I'll be alright. And what does it matter, any road? It's only a matter of time for all of us. One day they'll find me. 'It's old Solomon,' they'll say. 'The last of the old pedlars.' "

"That couldn't happen, Solomon. Someone will take care of you. Have you nowhere to go? No home?"

He shook his head.

"This has been my home. These hills. A cottage here and there. All I wanted. I won't be the first to end my days by the roadside like an old lost sheep. Food for them crows."

A memory stirred. What was it he had been saying that time in the courtyard at the Mill—or rather had begun to say when he was interrupted? Suddenly I remembered what it was —and who had interrupted him.

"Didn't . . . didn't they once find a body up here?" My knees trembled and I took a step toward the steep bank again, feeling almost unable to stand.

He looked somberly down at the river.

"Ay." He seemed to have relapsed into the exhausted state of a few minutes before. I waited, weak with anxiety, until he took a wheezing breath and went on: "Ay. There was quite a stir a year or two ago. Found a few miles back down there, lyin' among the bracken."

I moistened my lips.

"A woman?"

[246]

"Ay. A body could be lyin' there for years and nobody know."

He fumbled for his flask again. I leaned my cheek against the cool rock. It took all my courage to ask:

"Did they . . . did they find out who it was?"

He shook his head.

"It was too late. Some friendless soul, never missed."

He put the flask back in his pocket, took out a red-spotted handkerchief, wiped his face and blew his nose resoundingly.

"Most likely a tramp looking for work and lost in a storm. You don't find women wandering on their own, only lost creatures with some reason for separating themselves from their friends. Women in trouble."

Again his eyes darted from my face to my bag—my person —and suddenly I wanted nothing so much as to be rid of him, regardless of the lonely miles ahead.

"Goodbye, Solomon."

A little farther on I turned and watched him tramp stiffly down through the bracken, over the bridge and up to the sagging gate. It was a relief to think of him coming to rest at last by Jennie Armstrong's fire.

The raucous cawing of the crows recalled the sinister story of the dead tramp. There had been quite a stir, Solomon said. But not at the Mill. With a strange detachment as if I were looking at them from far away I saw the twilit rooms: the figures moving on the stairs, on the landing, in the hall; my stepmother skimming the pages of a newspaper, putting it down to take a restless turn or two, then picking it up again. She must always have been looking for news of the woman she had displaced. For the first time it occurred to me to wonder whether she had ever seen Cousin Rose, where and when their paths might have crossed or whether they had crossed at all.

There is nothing like exercise in the fresh air for clearing the mind. Tired though I was, I began to see, however imperfectly, through the tangled web of circumstance that had confused me for the last two days. One essential truth stood out with rock-like clarity. I had no proof that Cousin Rose had ever come this way. Cissie Pellow's lady could have been my stepmother, or indeed some other person. And nothing could be less tangible than the lady Lucy had seen at the cross-roads. I well knew Lucy's capacity for transforming the most trivial waking experience into dreams of such visionary power that she spoke of them solemnly for days after.

"When she was humble, kneeling down to ask for forgiveness." It was surely Alec's description of the Lady of Locarno that had fired Lucy's imagination—if she had been dreaming. If on the other hand she had—I marveled at the strangeness of it—been awake, it could still have been the Lady of Locarno in the person of my stepmother. Was it not more than likely that it was she who had spent the night on the moors? I remembered her distressed state, her terrible pallor when she had first lifted her veil.

Then just as I consigned Cousin Rose once more to the grave, a quiet resting place in the churchyard at Appleby End, I recollected the earring and the mountain of luggage, each piece laboriously corded and labeled, "Miss Rose Warden, Passenger to Saxelby Mill." "The Miss Warden who used to live at Appleby End." How eager, how anxious he had been, the stranger who had ridden by. I interpreted his search for her as positive proof that she had indeed left home. The memory of his bitter disappointment was a reproach. Unconsciously I had misled him. There remained the faint hope that he might somehow be found. Yet I would have little consolation to offer him.

As a result of all this mental wavering, with its chameleon-like power of change Cousin Rose's image once again transformed itself in my mind so that I became curiously obsessed with an idea of her as humble and contrite, begging for forgiveness.

I came to myself with a dismal sense of being wet through, my hair lank on my cheeks under my sodden hat brim. It was the distant bark of a dog somewhere to the right that had roused me.

Through the curtain of fine rain I could just make out the gable end of a farmhouse two or three hundred yards from the road. As I hesitated, the light of a newly kindled lamp appeared in the window. Without anything more to impel me than a longing for warmth and shelter, I followed the farm track to the door and knocked.

At first I heard nothing, then footsteps on a flagged floor, and a woman's voice, "Yes. Who is it?"

"Please can you help me? I'm on my way to Kindlehope and I can't go any farther."

The bolts were drawn and the door opened to reveal a pale-faced, middle-aged woman. She was plainly astonished.

"Are you on your own? Where've you come from?"

"I've come from Saxelby Mill. Please may I come in and rest? I'm Ellen Westerdale."

"Well, if that doesn't beat all! You'd best come into the kitchen, Miss."

It was a barely furnished room with oil cloth on the table, a luridly flowered wallpaper, a portrait of the queen in a tartan border, plain wooden chairs and a settle, but the black-leaded range reflected the light from a cheerful fire and a savory smell rose from the iron pot on the hob.

"My, but you're soaked very nigh to the skin."

It was a few minutes before she could recover from her surprise. She had pushed me into a chair by the fire where my damp skirt soon began to steam. "Had you better slip your things off, Miss? There's no one here but Lizzie and me. Mester's away at Saxelby seeing his old mother. I'm not expecting him till last thing. I could find you something . . ." For a moment she was nonplussed. "You could mebbe wrap a quilt round you till your dress and jacket dry."

Lizzie, who had appeared from the scullery to eye me in amazement, was dispatched upstairs for the quilt.

The sudden warmth made me so languid that I could scarcely unbutton my dress, but my hostess, once having recovered her wits, showed every sign of treating my arrival as a rare adventure. Wrapped at last in the quilt and wearing my own spare pair of stockings, I listened to a stream of talk while she trotted between kitchen and scullery.

"It's the only chance he has to see his mother—of a Sunday —or sometimes of an evening. It'll be midnight afore he's back. You'll be related to them at the Grange, I dare say?"

I murmured something about family friends which evidently satisfied her. It certainly did not interrupt her flow of conversation.

"Things are very comfortable up there now, they tell me. Not like what they used to be." She shook her head reminiscently. "But it's a tidy step from here to the Grange."

"I didn't realize how far it was. I mustn't stay too long. As soon as my things are dry . . . Mrs. . . . ?"

"Amblethwaite, love. It isn't fit for you to turn out. You could stay here but . . ." She hesitated. "It isn't that we haven't the bed, but it's never been aired since Grandad died three years gone Michaelmas. Not a soul has laid their head on the pillow since then and the room's that damp."

Drugged with warmth, I forced myself to look out of the window and saw with a sinking heart the drenched panes and blurred hills beyond.

"If you would just let me stay here by the fire . . ."

"I'll tell you what," she said, flushed at her own initiative, "you can sleep on the sofa in the front room. Lizzie, get some kindling and light the fire in there."

My apologies and protests were swept aside; nothing was too much trouble. In return I listened to a torrent of information about her family, her relations at Cross Gap, her daughter in New Zealand, until the fire in the sitting room had burned up sufficiently for me to retire.

Even so the unused room struck cold as a vault. Grateful though I was, I spent an uncomfortable night between extremes of burning heat and deathly cold, spells of anxious wakefulness alternating with feverish dreams. More than once I woke in the darkness, wondering confusedly what I was doing there—or half-asleep, fancied there was someone with me. Sometimes it was Lucy, sometimes a tall woman, vague as a will-o'-the-wisp with a disturbing tendency to become two separate people. I woke at last to see daylight creeping through the shutters and Mrs. Amblethwaite bringing in my dry dress and sadly shapeless hat.

Her husband was finishing his breakfast when I went into

the kitchen. No wonder he looked astonished when I burst out without preamble:

"Mr. Amblethwaite, when you found a—a body on the moors—who was it? Did they ever find out?"

"Nay. It were too late for that, love. She's been there over long. Years, I reckon. There were nought but a few rags and a skeleton. I thought it were no more than one o't sheep at first."

It was scarcely a topic for the breakfast table. He emptied his cup, called his dog and went off with a nod.

It was a relief to know that she had found a resting place at last, for I never doubted that it was the woman from Chantry Cottage. She may even have found the bare hills friendlier than her neighbors.

I could eat little. The heavy aching persisted in my head. My throat was aflame.

"I doubt you've catched cold, love," said Mrs. Amblethwaite and she refused absolutely to take any payment when I held out the sovereign. Instead she stood looking at me for a second or two, then said suddenly, "You're not running away, love, are you?"

"No, Mrs. Amblethwaite, of course not."

"Because there isn't a man in the world that's worth leaving your home for. And if it's . . . anything else . . . whatever trouble you're in, home's the place for it. There's plenty that have lived it down before today."

Feeling her concern without immediately identifying its direction, I said quickly, "I've had an anxious time and I'm going to seek advice because my father is dead and there's no one. But I won't do anything foolish and I'll come back and see you if I may."

"And welcome. This'll be something I'll not forget, for I haven't seen a lady like you since . . ."

She broke off as a coal exploded into the white-stoned hearth, and bent to replace it with the tongs.

"You were saying . . ." I was suddenly alert.

"I haven't seen a lady like you since I was in service down at Cross Hall before I was married. The sweet way you have of speaking took me back a few years, I can tell you."

So much for the Miss Pritts, I thought, making up my mind to tell Lucy.

I went out into a morning of sparkling grass and the chatter of sunlit becks. But the sun could not warm me, nor could I walk quickly enough to set the blood flowing in my heavy limbs. The very brightness of the morning made my headache worse and the farther I went, the more confused I became as to why I was going to Kindlehope at all. Moreover a kind of uneasiness troubled me. It was something Mrs. Amblethwaite had said, echoing a phrase of Mark's.

"We were living a bachelor sort of existence, but that's all changed."

I stopped dead, seeing him at the toy-stall with a doll in his hand. Incredulously I faced the possibility—more than that, the strong likelihood—that Mark Aylward was married.

The thought took away all my strength, all my hope. I had come to a spot where a green bridle-path climbed between leafy hedgerows to a clump of Scotch firs on the crest of the hill. Ahead stretched the hateful road. I could bear it no more. I could bear nothing anymore.

I dragged myself along the bridle-path for a little way and sank down by the margin, not caring any longer about the damp grass and the creeping cold. I remember with a sob of regret taking out the hagstone and holding it in my hand, seeing it through a haze of tears.

It was through the same haze that I saw a faint movement on my right, a gray ripple gradually recognizable as a flock of sheep coming down the track.

I felt a rustle beside me, heard a soft whine and excited bark, smelt the damp warmth of a dog. Then the sheep were all about me as I lay unprotesting even when a dark figure bent over me, knelt beside me.

"Ellen! My dearest Ellen!"

It seemed important that I should show him the hagstone but it was terribly heavy and I was not sorry to let it slip from my hand.

I heard a piercing whistle, other voices and the light wheels of a gig. Then I felt myself lifted gently in strong arms.

Chapter Twenty-three

Nothing in the room was familiar but the window. From the curtained bed it had been the limit of my view for what seemed a long time. I had watched the daylight drain from it, the twilight fall and moonlight slowly fade into dawn. There had been people in the room. Someone had given me water and draughts of medicine, had bathed my hands and face and brought a lamp.

The fever had quite gone. I struggled to sit up, aware of the snowy sheets, the frilled edge of the pillowcase. My hair was tied back. I wore a fleecy white wrap, soft as down. Gradually I discovered a girl in a cap and apron sitting by the fire.

"Where am I?"

"You're at the Grange, Miss, at Kindlehope. My, but you're looking better."

She arranged the pillows and disappeared. I closed my eyes, afloat on a stationary cloud in a peaceful sky, hearing all the time the magic words which had lingered in my memory even in the height of the fever. "Dearest Ellen."

Yet as consciousness revived, misgivings were reviving too. When presently the maid returned with a bowl of broth I ventured, "Perhaps I ought to speak to Mrs. Aylward."

"Mrs. Darwen, you mean, Miss. There's no Mrs. Aylward and hasn't been for nearly twenty years. Mrs. Darwen has been with you all the time, very nigh. She sat up with you when you were wandering a bit. She's lying down now. Shall I call her?"

"No, no." I felt a revival of strength that owed nothing to the broth. "I'm afraid I have been a great trouble to you."

"No trouble, Miss. I'm sure it makes a change. There's nothing much happening up here as a rule. Only we was worried about you. You seemed starved like and overdone. The dog found you. Old Sweep. Providential I call it. You'll be all right now. Mrs. Darwen's a rare nurse. She saved Mr. Aylward's life a year or two back when he had congestion. It was like a miracle . . ."

Later in the day Mrs. Darwen herself came to see me. She was a fresh-faced woman of about forty with fair hair fading to gray. She wore a plain housedress with a bunch of keys hanging from a housekeeper's chain.

I told her who I was, of my father's death, my sister's illness, the absence of my friends.

"You've been overtaxed, my dear. Had you no one to turn to? We had heard . . . Mr. Mark has often spoken of you— that there was an engagement with a Mr. Southern."

[256]

"Oh no. There was no engagement. How could you hear such a thing, I wonder?"

Then, unable to resist the pleasure of hearing it again, I asked, "Did he really speak about me?"

"He spoke of you a good deal until the news—or rather the rumor—of your engagement."

"There were things I needed to ask him about. I knew that he would help."

"I'm sure he will. But I understood that you have a step-mother."

"She went away."

Mrs. Darwen probably saw my distress. She turned away and presently laid a handkerchief soaked in cologne on my forehead.

"You have come to the right place. You may talk to Mr. Aylward in absolute confidence, as well as to Mr. Mark. To-morrow we shall see whether you are strong enough to dress."

Her voice was low-pitched and slow. Before I could thank her for all she had done, she went quietly away, leaving me astonished—as I recovered my wits and judgment—that these people should be so good to me. I was conscious of no intrusion. They might almost have been expecting me.

The next day Kate, the maid, helped me to dress and put a chair for me by the window in the adjoining room. It was furnished as a sitting room with a walnut chest of drawers, a green couch and a work-table with a sewing basket. It occurred to me that Mrs. Darwen had given up her own rooms for me.

The window looked out on a wide expanse of hills and sky, shimmering green and blue in the May sunshine. About half a mile away through the young foliage of a pair of elms,

I saw gray roof tiles and a church spire. Watching the rooks circling above it gave me the feeling of reassurance one has on waking from a nightmare to find the world restored to its natural order. I had not known such tranquillity since childhood; surely not even then. Only the sorrows of the past year could have made me so deeply sensitive to the peace of Kindlehope Grange.

There came a knock at the door. Mark stood there, smiling. He had haunted my imagination for so long and so persistently that I felt no strangeness.

"They won't let me talk to you," he said.

"But that was why I came."

"You did?" He took an impetuous step into the room, then retreated. "I'll talk to you for the rest of my life if only you'll get well first."

There was something deeply satisfying in this remark. Exhausted by the sheer bliss of it, I closed my eyes. When I opened them again, he had gone.

But the next day he came again. Mrs. Darwen was darning linen at the table but she discreetly withdrew into the bedroom, leaving the door ajar. Mark sat down on the broad windowsill. We looked out together toward the blue hills.

"Ellen!" He leaned forward, "I shouldn't speak to you now, not while you are ill and while you have no choice but to stay here. But there is something I must say."

It seemed so natural for him to take my hand that I might have been used all my life to the entrancing happiness it gave me.

"I've dreamed of seeing you here," Mark went on, "but I was sure that it could only be a dream. After that day at Stanesfield I knew for certain that it was what I wanted, though the feeling had been growing for years. In fact I had always known from first seeing you and your sister at Cross Gap. I used to look forward to May Day, planning it all day before. I used to get up at dawn and walk, instead of riding, in the hope of perhaps walking along Plum Lane with you. But I never had the courage to suggest it. Sometimes you weren't there and I would face a whole year stretching ahead without an opportunity of seeing you. Even last week I went, though by then I had given you up to Southern. It serves me right for paying any attention to that old rogue Solomon."

"It was a mistake."

"You're sure? After that meeting at Stanesfield I had made up my mind to find an excuse for calling. Then one day I found him sitting in the kitchen. Solomon, I mean. He mentioned having come from Saxelby. I couldn't resist saying that I had friends at the Mill. That was when he told me that you were going to marry Southern. It seemed only too likely."

"He was Father's dearest friend."

"No one could know you and not love you," said Mark sweepingly. "Grandfather knows Oliver Southern. They're both founder-members of the Mechanics Institute. He thinks him a good sort of fellow."

"He is . . . a very good man." From the immense distance now yawning between us, I could esteem Mr. Southern as never before, only to forget him completely when Mark said, "I was a fool to listen to that gossiping old rascal. More than a fool. I might have been of some help to you. Actually I've ridden over to Saxelby several times—even though it seemed hopeless—and gone no farther than the cross-roads. From there one can look down on the Mill. It was like looking into an enchanted garden where I had no right to go."

[259]

"I didn't know."

"One afternoon a few weeks ago I actually did get as far as the pack-bridge and stood there for a while as miserable as sin. Everything was so still I felt sure you had all gone away. Not a sign of life. It's a lovely old place, isn't it?"

"Yes," I said, my throat aching. "It's lovely."

He had let go my hand but now he leaned forward and taking it again in his, he said, "What was it, Ellen? What went wrong?"

It was strangely difficult to begin.

"When Sweep found you," Mark said as I groped for a beginning, "out there on our own bridle-path, bless his heart, I could hardly believe it. It was one of those absolutely breathtaking things that make one believe in a benign Providence. But of course I knew there was something wrong. You were light-headed you know. You were talking about some women. 'There are two women,' you said. 'Where are they?' What was it all about? Or ought I not to have mentioned it?" He glanced uneasily at the door behind him. We could hear Mrs. Darwen's quiet movements as she tidied the room. "I said I wouldn't talk."

"No, I must. It was to tell you about it that I came," I said, seeing though at a distance, the phantom figures reappear. He must have felt my agitation. He took something from his pocket, the hagstone.

"It was a strange love-token," he said. "I must give you another, if you will let me. But there was something in it. It brought us together."

"You said there could be evil spirits."

"I said that I knew there were good ones and now I'm more

[260]

certain of it than ever. As a matter of fact on that very same day, I had proof of it. But that can wait. . . ."

"Are they just people?"

"I don't know. Who was it, Ellen, or what was it that frightened you?"

"I want to tell you. She came—instead of Cousin Rose."

Slowly, incoherently, I told him. He listened with the sympathetic attentiveness I had noticed in him from the beginning in the old childish days, but now his interest was deeper, warmer, intensified I knew, by love. Even so I had not been prepared for the effect my halting story had on him. He seemed quite hypnotized. I too was absorbed, strengthened by his presence, soothed by the dreamlike peace of the room, of the whole new world of Kindlehope, so that I could speak of our life at the Mill almost without pain. Stumbling at last to the end, I found that Mark had released my hand and with his face half turned away from me was looking out of the window with a curious expression of indecision.

"When your stepmother came," he said suddenly, "that was two years ago?"

"It was May Day. The day you gave me the hagstone. Such a long time. It's hopeless to look for her now, for Cousin Rose, I mean, isn't it? Do you think she can be—alive? Surely we would have heard from her."

There was one more thing. I had not yet found words for it, even to myself. But to Mark I could say it though in no more than a whisper.

"Suppose they met, Mamma and Cousin Rose. Could she have . . . come to some harm?"

Half-formed images of some fearful encounter, though instantly suppressed, made me catch my breath. I felt stifled.

"You must rest. I shouldn't have let you talk. Not yet. Mrs. Darwen will give me a dressing-down for tiring you." Again he looked guiltily at the open door. It was still ajar, but the housekeeper must have come to the end of her tasks for there was no sound from within. "You mustn't worry about it any more. It seems to me much more likely that your stepmother's arrival was no more than a coincidence. You say these actors were penniless and stranded. She had probably left Stanesfield just trusting to luck."

Then Mrs. Darwen came in firmly with a rug and at her look Mark melted out of the room but not before he had whispered: "May I tell Grandfather?" and when I nodded, he said, "We'll straighten the whole thing out, never fear," with such conviction that I was comforted, not with the slightest hope that he could solve the mystery of Cousin Rose's disappearance but simply from the exquisite relief of having confided in him.

On the following day Mark and his grandfather came together to see me. Mr. Aylward was tall and white-bearded, with the easy confidence of a man who had lived all his life on the acres where generations of his forefathers had lived before him.

When I thanked him for his kindness and hospitality and began falteringly to speak of my plans for leaving, he interrupted: "You must not think of leaving until you are quite recovered. From what Mark has told me you have been through a time of great stress. I shall consider myself responsible for your welfare until we can see you safely into the care of your aunt—in the Isle of Wight, I believe."

Seeing that I was too overwhelmed to speak, he went on: "You realize, my dear young lady, that whoever the person may have been who imposed upon you, she is not your step-mother. She must have married under a false name and made a false entry in the register. The marriage was therefore invalid."

Despite the now-familiar irrational impulse to defend her, I felt an immediate sense of release.

"She must have drawn money from the Bank against your father's estate, besides as you say, converting valuables into money which she has appropriated. She is not entitled to any legacy your father may have bequeathed under the misconception that she was his lawful wife. Indeed, the whole matter should properly be in the hands of the police but . . ."

"Oh no, please. We couldn't do that to her."

Someday perhaps I would be able to estimate all that she had taken away from me, the money being the least of it, but now I was chiefly concerned about Cousin Rose.

"I must find out what became of her. There is no one but me to care about her. I believe that no one knows where she is."

I told them about the stranger, the farmer, whom I had misled into believing that she had married.

"He must have cared for her and now he may never know the truth about her."

Neither Mark nor his grandfather spoke. Mr. Aylward had been standing with one arm on the mantelpiece. Now he brought an upright chair from the table and sat down at my side.

"As for your relative, that is quite another case. We must assume, I think, that she kept away from you deliberately or was obliged by some unknown circumstance—unknown to you, that is—to do so. You have talked enough, Miss Ellen. You

look pale. But when you are stronger—if I may advise you—
it would be well to give serious thought to the kind of circumstance which could have induced your cousin to behave as she
did."

The effect of this was only to increase my perplexity. I could
think of no circumstance that would in any way account for
Cousin Rose's extraordinary absence. At the same time Mr.
Aylward had contrived to cast a more rational light upon the
affair and the darkness in my mind was lifted a little, so that
it was chiefly for reassurance that I said, "You don't think . . .
she may be dead?"

"We must assume that she is alive in the absence of any evidence to the contrary." He was not speaking at random but
slowly, with deliberation. "Let us suppose that she chose at the
last minute to refrain from coming to the Mill. You say that
she had commissioned the carrier to take her there and then
changed her mind. Have you given any thought to the possible
reason for such a change of plan?"

"I believe it was always in my mind, only now I cannot dis-
entangle my thoughts about Cousin Rose from my thoughts
about Mamma—that there might be something odd about her.
A sort of insanity. There was a strangeness in her letter, as
if she had almost"—what was the expression I wanted?—
"broken down, or given up."

"A person may act on a sudden impulse, or may reach a
decision after a long period of indecision. In your cousin's case
it might well have been the second."

"So many things . . ."

Indecision had certainly been the keynote of that smudged
letter, undated, incoherent—yet containing all that I knew of
whatever dilemma or disaster had overtaken its writer.

"Strangely, no doubt," Mr. Aylward was saying, "but not necessarily in madness, unless perhaps the temporary derangement which fear, loneliness, exhaustion, despair, can induce. There are few human situations, however, which do not resolve themselves through time, as your own unhappy experience has in part, at least, proved." He got up. "I should like a word with you, Mark, if you don't mind," and they left me.

Apart from the slightly dispirited feeling I already suffered whenever Mark went away, I was not sorry to be alone for a while. The conversation had tired me. I went back to the bedroom intending to lie down, but sank instead into the chair by the window, too listless to undo my dress.

It was a soft gray afternoon. I looked about the room, trying though in a vague, inactive way, to define the particular quality which gave to the Grange its aura of peace. Nothing, it seemed, could ruffle my spirits for long in this sanctuary. Imperceptibly my melancholy was lightened; the threads of perplexity quietly unraveled so that I felt again a mood of tranquil emptiness like a healing trance. A faint breeze, cool and lilac-scented, stirred the muslin curtains and the spotless valances on the bed. From the grate came the whisper of a wood fire burning clear above the shining hearth-tiles.

Presently Kate brought a tray of food. I noticed her quiet tread, the unobtrusive way in which she drew up a table, every movement that of a well-trained servant. Her streamered cap and frilled apron were as fresh and white as the moorland breeze could bleach them. I had noticed the same crispness in Mr. Aylward's linen, and Mark's.

Everything was as it should be. The intricately carved bedposts harbored no speck of dust. Meals appeared with effortless regularity. When Kate had taken away the tray, I thought of Mrs. Darwen with growing respect, seeing in this well-conducted household the refinement and elegance I had always longed to establish at the Mill.

My musing was unexpectedly interrupted. Small unaccountable movements in the next room were followed by the appearance in the doorway of the last thing I expected to see, a little girl, a fair-haired mite, still sufficiently a baby to fall over her pinafore and subside into a comfortable bundle on the floor. She had lost one shoe and now began to pull off her sock, gurgling happily to herself.

"Come to me." I held out my arms but she staggered to her feet and stumbled away. I waited, hoping that she would come back. She had a look of Lucy as a little girl, long ago, before Mother died.

The thought brought with it the clearest memory I had ever had of my mother. She had seemed tall to me in her sweeping dresses of gray and blue, as I had sat by her chair listening to stories of Appleby End, of Uncle Adam and Aunt Ann, of Cousin Rose . . .

I must have fallen asleep, to dream again of the lullaby she used to sing to us, a long, rambling ballad with a refrain, something about the Green Broom-O. It came to me now, soft and low, echoing wistfully down through the years. But now I was quite awake, for I saw that the sun had come out and was sending a long westerly beam into the heart of the fire.

Yet the crooning voice went on, verse after verse. It came from the next room. I went to the door and saw Mrs. Darwen in the act of laying the child on the couch. She sat down in a low chair and took up her needlework.

At the sight of me, she stopped singing. Was it her look that made my heart beat faster?

"She's your little girl?" I said.

"Yes."

I went over to the couch and looked down at the sleeping child.

"What's her name?"

She caught her breath. There were tears in her eyes.

"Lilith," she said.

"That was my mother's name."

"Yes, Ellen. It was your dear mother's name."

I went down on my knees and laid my head in her lap.

"Cousin Rose," I said. "Where have you been? Where have you been all this long time?"

Chapter Twenty-four

It was to be days, weeks, months before I knew the whole of Cousin Rose's story. Indeed it is only after years of security and happiness in my own marriage that I have been able to understand the agony of the dilemma in which she found herself, when, almost middle-aged, she faced the disaster which would set so immense, so insuperable a barrier between her and her kind.

I remember how clumsily in my ignorance I forced her to speak of it.

"I wish there were someone to tell," I said, "that I have found you at last. I wish Lucy were here."

"You must go to her as soon as you are well enough. You

should never have been parted. Perhaps I will go with you. I ought to see Aunt Lumley."

"You have heard everything?"

I remembered the stillness in the inner room while I was talking to Mark, but she did not confess to having overheard.

"Mr. Aylward told me this morning. Until then I only knew, when Mark mentioned your stepmother, that your father had married again. But I knew nothing else, nothing about this impostor."

"She wore your clothes," I said, "and used your things." How trivial I made it sound when she had taken so much besides.

"Poor creature! Don't be too hard on her. Until you have known what it is to be quite alone without friends, without a future, you cannot know what it means to be taken in without question as you took her in—and as the Aylwards took me."

"Mr. Aylward knows who you are?"

"He knows now."

I looked up and saw the tension in her face. She was very pale.

"And you've been here all the time? I never dreamed, never even guessed that you might be married."

"I am not married, Ellen."

The simplicity of it! The one possible explanation! And yet disbelief kept me silent.

"Do you understand?"

Yes, I understood. Binnie was not one to mince words. Death according to her was the alternative. "And death," Binnie had said, "is what most of them prefer, excepting a few brazen ones that nothing could shame."

I knew all about the servant girl thrown out into the street with her box, the irate father, the door closed against her, the dragging of ponds. A fleeting vision came to me of Cissie Pellow, framed in the yellow hazel leaves, cradling in her arms the substitute for her dead baby. Poor crazy Cissie! But Cousin Rose!

"What right had I to impose on your father, Ellen? Was I fit to bring up his daughters? How can you possibly understand. You are young, you know nothing of life."

"Oh Cousin Rose," I burst out, "why did you not come? You were so near and so unhappy. It could have done nothing but good. Lucy and I would have loved the baby. She's like Lucy. Father would never have gone back to sea and . . ."

I stopped, realizing how I hurt her.

We must have talked for hours, then and in the days that followed. Rose's voice and manner were quiet and unemphatic so that it was not easy to reconstruct from her rather prim understatements the drama, near tragedy, she had undergone. But bit by bit I learned the painful story and after all it was no more than a tale of faithful love. John Bishop had been "promised" to someone else when he and Rose first met. The Bishops were neighbors who had suffered like many other farmers from the decline in prices and the rise in costs. They had been saved from ruin by John's uncle, who had a daughter in delicate health. Somehow an obligation had been imposed. It was understood that the cousins would marry.

When John had begged to be released, he had found that a frail woman can be as hard as steel, that family ties can strangle as well as bind. He had married in misery and never ceased to repent. After Uncle Adam's death he and Rose had met again, by chance.

"The bitterness of shame I felt, Ellen, when I knew what I had done. To have lived all those years, following a quiet duty—I was happy with Father, apart from the one blessing I couldn't have—and then to bring such a thing on myself." The knowledge of her condition had a curiously isolating effect. Other people, even the child's father, simply receded. But the dreamy vagueness imposed by her physical state made her almost incapable of action of any sort.

"My first thought was that I must leave Appleby End where everyone knew me. Your father had often offered me a home and the Mill seemed the obvious refuge. It was only gradually that I began to see the impossibility of going there either."

I suppose my own emotions were principally of incredulity. Looking down at Lilith chubbily asleep with one sockless foot protruding from the rug, I found it impossible to connect her with the agony of that vigil at the cross-roads. It was equally impossible to see in Rose's neat person, smooth hair and placid manner the half-demented creature she had been when Babbitt had set her down a mile or two from the Mill.

"I could have taken a cab from Stanesfield but I chose the carrier because it would be so slow. I don't know how long I spent up there on the moors. It was evening when I saw a house by the river and knew that it must be the Mill. The lamps were lit and it looked so peaceful, so undisturbed, that I couldn't come. I couldn't face it. And yet where else could I go? I slept a little under a wall and then the next morning I set off along the road away from the Mill. It was a lovely morning with the larks singing and I thought I would die of grief. There was a spring by the roadside . . ."

As she had rested there Tom Amblethwaite had come along in his trap.

"I told him I was going to Kindlehope. It seemed a friendly name, and there was nowhere else. He put me down about half

[271]

a mile from the gate of the Grange. I came up the drive, thinking to go round to the back door and ask for a bit of bread
like a pauper. But as I passed the front door—it was standing
open—I saw Mr. Aylward lying in a chair, gasping for
breath. . . ."

She told me how, miraculously, the sight of him had
changed the whole course of her life. As soon as she crossed
the threshold, her confidence returned. With all the conventional values suspended, she fell back upon the practical things
she understood so well.

"I knew just what to do from having seen Father in the same
state. There was no one about. You never saw such a place.
The neglect! They were living like gypsies, the two of them,
with only an old woman from one of the cottages to see to
things."

When Mark came home, the atmosphere of the house had
already changed. By the time the old gentleman was nursed
back to health I suspected that Rose had established herself.
Small wonder that they saw her as a ministering angel and
begged her to remain. She had told Mr. Aylward that she was
expecting a child but no other details. Characteristically he had
offered them both a home.

"My mother always said, 'When one door shuts another door
opens,'" Rose said reminiscently. "It was so for me. Sometimes
I have missed all my things. . . ."

But she had found plenty of other things at the Grange and
had fashioned them into a home for the Aylwards, for Lilith
and herself. If Cousin Rose had been inconveniently set down
in a desert, she would have made a home there without too
many regrets for the one she had left behind. As it was, she

had suffered, but in moderation, at the thought of the older Lilith's motherless girls at the Mill.

"Then when Mark told us that you had a stepmother," she concluded, "I thought 'Everything works together for good.'"

Another of Aunt Ann's sayings, I supposed, with just a touch of resentment. Nature had not cast Cousin Rose in the heroic mold. She was one of those whose destiny and disposition seemed startlingly at odds, and yet, seeing how she had rescued Kindlehope Grange from neglect and herself from social ostracism, I gradually came to recognize in her one of those quiet women who can take destiny in hand with surprising tenacity. She had well-shaped, capable hands, rather wide in the palm.

"It was you who sent the dress, wasn't it? It's beautiful, the most beautiful dress I ever had."

For the first time she looked happier, as with an air of almost complacent triumph she said, "That was something at least I could do for you. When Mark told us that he had seen you in Stanesfield and heard the sad news about your father, I thought 'She shall have a lovely dress,' knowing from experience how difficult it is to get good mourning in the country. I sent it over by Tom Amblethwaite. He goes that way to see his mother at Saxelby and Tom isn't a man to talk. The fit was just a matter of guessing. I don't think it can have been far out."

In speaking of the dress she became sure of herself. Illogically perhaps, I felt irritated. Though I thanked her and reassured her about the fit, I detected in her and resented, a hint of self-congratulation as though in sending the dress she had atoned in some way for not coming herself.

"That was one thing I could do," she repeated, "after the way I disappointed you."

The phrase was typical of her. With reference to the cataclysm she had wrought in our lives it seemed inadequate. I do not believe she ever understood what she had done to us. It was as though all her emotional reserves had been exhausted in her own private turmoil, leaving her insensitive to ours. Or perhaps she had always been insensitive.

Nevertheless, because I needed her, because she was, unfailingly, at last, my mother's cousin, I loved her, and when she said, "Poor John! After all he has had the worst of it. God has been good to me," it was wonderful to be able to tell her that he had come to find her.

"Then Bella has gone," she said, and I saw how shaken she was. "She was always a creaking gate and she's gone at last. Otherwise John would never have come for me."

"Did he know—about Lilith?"

"He knew nothing. What was the good of adding to his misery, poor fellow? He had enough."

"How pleased he'll be!"

I left her tearful and incoherent and for the first time I dare say since she came to the Grange, dinner was late that evening.

I was well enough to join them in the dining room. We sat on at the candlelit table after Kate had cleared away until the sky deepened to purple and a second cluster of candles glowed yellow in the windowpanes. But we did not talk much. Rose was so absent-minded that she sat motionless as a waxwork figure for minutes at a time, forgetting to eat. Mr. Aylward made one or two attempts at conversation, but arousing little response in either Mark or me, composedly ate his meal in silence.

[274]

At last Rose withdrew to the kitchen and Mr. Aylward to take a turn in the garden. Mark drew me into the window, where suddenly there was so much to say that we did not notice the arrival of a visitor. We were still standing in the deep embrasure when Mr. Aylward opened the door and ushered in . . . Mr. Southern.

With a rush of pleasure and affection, I said, "Oh Mr. Southern! How very good of you to come!"

I saw his eyes rest for a second on Mark and a kind of bleakness came into his face. I must have spoken warmly, but he only bowed without smiling and said, "I'm relieved to find you safe and well, Ellen. Mr. Aylward has told me everything."

The Aylwards left us together. We sat by the fire and talked.

"That was the thing I never guessed, that she might be the wrong woman. I should have known it. I blame myself. The voice, the manner . . . There was a sophistication I could not account for. Perhaps if I had seen her when she first came, but unhappily, as you will remember, I was away from home. Though as it happened, I did see her on the day she came, without knowing who she was."

"When you rode into Stanesfield?"

"We stopped at the Moorcock for something to eat. It was just as we were leaving that the dray went by with the luggage. From there to Stanesfield I didn't meet another soul or a vehicle of any kind. But I did see a woman sitting on that seat about a mile past the Moorcock. Except that she was in black, I formed no clear picture of her but somehow I had the impression that she had been disappointed in a rendezvous. When I first met your stepmother at the Mill I had a sudden conviction that she was the same woman. I could not be sure and it seemed so unlikely. But I mistrusted her from the first. . . ."

He had even come to suspect, as I had done, some guilty secret or mental aberration and had gone to Appleby End to find out more about the circumstances of Miss Warden's life and her departure from the district. But he had learned nothing except that no one had heard from her. Even a chance meeting with John Bishop had revealed nothing, though he had become almost confidential when he heard of Mr. Southern's acquaintance with the family.

"It puzzled me that a decent honest man like Bishop should care for such a woman. But even then I did not guess, and after all your father . . . At best I thought she had suffered some change of personality."

He passed his hand nervously over his hair. He seemed to have lost the composure I had always known in him. I thought he looked older, and tired, as he sat staring into the fire, his shoulders drooping a little.

"By the way, Nancy gave me some letters for you. They came a day or two ago. Lucy has written herself. I think you will find that she has good news."

"She is better." I handed him her letter and then Aunt Lumley's, which confirmed the news of her recovery. There was no damage to the lungs, though she must always lead a quiet life, preferably in a mild, dry climate.

Mr. Southern folded each of the letters slowly and placed them with laborious care back in the envelopes. It took him a long time.

"Things should be better for you now, Ellen," he said at last. "I'm glad."

Lost in rosy dreams of a future suddenly too promising to be believed, I was vaguely aware that he had got up, heaving himself out of the chair as if it cost him an effort.

"You're not going?"

He looked down at me as if he found it difficult to speak. "You have forgiven me, Ellen?" he said at last.

"It isn't a question of forgiving," I blurted out. "I have so much to thank you for. I'm ashamed of the way I behaved and I wish . . ."

"You understand a little better now—how I felt."

"Yes. I understand."

"But only because you have felt it for someone else. I always hoped that in time, if I came back, things would be different. I thought you might find that you could not live without me. . . ."

"At first," I began, then stopped, longing to tell him how much he had meant to me, yet afraid of saying too much. Besides, he knew me well enough to be aware that a few short meetings had brought me closer to Mark than I had ever felt to him who had known and loved me all my life.

"But I left it too long. I am too late, am I not, Ellen?"

I could only nod.

"But I shall see you?"

He shook his head.

"We may meet from time to time, I dare say, but I shall try not to see you. Since I cannot have what I wanted, I will have nothing else. If only things had gone on as they were, if only your father had lived. . . ."

But just then Rose herself came in with a tray of food for him. I made the introductions. Mr. Southern bowed coldly and declined to eat. He refused even a glass of wine but took up his hat and gloves and went into the hall. When he had said goodbye to Mr. Aylward, I went with him to the gate.

"You mustn't come out. It's quite cool," he said. But I insisted; there was so much I had not said.

Mark brought round his horse. In the west the sky was still streaked with silver but it would soon be dark. As Mark and Mr. Southern shook hands I became aware of a warm glow from the house, and turning, saw its windows one by one infused with yellow light, like golden flowers opening in the dusk. Rose was going from room to room, lighting the lamps. Through the open door we saw her cross the hall and go steadily up the stairs. There was a kind of assurance in her unhurried pace, like that of a priestess secure in the fulfillment of a necessary ritual. In her plain dress with the lamp in her hand she might have been a beneficent spirit presiding over hearth and home. We all three watched her until the turn in the stairs took her out of sight and the windows above in their turn grew yellow.

Suddenly Mr. Southern spoke, his tone in such marked contrast to the serenity of that lamplit scene that it shocked and saddened me.

"What harm could she have done in coming to the Mill," he said bitterly, "compared with the harm she did in staying away?" He took my hand and his voice changed. His eyes were tired but I saw in them a depth of feeling I shall never forget. "She couldn't have changed you, Ellen. Nothing can change you." Then he mounted and rode away.

We watched him riding eastward where the white road dipped between deeply shadowed hills.

"He'll never forgive her," I said. "He'll never forgive either of them."

"Can you blame him?" Mark said as he put his arm round me and drew me close. "After all, he has lost more than anyone else."

Chapter Twenty-five

Mark and I were married from Appleby End, an unpretentious farmhouse overlooking flat pastures and prim pollard willows. Perversely, after dreaming of it so long, I had found the place dull and spent my time there longing for the open moors of Kindlehope—and for Mark.

The dullness of Appleby End was equalled only by the dullness of the Bishops. They had settled down instantly into a life of such unrelieved mutual contentment that an outsider, ignorant of their history, might have been forgiven for thinking them smug. Their very kindness seemed preoccupied. I felt like a stray pigeon perched on their roof and waiting for the right weather to wing my way home; waiting with an impatience that made the two years before our wedding seem interminable.

"How strange it all was, Ellen."

We were standing on the bridge, taking our usual last look at the Mill before climbing the hill. Lucy liked to spend a day there occasionally during her annual visit to Kindlehope.

She spoke with almost all her old gusto; but not quite all. She was calmer in manner now and had learned to pitch her voice a tone lower. Her hair was a shade darker. We were thought to have grown more alike. But she was not too much changed as she stood, eyelashes fluttering, lips thinly compressed, her whole being absorbed in delighted contemplation of the strangeness of it all.

Some response was obviously expected but it was with reluctance that I said, "What was strange?"

Lucy looked at me reproachfully.

"You know what I mean. It makes me a little sad sometimes, Ellen, to see how you've changed. I don't believe you would ever come here at all if it weren't to dig up herbs for your garden at the Grange. The last time you could think of nothing but marjoram and fennel and this time you've spent the whole afternoon rummaging in the cellar for that old iron griddle just because Mark likes griddle cakes. And the weight of it!"

"I'll leave it with Nancy. Tom Amblethwaite can fetch it for me some time."

"No, indeed. I have no wish to withhold from Mark his griddle cakes. But you know, Ellen, it was the same in Switzerland. The hours you spent watching for the postman! I don't believe you even saw the mountains. In some ways," she eyed me reflectively, "you are very like Cousin Rose. What are you laughing at? Only in some ways, of course."

"Of course. But what was it that was so strange?"

"I know you don't feel it as I do but sometimes I'm inclined to look upon the whole thing as—a visitation." She lingered over the word appreciatively. "For instance, it was quite re-markable the way I suddenly got better on the very day she went away."

The idea was not new to me. Lucy had already aired it many times. I had heard her say the same thing that very afternoon as we drank a cup of tea in the Kirkups' cottage. Nancy's response had been more sympathetic than mine.

"Not really," I said briskly. "After all, you had had a long rest. It probably took a few weeks for the sea air to take effect. There couldn't really be any connection."

Lucy only smiled inscrutably, looking quite beautiful enough to account for her success at the Ventnor evening par-ties, and the familiar surge of gratitude at seeing her restored to health made me smile too. I laid down the heavy griddle and put my arm round her. Together we leaned over the para-pet, looking down at the water.

"There was nothing strange about Mamma, not in herself," I said. "Only in her coming."

I watched a sycamore leaf afloat on the smooth water slid-ing toward the weir. Over it went in a white froth, seemed momentarily lost, then emerged again to be washed by a capricious current into a tiny harbor between flat stones by the garden wall, where it lay, rocking gently, lit by a long shaft of sunlight.

"And in her going," Lucy said.

The light changed. A stronger ripple detached the leaf from its resting-place. It hovered uncertainly, almost sub-merged, but presently the current caught it again and I watched it sail gallantly away until the river curved out of sight.

"We never even knew her name."

I detected in Lucy's voice a note of regret but made no comment. Not even to her could I unburden my feelings about what she called the visitation—only to Mark, who, as always, understood.

"Taking everything into account," he once said, half teasing, "I think it was quite suitable for you to love her a little, as I believe you did, my darling."

I listened now for the sound of the gig, hoping that Mark would come himself and not send one of the men. It was growing cool as the last of the sunlight stole from the water and from the overgrown garden. More than ever aloof, its windows boarded against marauding village boys, the Mill had withdrawn into deep shade. According to Binnie, who kept house for Mr. Southern now that his sister had moved permanently to Ventnor, it would never be let again.

"He seems to have a feeling for it," she said. "And not only that—it isn't everyone that would live in it—not now."

What was there to keep them away?

As the cool air of evening crept up from the river and the tall trees closed in, I could almost have felt—once again—a wavering doubt, as if water and stones and trees had power to shift and regroup themselves in a new and more disturbing pattern. For a moment my shadow on the water was like the presence of a stranger. One could almost believe . . .

At that time of day one could believe anything.

"We must go," I said firmly. "You'll catch cold."

With relief I heard the sound of wheels. We hurried up the hill to save the awkward turn and found Mark himself already shaking out wraps and rugs.

As always I enjoyed the drive up the valley to the west where the sky was lighter.

[282]